Cover design by MiblArt

ISBN 978-1-952033-01-8 (paperback)

ISBN 978-1-952033-00-1 (ebook)

www.dskogler-books.com

THE HEART OF THE RADIANT

D. S. KOGLER

Chapter 1

An explosion jolted Jax awake as it shook his room. An orange flicker from the window lit the bedchamber with an unnatural light. Before he could even climb out of bed, his father Ronan, fully clad in armor, burst into the room with his sister Ev in tow.

"Jax! Take Eveline and get as far away from here as you can."

Jax leapt out of bed. "What? Why? What's happening?"

"We're under attack. Now take Eveline and get to safety."

"What!? No way!" Jax ran towards his closet and began pulling out his armor.

"Jax!"

"I can fight, too!" he insisted, stripping to put on his chain mail. "I—"

"This isn't up for discussion!"

Jax fumed.

His father's face softened as he walked over. "Jax," he said, placing his hand on Jax's shoulder, "you are strong, but this isn't a fight we can win."

"What are you—"

"Use your strength to protect your sister. She'll do the same for you. I have to defend the Heart. You have to live."

His father squeezed his shoulder before turning to leave. He hugged Ev and whispered something in her ear, then left them alone in the dark room.

Jax stood in silence. His father was acting like the fight was already over, but they were part of the Maristol Light Guard — soldiers of Supreme Lord Grandis himself! No one was going to take this city as long as it was under their protection.

"Jax," Ev said after a moment, "we need to go."

Jax looked at his sister. She was only fourteen, but already a competent healer. Still, she hadn't had much training in combat. Perhaps it would be best if she didn't get involved in the battle.

"You're right." Jax continued changing into his chain mail. Mail didn't offer as much protection as plate, but the Guard only offered plate to soldiers who'd reached the rank of elite, or else were willing to shell out for it.

"What do you think you're doing?" Ev asked him. "Father said—"

"We're under attack. Do you want me to go out there without any protection?"

Ev didn't answer.

"You should put yours on, too. I'll meet you downstairs."

Ev frowned, but acquiesced.

The sounds of battle grew louder now. More explosions echoed into his room. He could hear shouting, screaming, the clang of metal against metal, and something large roaring in the distance.

Jax finished suiting up and sheathed his sword, then headed downstairs where he saw that Ev had changed into her day clothes.

"Why aren't you wearing your armor?" he asked.

"I'm wearing it underneath."

Jax wanted to ask why, but it wasn't important at the moment. He could hear the sounds of a skirmish out on the street. He made his way to the window and peeked out to see if they had a shot of getting out that way. He barely had time to register a flash of light when the body of a knight crashed through the front door.

The knight didn't even have a chance to push himself up before a wave of fire enveloped him, setting the place ablaze.

Jax locked eyes through the window with a hooded figure holding a twisted staff. The figure yelled and pointed his staff at the window.

"Run!" Jax yelled as he pulled Ev out of the way of a second wave of flames.

The two of them ran for the back of the house. Jax took a quick peek out a back window and saw no sign of immediate danger. He helped Ev through before climbing out himself.

Ev gasped. Her eyes were fixed on the sky.

Jax looked up to the sight of dragons and other winged monstrosities converging on the center of the city.

"They're heading for the citadel," he muttered.

"There's too many of them," Ev said. "Father..."

"Will be fine," Jax finished for her as he looked both ways down the street. He was torn between rushing to help his father and getting Ev to safety.

A group of enemy soldiers rounding the corner decided for him however. "This way!"

He grabbed his sister by the arm and started running towards the center of the city. The enemy soldiers followed them, and Jax pulled Ev into an alley to try and lose them. For whatever reason, the soldiers didn't follow, carrying on towards the city center.

At the far end they stumbled into the final moments of what must have been a fierce battle. Bodies of soldiers from both sides lined the street, most of them belonging to the Light Guard. Only a single enemy soldier remained standing, but the last two Light Guard appeared on the verge of defeat. Jax recognized one as his friend Gare, and instinctively drew his blade to help.

Before he had a chance to act, however, the enemy soldier lunged and struck down the accompanying Light Guard. Gare swung his ax with all his might, but the invader swatted him to the ground and raised his twisted blade for the kill.

Jax knew he couldn't close the distance between them in time, so he did the only thing he could. He raised his hand and fired a blast of light at the assailant.

His magic was weak, but it served its purpose. The light connected and knocked the attacker off balance. Gare took the moment to swing his ax once again, connecting squarely with the enemy's leg. The enemy soldier buckled, but didn't fall.

In retaliation the invader thrust his blade down and clean through Gare's chest plate. Gare screamed, and a fury boiled up inside of Jax.

He charged the enemy soldier. The soldier wheeled around, revealing an emaciated face that was little more than skin hanging from bone. The dead-eyed warrior swung his weapon. Jax dodged the blow and fired another blast of magic at his opponents head, hoping to gain an opening.

The enemy soldier recovered from the blast almost immediately and launched into a flurry of attacks.

Jax lifted his blade and parried swing after thrust after swing, but his foe struck with such force and speed that Jax soon found himself overwhelmed.

The undead soldier pulled back for a massive strike but stopped in his tracks as Gare lodged his ax deep into the soldier's skull from behind. The soldier staggered but remained standing, then spun around and dashed Gare to the ground once again.

Seizing his chance, Jax fired one more blast at the enemy soldier. Predictably, the soldier spun back, arcing his blade though the air. Jax ducked under it and thrust his sword up into the chin of the soldier, clanging against the ax still lodged in his head.

The undead soldier dropped his blade and stumbled backwards. With a shout Jax channeled a beam of light through his sword and the monster finally fell. A feeling of strength welled up inside of him as the warrior crashed against the ground.

Sheathing his sword, Jax hurried over to Gare. Ev rushed to join them. Blood was seeping out of the gash in Gare's armor.

"Gare, hold on!" Jax shouted as he hoisted his friend to his feet.

"Jax," Ev tugged on his arm, "we need to get out of the street."

Jax half-carried Gare back to the alley where they'd come from. Seeing no enemy forces nearby, he set his friend down and positioned himself where he could keep an eye on the street.

"Ev, I need you to..." he started, but she was already casting one of her healing spells.

Gare coughed up blood, then wiped it from his mouth. "Th-thanks," he managed to get out.

Jax glanced down the alley, then back towards the street. This was taking too long. "How much longer?"

"I don't know," Ev answered. "I can't see the wound."

That wasn't the answer Jax wanted to hear.

Gare reached out and pushed Ev's hand away. "I think that's good enough for now," he said as he started to push himself up, but he winced and quickly fell back down again.

"Don't move," Ev said, "it just makes it harder."

Gare nodded tiredly. The roar of a dragon echoed down the streets.

Jax stood and gripped his sword's hilt. "Gare, do you know what's going on? Who's attacking us?"

Gare looked up at Jax with concern. "It... it's Dezeroth."

Jax froze. That was impossible. The Undead King and his horde had vanished after the last awakening of Apollyon. Lord Grandis himself had confirmed their disappearance.

Jax locked eyes with Gare. "You're sure it's him?"

"My entire barracks was just killed by revenants, Jax. Who the hell else could it be?"

Jax didn't answer. He walked to the edge of the alley and gazed over at the soldier they'd just slain, Gare's ax still lodged in his cranium. Necromancers were far from unheard of, but undead with the strength that soldier had possessed...

"Do you think you're recovered yet?" Jax asked, looking back over his shoulder.

Gare stood up, and Ev removed her hand from his chest. "I think I'm good, yeah." He pounded his fist against where he'd been wounded. "Your sister's got talent."

Jax focused on the towering citadel at the center of the city. "Good." He turned back towards his friend. "In that case, I need you to do me a favor."

"A favor?"

"Yeah." Jax looked at his sister. "I need you to get Ev out of the city. Take her somewhere safe."

"Jax, no!" Ev yelled. "Father said—"

"I know what he said," Jax interrupted.

"Jax," Gare began, "whatever the hell you're thinking of doing—"

"My father went to the citadel to protect the Heart. If Dezeroth is really here he's going to need all the help he can get."

"Jax, wait!" Gare called, but Jax was already running.

* * * *

Jax sped towards the citadel, the sounds of combat intensifying with every step. The roar of dragons and explosive spells accentuated the shouts of legions clashing against one another.

Jax rounded one final corner and found himself facing the backs of a hundred undead soldiers. Beyond them, at the steps of the citadel, the Light Guard held strong against the horde. Bolts of magic and arrows rained down from the windows of the citadel on the invading army. The corpse of a dragon lay sprawled across the left third of the steps up to the citadel. Two more dragons circled high above around it, scorching the citadel with their flaming breath. A fourth slammed into the loft of the citadel, raining stone down upon the fighters below. It tried to claw its way in through the stone structure, but was quickly driven back by a volley of magic and arrows from within. The most powerful warriors and mages in the land protected the citadel, and not even Dezeroth's forces would penetrate it easily.

There was no way Jax could do anything where he was. He needed to find higher ground so he could gauge the situation. A complex of buildings surrounded the citadel, several of which had balconies facing the citadel's court. Perhaps he could find a better position there.

Jax took off down the street to his left, then promptly changed direction as another group of undead rushed towards him. He followed the row of buildings around until he found one he knew would have a good view from the upper story.

The door to the building was ajar. Before entering, he looked back to see if he was still being followed. Thankfully, the enemy soldiers seemed to have decided chasing a single paladin wasn't worth their time.

Jax cautiously made his way up the stairs. At the top, he could see two enemy soldiers — an archer and a mage — out on the balcony. They were completely focused on sniping the Light Guard and didn't notice as Jax crept up behind them. If they were like the warrior he'd fought earlier, he'd need to attack with everything he had to bring them down.

He wound up to strike, and with all his might cleaved the head clean off of the mage's shoulders.

The archer turned at the commotion, but Jax struck before she had time to react. He attempted to repeat his attack on the archer, but was only partially successful.

The archer's head hung lopsided off her neck as she fired an arrow at Jax. The black arrow sliced through his armor like butter, lodging itself deep into his shoulder. Jax swung again as the archer dropped her bow and pulled out a dagger.

She dodged Jax's attack, but the motion swung her head around backwards. She swiped blindly at where Jax had been, leaving herself exposed. With a final sweeping blow Jax finished what he'd started and claimed the balcony.

Fortunately, none of the other invaders seemed to have noticed his little skirmish, which gave him a moment to survey the situation. What he saw wasn't good.

The rain of magic and arrows from the citadel had all but disappeared. Two dragons had broken through the loft and had set the building ablaze. On the ground, the Light Guard had been backed all the way up the steps of the citadel. Jax could see his father among the survivors behind the front line, protecting the spellcasters with his light shield.

Desperate to find some way to turn the tides, Jax scanned the battlefield up and down looking for anything that might give his side an edge. That was when he noticed the dark figure making its way up the citadel steps. A hulking figure in black, twisted armor, with a face as gray as his beard and eyes glowing an unholy orange light — the Undead King, Dezeroth.

Dezeroth cut through the ranks of the Light Guard as a child would daisies in a field. He shrugged off every blow and struck down warrior after warrior.

As Dezeroth approached the top of the citadel steps, Jax's father turned his shield into a weapon, unleashing a powerful blast of light onto Dezeroth. The Undead King was knocked back, then responded by unleashing a wave of darkness that dropped all in front of him to their knees.

Jax watched from afar as Dezeroth stepped calmly towards his father.

"Get up!" Jax screamed in his head.

His father gripped his sword and started to rise before crumpling helplessly as Dezeroth bore down on him.

In a fit of desperation, Jax fired the strongest blast he could manage at Dezeroth. His aim was true, but the light petered out just as it reached the warlord. Dezeroth didn't so much as glance in the light's direction as he plunged his blade into Jax's father.

Jax stood frozen, arm still outstretched as he watched his father's body fall. Try as he had to make a difference, Jax had been useless. Helpless to even save his own father. His breathing quickened. He would make these monsters pay. He would slaughter every one of them. He prepared to fire another blast straight down into the horde when a sharp pain shot through his left side. Instinctively, his hand reached for the source of the pain, where he felt the feathers of an arrow barely protruding out from beneath his armor.

Jax had completely forgotten about the neighboring balconies. An enemy archer to his left nocked another arrow as a third pierced his back from behind. Jax suddenly had trouble breathing. The first archer took aim once again.

Jax couldn't stay here. If he died now, he'd never avenge his father.

Ignoring the pain, Jax dove back inside and down the stairs. He tumbled back out onto the streets and stopped to catch his breath. Every inhale and exhale was excruciating. He hadn't realized how badly he'd been hurt, but each breath was more difficult than the last.

He needed a healer.

"Jax!" came a shout from down the street.

Jax looked up to see Gare and Ev running towards him.

"Lords," said Gare when he arrived, looking at the arrows sticking out of Jax. "What the hell were you thinking!"

"They've taken the citadel," Jax panted.

"What? No!" exclaimed Gare.

"What about Father?" asked Ev. "Is he…"

Jax shook his head. "Dezeroth," he clenched his fists as he said the name, "Dezeroth killed him!" He slammed his fist down and immediately regretted the action as his body filled with pain.

"Oh, lords, bud, I am so sorry," Gare said. A loud crash caused him to look over his shoulder. "Listen, we need to get out of here."

"We need to get those arrows out of him," demanded Ev.

"Oh, right," remarked Gare. "Hold still, bud, this will just take a second."

Before Jax could say anything, Gare ripped an arrow right out of Jax's back. The entire world went dark, and the next thing he knew he was on Gare's back hurtling down the street, Ev keeping up right along side him. Jax realized she was taking care to keep her hand on his back, then realized the pain from his wounds had significantly subsided.

Jax lifted his head to see where they were going and Gare stopped.

"Hey, man, you back with us?" he asked.

"Yeah," Jax answered, and Gare let him drop to the ground.

"Thank goodness. Another mile or so, and you might have started getting heavy," Gare quipped.

"We can't stop now," Ev said, urging them forward, "the stables are just a little further down."

"Stables?" Jax stopped. "No! I'm not running away."

"Yes, we are," Ev retorted.

"No, we aren't! Father—"

"Told us to get to safety!" Ev yelled. "The last thing he told us was to live. Are you just going to ignore that?"

Jax didn't have a response. He knew his father had told him to protect Ev, but he had a duty to stay and fight. Even if it was a losing battle, he had to at least regroup with the rest of the Guard to prepare a counterstrike. If he ran, he'd never get a chance to get back at Dezeroth.

Gare put his hand on Jax's shoulder. "Jax, I get that you don't like running, but if your father told you to watch out for Ev, then you owe it to him to do that."

"...yeah," Jax agreed reluctantly, "I suppose you're right."

"Then come on!" shouted Ev, and the three of them made their way to the stables.

They arrived in time to see a large group of Light Guard mounting their steeds. Eighteen fully armored soldiers — all facing towards the city gates.

A new rage bubbled up inside of Jax at the sight of these cowards. If they'd fought back at the citadel, his father might still be alive right now! He rushed over to the woman in front and blocked her horse's path.

"What do you think you're doing?" he shouted, recognizing the woman as Captain Kelva, her white armor a full tier above the rest of those present.

"Step aside, cadet," Kelva commanded as she nudged her horse to sidestep Jax.

Jax was having none of it and blocked her path again.

Gare and Ev both ran up and tried to pull him aside. "Jax, now isn't the time for this," Gare started, but Jax pushed him away.

"It's the only time! These cowards are running away! If they had been at the citadel—"

"We were at the citadel," Kelva interrupted.

"Oh really, then what are you doing all the way out here?"

"Captain," another guard approached the group, "we're ready."

Kelva looked down at the trio. "We are protecting the Heart. The only ones I see running away are the three of you."

"We're not—" Jax began.

"As soldiers of the Light Guard, we have a duty to defend the Heart with our lives. If you want to make amends for your cowardice, mount a horse and ride with us."

"We...!" Jax blinked. "Wait, what?"

"There are still a few steeds in the stables. We need as many riders as we can muster. The more of us surrounding the one who carries the Heart, the more likely they will make it through the enemy lines surrounding the city."

"Whoa, whoa, whoa," Gare waved his hands. "You want us to ride with you just to be meat shields?"

"If you wish to fulfill your vow to protect the Heart as a servant of Lord Grandis," Kelva began, "then yes." She then looked at Jax with narrowed eyes. "And if you want to escape from the city, doing so will be your only chance."

Jax clenched his fist, but after glancing at his sister he looked back up at Kelva. "We'll ride with you for the honor of Lord Grandis." He placed his arm across his chest.

Gare and Ev did the same.

"Good," responded Kelva. "We ride immediately."

Jax started towards the nearest stable that was still occupied, but Kelva stopped him.

"Wait," she said, looking at Ev.

"What now?" Jax asked.

"That girl is not part of the Guard."

Before Jax could answer Ev stepped towards Kelva and pulled down on her tunic, revealing her mail. "Yes, I am," she said defiantly.

Kelva examined Ev. "And what exactly is your field of training?"

"I'm a cleric," Ev responded.

"And a damn good one at that," Gare added.

Kelva considered this information for a moment. "Alright then. You will ride next to the bearer of the Heart and heal her if she is injured. You two," she directed her attention to Jax and Gare, "will take up the left flank. Any objections?"

"No ma'am!" Gare said quickly.

Jax looked at Ev. He was happy enough with this arrangement. At the very least Ev would have a decent chance of making it to safety, and he'd prove to Kelva that he was no coward.

"No ma'am," he answered Kelva, then headed over to mount one of the few remaining horses.

Once the three of them were up and out amongst the rest of the Light Guard, Kelva raised her sword and fired a beam of light into the sky. Shortly after, a second light from the edge of the city followed hers up towards the stars.

"Remember! Above all else protect the center rider!" She pointed toward a female soldier Jax didn't recognize. "We must protect the Heart at absolutely all costs! Now, we ride!" Kelva shouted, tightening her reins and waving her arm forward.

Her horse took off, and the rest of the company followed suit. They headed straight towards the east gate of the city. Jax and Gare took up their positions on the left flank as Ev slid into the relative safety of the center.

The gate was shut upon approach, but Kelva didn't slow. As the group drew near, guards hoisted open the gate to reveal an army of undead and other fiends on the far side. The Light Guard charged through the gate and towards the enemy line waiting in the distance. As Jax passed through the gate, he felt a strange power welling up inside of him as he and everyone around him began to glow with a faint aura. He looked back to see spellcasters atop the city wall bestowing enchantments upon the group as they galloped beneath them.

Looking forward again, Jax watched as Captain Kelva pointed her sword at the enemy line. Two mages and a knight who had been flanking Kelva moved forward to the front of the charge.

The enemy unleashed a barrage of flame and arrows upon the group. The frontmost mages cast a spell on the knight's shield that formed a large barrier, deflecting the projectiles.

A stone's throw from the enemy forces, Kelva fired a powerful beam of light from her sword that pierced several rows of the enemy line. Not to be outdone, Jax raised his sword to do the same, along with every other paladin riding.

He unleashed a magical attack more powerful than any he ever had in his life, taking out two soldiers with one shot. Gare readied his ax as the line grew ever closer. Just before crashing into the enemy, the mages turned off their protective spell and conjured a wave of fire and lightning that blasted through the bulk of the enemy's formation.

The horses plowed over the fallen and into those that remained standing. One of the horses in front fell. The rest jumped over it. Arrows that had been blocked by the mages' barrier now connected with their targets. Another horse to the right whinnied and toppled. The rider in front of Jax was thrown off when a spear connected with her. Jax fired a blast at another spearman aiming to do the same to him and rode on.

At last, the company made it to the other side of the enemy line. Jax wasn't sure how many of them had fallen, but he knew they'd made it through just in time. Already, he could feel the enchantment wearing off him.

A surviving knight and mage at the back put up another protective barrier, which they held until they were in the clear.

Jax looked back at Marisol, the city he'd been raised in, now engulfed in flames. Dezeroth may have succeeded in taking both Jax's father and home from him, but he'd failed to capture the Heart, and now Jax was one of the few left to protect it. He would carry on his father's legacy and ensure the Heart was never used. He would protect it with his life, and one day, once the Heart was safe again, he'd find a way to kill Dezeroth permanently, ridding the world of his evil for good.

Chapter 2

Captain Kelva led the group down the highway stretching away from the city for half a mile before making an abrupt turn into the forest. During that time, Jax had taken stock of those around him. Down from eighteen to a mere twelve, there was he, Gare, Ev, Kelva, a cleric, two mages, two knights, two rangers, and a spellcaster. Depending on individual specializations, they could very well have all they needed for a strong party.

A cacophony of roars from the city warned them all that Dezeroth had learned of their escape. The horses wouldn't be able to outrun his dragons. They might be able to avoid detection in the forest, but they wouldn't be able to hide there forever.

"Where are we going?" Jax shouted up to Kelva.

Kelva called back, "There are caves to the northeast that stretch to the far side of the mountains and valleys beyond them where dragons cannot fly. They are our only chance of escaping Dezeroth's forces."

The group continued through the forest until they reached the edge of a clearing. Kelva held out her arm in a signal to stop. Jax could see the entrance to a large cavern a hundred yards out, and above it, the looming figure of a red dragon.

The dragon spotted them and roared. Two dozen soldiers dropped from around the dragon to block the mouth of the cave, with one erecting a dark barrier blocking the entrance and a second launching a blinding flash into the sky. The light prompted more roars to ring from the heavens.

"They knew we were coming!" shouted Gare.

The dragon opened its enormous jaws — a fiery glow emanating from its throat.

"Diana! Huxley!" shouted Kelva, motioning forward.

A knight and mage rushed forward. The knight raised her shield as the mage cast a spell and the dragon unleashed its breath. A powerful barrier erupted from Diana's shield, redirecting the dragon's fire around them and setting the forest aflame.

"Go! Now!" Kelva yelled as she charged towards the enemy.

The Light Guard took off after her. Gare looked to Jax, unsure if they should follow. Jax wasn't sure either, but they didn't exactly have much choice. That cave was their only hope of escape at this point, and... Ev had already joined in the charge!

Jax tightened his horse's reins and waved his arm forward. The horse bolted forwards out of the woods, Gare following close behind.

Kelva had already reached the line of foes blocking their path, engaging a bulky warrior in combat. An undead sorcerer launched an ominous purple orb at her, but the mage called Huxley intercepted it with a spell of his own, creating a blast that caused one of the horses to panic, throwing its rider to the ground. The rest of the Light Guard quickly overpowered the blockade, the rangers receiving enchantments from the unnamed mage and spellcaster that caused their arrows to pierce the enemies' armor and explode.

Eventually, Kelva made it to the barrier and forced her blade through it, allowing her to fire a beam of light at the sorcerer on the other side. As the sorcerer fell and the barrier faded, the dragon reared back again, preparing to scorch the entire battleground. Diana and Huxley quickly put up their protection spell just as Jax and Gare made it into its glow.

The dragon's fire incinerated everyone who hadn't made it into the barrier, including its allies. When the flames cleared, only eight Light Guard and three of Dezeroth's soldiers remained.

"Get to the caverns!" Kelva shouted as she finished off the bulky warrior blocking her path.

The group rushed towards the cave entrance. The dragon snapped at the tiny warriors as they passed under it, killing the cleric but receiving a beam of light in one of its eyes as a reward. The dragon screeched horribly and shook its head, giving the others an opening.

Jax urged his horse towards the cave. Between him and safety stood a single undead warrior, the other's attention focused on shooting at those who'd already made it into the cave. It would have been a simple enough matter to go around them....

Jax brandished his sword and nudged his steed in the direction of the soldier facing him. The warrior raised his spear and Jax fired a beam of light into the revenant's face, throwing it off balance. Jax took a free swipe at the soldier as he rode past. A loud clang to his side informed him that Gare had taken out the other. Jax didn't know if either of their attacks had resulted in a kill, but it was satisfying nonetheless.

His victory was short-lived, however, as a powerful swipe from the dragon's claws threw him clear from his steed just before he'd reached the safety of the cave, his sword flying off to his side.

Dazed, Jax looked up to the sight of the dragon's gaping maw rushing towards him. He closed his eyes as he felt the dragon's breath surround him, only to open them to the sound of a roar that caused the mountain itself to tremble.

An arrow had lodged itself firmly into one of the dragon's eyes, sending the beast into wild throws. A second later, the arrow exploded in a ball of lightning, and the dragon's scream forced Jax to cover his ears. In the cave, Diana held a bow aloft, and Gare was running towards him, having dismounted from his horse.

Gare pulled Jax to his feet, and Jax grabbed his sword as the two of them bolted towards the cave.

A loud crash signaled that the dragon had climbed down from atop the cavern entrance.

Jax looked back to see the enraged beast charging up its breath. He and Gare ran with all the speed they could muster to get behind Diana's shield before the flames overtook them.

They passed through the barrier just as the flames reached their heels, the magic shield holding back the inferno. When the flames settled, a clear line was left between the cool stone that had been protected and the molten stone that had suffered the dragon's wrath. The heated rock began to crack and shatter, and the roof came collapsing down. Jax and the others scrambled deeper into the cave away to safety.

Deep inside, Huxley held the darkness at bay with the light from his staff, while Ev frantically attempted to heal a female ranger cradled in Kelva's arms.

The glow from Ev's hand was nearly as bright as the light from Huxley's staff as she strained with all her might to repair the injury to the ranger's head. "It... it's not working...."

Another few moments passed with no sign of improvement, and Kelva grimaced. "That's enough. There's nothing more we can do."

Ev hesitated before pulling her hand away. "I... I'm sorry. I tried..."

Kelva shook her head. "Not even a Radiant can bring back the dead. You tended to her as soon as you were able, and that's all anyone could have done." She turned to Huxley and awkwardly flipped the ranger around in her arms, revealing a small pack on her back. "Remove the bag. Do not let the Heart fall from it. From now on you will be its bearer."

Huxley obliged, cautiously slipping the bag off of the ranger's shoulders and onto his. Once the transition was complete, Kelva gently laid the ranger onto the floor of the cave.

"Farewell, Dame Mesmine," murmured Kelva. "May the light guide your spirit to the peaks of Ars Summis."

Kelva stood up and looked around at the surviving soldiers. "Come. We are not safe yet."

Jax looked back the way they'd come. The path back was completely sealed off. The party would be protected from further pursuit for now, but with dragons at their command Dezeroth's forces would likely dig through in less than an hour.

"Move, cadet," commanded Kelva, addressing him. "We still have a long road ahead of us."

* * * *

The party made their way into a large wet cavern, leading their horses behind them. The floor was pockmarked with interconnected pools of water. Covering every inch of the cave floor was a furry reddish-brown moss, stiff and crunchy underneath Jax's boots. Throughout the cavern were large, prickly plant-like structures that Kelva instructed the group to stay away from. The sound of running water in the distance grew steadily louder as the group ventured ever deeper into the caves.

Wondering what their end goal was, Jax decided it would be best to simply ask. "So, Captain, where exactly are we headed?"

Kelva turned and looked at Jax, Ev, and Gare. The rest of the group stopped. "We are taking the Heart to Roehelm. Where were you headed when we encountered you at the stables?"

"We weren't... we were just trying to get my sister to safety," Jax answered.

"So you admit you were running away." Kelva's eyes narrowed.

"No! I... my father..." Jax stammered.

Kelva raised an eyebrow. "Your father?"

Jax didn't want to say anymore. Honoring his father's wishes was still no excuse for cowardice.

"Father ordered Jax to protect me," Ev offered.

Jax glared at her.

Ev continued. "It was the last thing he told him before..."

"Before Dezeroth killed him," Jax finished for her, now glaring at Kelva.

Kelva's gaze softened, but only slightly. "And just who was your father?"

"Ronan Ruthoree, of the Shield," Jax answered.

"Ronan...." The sternness in Kelva's eyes dissipated. "So you're his children."

Jax and Ev nodded. "Yes ma'am. I'm Jax, and this is Eveline."

"And I'm Garrison, Garrison Hue."

"So Martin's son, then," Kelva said.

"Yeah," confirmed Gare. "You know him?"

"Of course. He's provided the Light Guard with equipment for years. And Ronan, he served under Treston, yes?"

"That's right," Jax answered. "He was Sir Treston's lieutenant."

"In that case, he should have been with the last line of defenders at the citadel."

"He was," Jax said, irritated that Kelva would imply otherwise.

"I didn't say he wasn't," Kelva replied. "I still wonder where you were during the attack, however."

Jax's face grew hot.

Gare stepped in. "Captain, Jax—"

Kelva held up a hand and shook her head. "It doesn't matter." She glanced over at the few remaining members of the Light Guard. "It doesn't matter where any of you were or what you were doing. Dezeroth's forces were too strong. Even if you had fought in the citadel itself, it wouldn't have gained us more than a few seconds." Kelva looked back at Jax. "Ronan was right to tell you to flee."

Jax was starting to dislike Kelva. It's not like she was in any place to talk about fleeing.

"What about you?" he asked. "Where were you when Dezeroth attacked?"

"Unconscious," she replied.

Jax didn't know whether he was impressed or disgusted with how quick she was to give that answer.

"You mean like, sleeping?" asked Gare.

Kelva ignored him. "I took a blow to the head from a dragon when the first wave of fighters struck. I came to being carried by Diana through the tunnels. Apparently Treston had given the order to evacuate the Heart while I was out."

"Tunnels?" Gare seemed as confused as Jax was. "What tunnels?"

"The evacuation tunnels, of course," Kelva answered. "You must also be a cadet if you didn't know that, despite your armor."

"Yeah," Gare replied, rubbing the back of his head, "my pops bought this for me back when I joined the Guard."

Kelva didn't seem interested. "Well, since you're part of our little band now, I suppose introductions are in order. You already know who I am."

Jax and the others nodded.

Kelva pointed to the bulky dark-skinned woman with the shield. "That's Dame Diana Erwood," she said, informing Jax of what he'd already deduced. "She specializes in defensive light magic," Kelva added before pointing at Huxley, who Jax just now realized was actually rather aged. "That's Sir Huxley Farrow. He's a master of lightning and protection spells."

"Howdy," piped Huxley, waving, and surprising Jax with his joviality.

Kelva continued, "And now that that's out of the way, we need to keep moving. I want to be out of these caves as soon as possible."

The party continued on in near silence for what seemed like hours, sloshing through shallow pools and avoiding the large plants, which Jax swore twitched from time to time. The mossy caverns gave way to great underground lakes fed by streams pouring in from above. Jax spotted something large lurking beneath the waters. It was too dark to make out the shape, even with Huxley's light, but Jax was quite content staying high up on the shore and well away from whatever it was. Dragons might be fearsome, but he'd take a dozen oversized lizards before facing off against giant underwater monstrosities.

Past the lakes were miles of long, drier tunnels. Twice in the tunnels their band was attacked by cave golems — living piles of rock held together by moss. Neither encounter was particularly memorable. The beasts were dumb and slow — the only reason they had to fight at all was because they blocked some of the narrower passages. Even to cadets like Jax and Gare they were hardly a threat and would fall apart simply by cutting or burning through the moss holding them together. Jax took advantage of the skirmishes to hone his magic skills, choosing to fight with light over his sword, not that the battles lasted long anyway. The scuffles did take some effort though, and by the time the group arrived at an eerily iridescent pool they were ready for a rest.

"Huxley," Kelva asked, "do you know if this water is safe to drink?"

"Hmm..." Huxley tapped his staff on the ground. "Well, if I remember correctly it is, but just to be safe I'd recommend drinking from one of the streams flowing into it."

"Right. Everyone, make sure your horses get some water, then take a break downstream if you need it. Be quick about it, though, we're moving again in fifteen minutes."

Gare scratched his head. "Why does it matter where we take a break?"

"Gare," said Jax, "what have you been asking to do for the last hour?"

"Oh. Yeah, that makes sense. Hey, do you mind watering my horse for me?" Gare offered his horse's reins over to Jax.

"You water your horse," Jax answered, taking his own horse's reins and walking away.

"Nah man, you got this," Gare said as he draped his reins over Jax's shoulder.

"Gare, I said—"

"Going now, talk later."

Gare hurried off back the way they'd come. Jax sighed and took both horses to the nearest stream, then took a drink from it himself.

A minute later Gare came clomping back. "Thanks bud, you're a pal."

"You seriously couldn't have waited thirty seconds?"

"What? Are you saying you wanted to go with me?" Gare asked with an obnoxious smile.

Jax rolled his eyes. "Here, you watch the horses now. They seem to be about done anyway."

Gare took the reins and Jax went off to do his business. When he got back, he spotted Ev and Gare both over by Huxley. Intrigued, he opted to join them.

"What's going on?" he asked.

"Gare wants to see the Heart," Ev stated, a tone of exasperation in her voice.

"Why is that so much to ask?" Gare complained. "We've sworn ourselves to protecting the thing. We should at least get to see what it looks like."

Huxley smiled and shook his head. "Sorry kid, but it's just not safe to take it out. Maybe you'll get a chance once things have settled down again."

"What do ya mean, 'not safe?'" Gare asked. "It's just a big rock! It can't do anything unless someone takes it to that Altar place."

Huxley leaned back against the wall of the cave, pressing the bag with the Heart against it. "True, true... except, not entirely. There is one thing the Heart can do if we take it out," Huxley teased while wagging his finger, "and that's disappear."

Gare looked around the room before turning back to Huxley. "Yeah, with all due respect, I don't think we've got much danger of losing it in here."

Huxley laughed. "It's not about misplacing it, Mr. Hue, it's about the rules of the Heart. Unless it's in the constant possession of a nepac or, lords forbid, its rightful owner, it will vanish and return to the place where it was split from its Divine. For this Heart, that place is the citadel."

"But I'm not asking to throw it away," Gare complained. "I just want to see it! We'd still have it. And since when has that been a rule about the Heart anyway?"

Ev answered for Huxley. "It's always been a rule, Gare. The Masters willed it so when they created the world. If a Heart isn't near its Divine, it must be held or it disappears. You'd know this if you ever studied the scriptures."

"Bah, the only books worth reading are the ones you need to study to get into the Guard," Gare retorted, "and that doesn't change the fact that we'd still be in possession of Heart."

Huxley shook his head again. "Sorry, Mr. Hue, but we can't risk it. Just dropping it on the ground counts as losing possession. If you want something else to entertain you while we wait, though, it looks like Dame Diana's found something of interest over there."

Jax followed Huxley's gaze and spotted Diana crouched over some odd rocks, having taken off her gauntlets to feel them with her bare hands.

"Uh, no thanks," said Gare. "I'm... just gonna go sit by the horses."

Huxley shrugged as Gare clomped off. Ev looked like she was bothered by the whole thing, and Jax figured it would be best to follow Gare to make sure he didn't cause any trouble.

"Hey," Jax offered once they were away from everyone else as he leaned against the wall, "what's going on with you? Why are you so obsessed with seeing the Heart anyway?"

"I'm not obsessed," Gare protested. "I just think it's not fair that they never let us see the thing back at the citadel, and now that we're actually in charge of it we still don't get to see it!"

"Most people aren't allowed to see it," Jax reminded him.

"Yeah, but we're the ones keeping it safe from Dezeroth. Don't you want to at least see what it is we're protecting?"

Jax had to admit he was curious, but he wasn't about to tell Gare that. "It doesn't matter what I want. We can't do anything that has even the slightest chance of allowing Dezeroth to get the Heart. Do you want him to restore the Dark Radiant to power?"

"Ya know, that's something I don't get," said Gare, resting his arm on one of the horses. "Why would he want to bring back the Dark Radiant?"

"For power, obviously. The Dark Radiant was the only being powerful enough to match Lord Grandis. If Dezeroth gains him as an ally, then no one will be able to stop them."

"I guess so," shrugged Gare, "but if Lord Grandis is split, then won't Apollyon destroy the world? That seems like a pretty bad plan to me."

"Well, maybe destroying the world is what he wants, have you thought of that?" Jax said. "Dezeroth is pure evil, and the Dark Radiant is said to have been even worse."

"I dunno.... I mean, I know Dezeroth is bad and all, but I have a hard time believing he'd want to do something that would kill him, too."

Jax stood up and took a step away from the wall. "Does it even matter what he wants it for? Whatever it is, it's bad, and it's up to us to stop him. And I don't want to talk about Dezeroth anymore."

"Wow, sorry man. I didn't mean to upset you."

Jax shrugged and looked away. "It's alright. I just don't want to think about any of that right now."

"Hey, I get you. And no worries. Once Lord Grandis finds out what happened, he'll fix everything."

Jax grunted an acknowledgment. He had no doubt that Lord Grandis would be able to handle Dezeroth and his army, but not even Grandis had the power to bring back the dead.

For the next few minutes he stood there with Gare, watching the ripples glide across the glowing pool nearby and observing the others. Huxley had joined Diana in looking at weird cave formations. Ev had gone off on her own away from the rest of the group, probably needing some time to herself, which Jax understood completely. Kelva stood on the opposite end of the cavern, glancing around at the connected tunnels. Eventually, she headed back towards the center and called everyone to her.

"Alright, break's over. I know that wasn't much of a rest, but we don't want to be in these caves any longer than necessary. If Dezeroth sends shades in after us, we won't stand a chance."

Everyone grabbed the reins of their respective horses as Kelva led them away from the luminous pool and back into the dark tunnels. The next few hours were a continuation from what they'd traveled through before. A few more encounters with golems, a lot more water, and several miles of crunching over stiff moss. When at last the group found their way out of the caves, it was already nightfall again.

"Great," said Gare, "we're finally out of the hole in the ground and it's still dark."

The caverns opened up into a forest. Hurricane winds tore through the valley overhead. Down in the forest, these winds were little more than a breeze, but the gale offered the group protection from pursuit by dragons and whatever other flying beasts Dezeroth may have had in his army.

Kelva led the group a short ways into the woods where they set up camp, not that there was much of a camp to set up. Kelva made it clear that they were not to have any fires, and they had no equipment for tents or even mats to speak of. They put together beds of leaves to provide a small barrier between themselves and the ground, but it hardly offered any comfort from the cold of the soil. Once the beds were in place and the horses were tied, Kelva set up a guard schedule. She and Ev would take the first shift, then Gare and Huxley, and Jax would stand with Diana for the third.

That settled, Jax pushed his little bed of leaves up against the trunk of a tree in an attempt to use its roots as a pillow. Gare made his bed on an adjacent side of the same tree. Ev put together hers on the far side of the camp, close to Kelva.

"Hey, bud," Gare whispered after they both lay down, "I know it's none of my business, but do you think maybe you should go talk to Ev?"

"About what?" Jax asked, though he already knew exactly about what.

"Well, you know. I mean, she didn't see it when... but it's still gotta be hard on her."

"I don't think she wants to talk about that, Gare," he replied flatly.

"Are you sure? I mean, you're kind of all she's got left—"

"Look, just drop it, okay?" Jax said as he rolled over to face the other way, not wanting Gare to see the tears building in his eyes.

Gare didn't say anymore for a minute, then, "Do you want to talk about it?"

Jax lay quietly for a moment before answering. "I just want to get some sleep."

There was a pause, then Jax heard Gare shift around on his pile of leaves, and after that there was only the sound of the wind rushing above.

After everything that had happened, Jax wasn't counting on getting any sleep. The exhaustion from the day's events had other plans, however, and despite the thoughts plaguing him of how he'd failed his father, he soon fell deep into slumber.

Chapter 3

A large hand jostled Jax awake. He opened his eyes to just barely make out Gare standing over him, his neck aching from sleeping on roots all night.

Gare reached out to Jax and helped him up. "Alright bud, your turn," he said. "You ready?"

Jax rubbed his neck and stretched his head to the side, trying to work out the cramp he'd gotten. "Yeah," he answered. "Do yourself a favor and find something soft to sleep on."

"Too late, man," Gare grinned. "I slept on a rock during first shift, and that thing was a perfect fit for my head."

Jax let a small smile slip out. "Yeah, well, I guess a hard head like yours would feel right at home on a rock, wouldn't it?"

"Ha! You know it! Anyway, I'm going to catch some more shuteye." Gare patted Jax on the back and slipped around to the other side of Jax's tree where he plopped down.

Jax shook his head, then headed over to where Diana was standing. "So, how do you want to do this?" he asked quietly.

Standing a foot above him, she looked down at Jax with a smile. "Where one is blind, the other sees."

"Uh... ok?" Jax replied.

Diana chuckled and pointed to the opposite side of the camp. "Stand over there and watch my back, and I'll watch yours."

"Oh, right, sure," said Jax before heading off. He still wasn't all the way awake yet, and cryptic answers weren't what he needed right now.

The job of standing guard soon proved to be more tense than he'd imagined it would be. The endless hurricane raging above them, the steady rustling of leaves, the sound of branches rubbing together — all worked together to create a note-less melody that would have been soothing, except it made it impossible to hear if anyone was sneaking up on them. Adding to that, the lack of light invited a darkness as deep as that cave's to creep in around the edges of the campsite. Jax could barely even make out Diana's figure on the far side of the camp. If anyone was sneaking up on them, they wouldn't know it until they were already under attack.

A flash of movement in the corner of Jax's eye set him on high alert. He peered out into the woods where he was sure he'd seen a shadow dash between the trees. He strained his ears to listen, but the only sound he could hear was that of the wind.

He placed his hand on the hilt of his sword and took one step into the woods, watching intently for anything out of the ordinary.

...Nothing. A good fifteen minutes must have passed before Jax felt the tension easing out of him. Whatever he'd seen must have been his imagination.

Another hour or so went by without incident when Jax noticed Diana spin around, an arrow nocked in her bow.

Jax tensed up again; his hand went back to his sword as he moved closer to the center of the camp to better observe the perimeter. Suddenly, Jax heard the sound of a scuffle punctuated by strange growls off in the woods.

Diana marched over to the edge of the camp nearest the sound, and Jax joined her. "Should we check it out?" he asked.

"No," answered Diana. "A rash move welcomes traps."

The growls escalated into roars and shrieks, waking the others.

Kelva jumped up and hurried over to Jax and Diana. "What's going on?"

"Unknown," Diana answered as the rest of the camp joined them in gazing out into the woods.

The beast causing the commotion let out a final scream and fell silent. Seconds passed and no further sound came from the forest.

Kelva drew her sword. "Stay here and guard the Heart," she instructed, stepping out into the trees.

"Wait," Jax said.

Kelva turned.

"This was my shift. Let me come, too. I can watch your back."

Kelva gestured with her head for Jax to accompany her, and the two of them headed in the direction of their mystery monster.

Not even fifty yards from the campsite, they found what had been causing the commotion. Three large figures each as big as Gare lay sprawled out on the forest floor. At first Jax couldn't tell if they were dead or even what they were, but then Kelva used her sword to illuminate the area.

The creatures were covered in a mixture of silky fur and scales, and seemed to blend into the ground almost as if they were invisible. As for whatever uncertainty there had been as to their being alive, that was cleared up as soon as the light hit them. One of the furry lizards had been thoroughly gutted. The other two were bleeding profusely from their necks. As nice as it was to know that these monstrosities didn't pose any threat, that didn't do anything to alleviate the bigger issue.

"What do you think did this?" Jax asked Kelva.

Kelva stooped over to the ground and placed her fingers in a puddle of inky black liquid near one of the carcasses. She then raised her fingers in front of her eyes and rubbed them together, causing a dark wisp to rise up off of them.

"Shades," she answered.

"Shades? You mean like 'shadow people' shades?"

"That's exactly what I mean," Kelva answered, standing up and looking around. "If we've been followed by shades, we need to get moving immediately. Dragons might not be able to fly in these mountains, but Dezeroth will send other forces after us the moment he learns where we are."

She turned, and Jax followed her back to the camp. "Breaks over, everyone," she announced as soon as they got there. "Mount your horses. We ride immediately."

* * * *

The group exited the forest and stumbled upon an old road running through the center of the valley. The morning sun illuminated the clouds above but had yet to peak up over the mountaintops. Beyond the cover of the trees, the wind was much stronger, though still nothing compared to the howling gusts high overhead. The party settled into a steady trot up the path to the east, following the road before them.

"You know we can go faster than this, right?" Gare shouted over the wind. "Aren't we kind of in a hurry?"

"If we work the horses too hard we'll have to break more often," Kelva answered. "We'll make the best distance at this pace."

Gare didn't look convinced, but he didn't press the issue further.

As the day wore on, the sun eventually overcame the crest of the mountains, bathing Jax in its light for the first time in what felt like days. The warmth was more than welcome.

The relief was short-lived, however. Soon after reuniting with the light Jax was torn from it once again when the road split into two paths. The first rose up to very near the top of the mountain before curving back down out of sight. The other dipped down into a narrow, muddy crevasse. Naturally, they took the shaded path.

"Okay," said Gare as soon as they left the sun, "I get the 'don't make the horses tired' thing, but is there a reason we're going down gloomy gulch instead of the open road?"

"Let it go, Gare," Jax responded. "Huxley just said this is the best way."

"No," Gare retorted, "he said we should go this way. He never said anything about it being the best way."

Jax rolled his eyes. "Don't you think that if he said we should go this way then it's probably the best way?"

"Why? Why is this the best way? It's barely even a road!"

Huxley overheard the conversation and called back to them. "Well, if you'd rather go the upper path then be my guest. You'd be able to make it to the far side of the mountains days before we would."

"Then why the heck are we going this way if the other way is faster?" asked Gare.

Huxley smirked. "Well, personally, I'd prefer to ride on the back of my horse to Roehelm rather than in the belly of a roc."

Gare was thoroughly confused. "What the heck are you talking about? How is a rock going to eat someone? They don't even move!"

Ev, who'd been quiet up until then, decided to help Gare out. "Not a rock,

Gare, a roc. It's a giant bird the size of the citadel."

"Yeah, right," replied Gare. "Have you been listening to that wind up there? There's no way any birds are flapping around out here."

Huxley spoke up again, raising his hands exaggeratedly as he spoke. "Oh, it's true, the gusts that blow through these valleys prevent most any creature of the air from entering them, but the might of the roc exceeds even that. It soars high above the clouds as King of Land and Sky. The wind from a single flap of its wings can topple the mightiest of trees. Its talons can crush boulders; its beak can cut through steel like paper, not that any of us would have to worry about that, seeing as it could swallow each and every one of us whole and have our horses for dessert! Stories say it doesn't often enter the valleys, but it's more than happy to snatch up any unwary travelers foolish enough to venture up to the mountain peaks."

As Huxley finished speaking, it was as if the mountains themselves had heard their conversation, for just as they turned another corner they stumbled upon a single feather wedged between a rock and the side of the gully. Actually, "feather" did not do justice to what they saw before them. The quill was as thick as Jax's leg; the vane nearly twice as wide as he was tall; and the entire thing must have stretched over forty feet in length. Jax and Gare stared in awe of the massive piece of plumage. The rest of the guard seemed equally impressed.

"Haha! You see?" said Huxley, turning to Gare with a smile. "Still interested in taking the other path?"

Gare closed his open mouth and silently shook his head "no." Jax also was more than happy to spend a little extra time slogging through the mud if it meant less chance of encountering anything as big as what would have left behind that feather. Travel through the ravine was slow, though. The road had long been washed away, leaving great patches of sticky mud behind that they had trouble getting the horses through. In the time it took for them to make it from one end to the other, the sun had made a similar journey, going from the eastern sky to the west.

Covered in mud from the hips down, the group pulled their horses up a steep incline at the far end of the gully and back onto dry road. After coming across the roc feather, Jax wasn't particularly comfortable being back out in the open, but at least they were still down in the trough of the valley. Hopefully now that they were out of that muddy pit, they'd find something to eat soon, too. Jax hadn't had food in nearly two days, and he was starting to feel it.

His prayers were soon answered, as a short ways down from where they exited the ravine they stumbled across the carcasses of a pair of large beasts amongst some dead trees not far from the road. The monsters, which looked to be a an ugly cross between a toad and a dragon, seemed to have been freshly killed — the blood still dripping from their wounds. Most of the blood was coming from the creatures' necks, but their faces and hands were also bleeding. On closer inspection, Jax noticed that the eyes, teeth, and claws had been removed from the corpses.

"Hunters," was all Kelva said.

"Hunters?" asked Jax, though he supposed that was the logical conclusion. "What hunter would be crazy enough to come all the way out here?"

"Certain monster parts can fetch a high price on the right market," Kelva answered. "Back before they disappeared, Divine often hunted in these valleys, occasionally alongside nepacs. I wouldn't be surprised if some have continued hunting without them."

Diana saddled up alongside them. "Truly awful," she said. "I hate seeing such pointless slaughter."

"Good riddance," Ev piped from behind.

Diana turned around. "How can a cleric say such things. These creatures were created by the Masters themselves."

"They were created for Divine to slay so they could grow stronger," Ev countered. "With the Divine gone, they serve no purpose; they just run around bringing devastation to the natural world."

"A monster, a beast, a bird or a tree, what makes any of these things different from one another?" asked Diana.

"Monsters are revived every new moon while the rest stay dead, that's what's different!" Ev retorted.

Jax figured it would probably be a good idea to step in at that point. As tempting as it was to remind Ev that nepacs could also grow stronger fighting monsters, this wasn't an argument they needed to pursue. "Yes, Ev, we all know monsters are a big problem, but that's not something we need to concern ourselves with now."

"Agreed," said Kelva, speaking up before Ev could further protest. "What's important is that we now know there are others out here. We should remain vigilant as we move forward. They may very well be opportunists who would see our horses and equipment as a quick ticket to wealth if they could take them from us."

Gare joined in as well. "Yeah, but at least we can finally eat something. Looks like they left all the good stuff for us!"

Huxley laughed. "Hate to disappoint you, Mr. Hue, but beaded zilas are toxic through and through. Your first bite of that meat may well be your last."

"Oh, come on, seriously?" responded Gare. "We haven't eaten in over a day!"

"Well, sorry kiddo, but..."

Huxley trailed off, distracted by the sound of an animal's squeals coming from the direction they were heading.

"Looks like we might run into our hunters sooner than I expected," Kelva stated. She pointed her mount in the direction of the noise and started off.

Jax pushed his horse to follow her and called out. "Wait, I thought we wanted to avoid the hunters."

Kelva looked back. "Do you see another road to take that would let us do that?"

Jax didn't. The sides of the valley were steep and rocky, even where trees were growing, which meant the road they were on was really the only path their horses could travel.

Following a short distance from Kelva, he rounded the corner and arrived just in time to see a black haired woman drive a dagger into the neck of a downed beast that was cross between a bear and a wild boar. She had a small bow and quiver on her back, but there wasn't any sign that she'd used them to take down her quarry. The woman looked up at the group of soldiers approaching her and casually wiped her blade on the beast's fur.

"Well, well, well," the woman called as they drew near. "Isn't this an unusual sight. What brings a small band of knights into these valleys, hmm?"

Kelva spoke for the group. "Are you the one who killed those beaded zilas back there?" she asked, gesturing back the way they'd come.

"Sure am. Name's Birdie, and there isn't a monster in all of Doxla that's a match for me," the woman answered, flipping her dagger up into the air and catching it.

"You're kidding," stated Gare. "You killed both those monsters."

Birdie raised her eyebrow, looked at her blade, then the dead beast beside her, then back at Gare with a smirk. "Nah, you're right. I was just wandering through the mountains when I tripped and fell on this big dead animal."

Kelva spoke up before Gare could say any more. "I think what he's trying to ask is if there is anyone else out here with you."

Birdie pointed her dagger back over her shoulder towards a horse a fair distance away. "Well, there's old Meathead over there."

"And what about other humans?" Kelva pressed.

Birdie placed her dagger back in its sheath. "You're the first humans I've seen out here in a long time," she answered. "Which, now that I think about it, has me wondering what you're doing here. Not hunting, I'm sure."

"No, not hunting," Kelva replied, "but our purpose is not of your concern."

"Mm, maybe not," said Birdie, head cocked, "but we can make it my concern."

Kelva sat up straight and looked Birdie in the eye. "I think it would be wise of you not to get involved with our affairs."

"And I think it would be wise of you to take someone who knows about these mountains with you. If you make it worth my while I can guide you. What do you say to eight hundred a day?"

"Eight hundred?" Jax exclaimed, interrupting. "Gold? You're insane! No one would pay that kind of money for a guide!"

"We aren't paying anything for a guide," Kelva stated before turning her attention back to Birdie. "While we appreciate the offer, we are more than capable of taking care of ourselves, thank you."

"That so?" said Birdie. "Because it looks to me like you don't have any supplies whatsoever. No food, water, equipment — and the closest town is more than a day away. I'd say you've got a pretty rough road ahead of you."

"We'll manage," said Kelva as she turned her horse away from the hunter.

"Wait," said Birdie.

Kelva looked back, though she didn't look happy about it.

"Tell ya what. You could probably do with some food, right? Well, I could make use of that ax." Birdie pointed at Gare.

Kelva eyed Gare's ax as if she was considering Birdie's proposal. Gare noticed.

"No way," he said. "She's not getting my ax."

"Pfft, I don't want your ax." Birdie pointed at the dead bugboar. "I want you to help me chop this thing up. Do that, and you can take as much of the meat with you as you want. It'd go bad before I got back home anyway."

Jax was still hungry, and he didn't wait for Kelva to answer. "That sounds like a pretty good offer, actually. Captain?"

Kelva also seemed interested, albeit reluctantly so. "Very well. Mr. Hue, help her carve up her beast."

"Seriously?" he asked, but Kelva gestured with her head, and he dismounted his horse and approached Birdie. "Alright," he sighed, "what do you want me to do?"

"Chop off its head for me," Birdie gestured with her dagger.

"Why do you want to chop off its head?"

"Because it takes a while to saw off the tusks, and I'd rather not do that out in the open."

"Wouldn't it be easier for me to just chop off the tusks?" Gare asked.

"Oh, sure, it would be easier, but then we'd risk breaking them, which would make them worthless."

Gare eyed Birdie for a moment, then grunted and started hacking at the bugboar's neck. It took several swings before its body was finally separated from its head.

"Perfect!" Birdie exclaimed as she bent down and quickly sliced off the beast's claws with her dagger. In less than a minute she'd scooped all of the bloody nails into a bag and hefted the bugboar's head up over her shoulder, holding it by one of its tusks.

"Right then, the rest of the bugboar is all yours. En-joy!" She turned and strolled off back towards her horse.

Jax hopped off his own mount as he watched Birdie climb atop hers. He headed over to the bugboar to help Gare clean it, but the two of them quickly realized they had no idea what they were doing.

"What are you waiting for?" Kelva asked. "That woman was right about one thing. We shouldn't stay out in the open with a large carcass like this."

"Right," said Jax, and he swung his sword hard in an attempt to cut off one of the beasts legs.

The blade dug in deep, but stuck in the bone. Jax yanked it back out and Gare pulled Jax back.

"Hey bud, just leave this to me."

Gare wound up and struck the beast's leg with tremendous force. There was a loud crack as the ax snapped the bone. Gare grinned, then prepared to swing again before Huxley halted him.

"Stop," he said, joining them on the ground. "Lords, just, stop."

"What wrong?" Jax asked.

"Oh, nothing, it's just... you two have clearly never cleaned any game before. Let me show you how it's done before you butcher the whole thing. Mr. Ruthoree, may I borrow your sword?"

Jax reluctantly handed over his blade and Huxley went straight to work slicing off strips of meat. He handed the meat to Jax and Gare as he worked until they were both holding about as much as they could carry in their arms.

"There," he said, "that should be plenty for now. Sorry for not letting you boys join in, but like the Captain said we probably want to hurry."

Jax looked down at the big beast. Most of the animal was still there. It almost seemed like a waste to leave so much of it behind, but they didn't have any way to keep the meat fresh, or even carry it, really, so he didn't oppose moving on.

Jax brought the meat back to his horse and climbed back on, placing the bloody chunks between his legs on the saddle.

"Alright," said Kelva, "now that we have food, let's keep an eye out for any caves we can camp in. Even nonpoisonous monster meat isn't safe to eat uncooked, and we'll need to keep any fires we make hidden."

Jax hadn't seen any caves since the one that they'd left. He was also hungry, and wasn't too keen on the thought of them not eating because they couldn't build a fire. He noticed Birdie hadn't traveled too far from them yet — just barely into the woods a tad further down the road. "Do you think that hunter would know of a good spot?" he asked.

"I'd rather not have her involved any further than she's already been," Kelva replied.

Huxley seemed to be thinking along the same lines as Jax. "With all respect, Captain, night will soon be upon us, and it has been years since I last traveled these mountains. Surely it wouldn't hurt to at least ask."

Kelva looked up at where the sun had just gone back down behind the mountains, then back towards the road they had yet to travel. "Very well. We can ask for her help, but I will not allow her to accompany us as a guide."

"I'll go ask her," Jax offered.

"Fine," said Kelva. "Just be clear that we don't need a guide. We'll be on up ahead so that we aren't just standing around exposed."

Jax rode his horse over to where Birdie was busy sawing through the bugboar's tusks. She looked up at Jax's approach.

"Well, well," she said. "Changed your mind about my offer?"

"Not exactly," Jax answered. "We were just wondering if you knew of any nearby caves where we could camp for the night."

"That so?" Birdie stood up and sheathed her dagger. "Funny, that sounds almost exactly like the kind of help I just offered you, only..." Birdie tapped on her chin in mock thought, "oh yeah... free."

"Look," said Jax, "I'm not asking you to take the time to help us through the mountains. I'm just asking if you know a place where we could set up camp."

"Alright, fine. You want a cave to camp in? There's one behind a waterfall about thirty minutes ride that way," she pointed in the direction they were already headed. "Just follow the third stream you come across up for a ways and you can't miss it."

Jax had trouble believing she'd give him an answer so quickly without a price attached to it. "So there's a cave three streams down. What's the catch?"

"Catch? There's no catch. I just figured I might as well do you a favor since, without me, you're basically a dead man walking."

Jax decided he might not be very fond of Birdie. "Listen you, I'm a paladin of the Maristol Light Guard, and I'm more than capable of taking care of myself."

"Oh, I'm sure you think that, but there are places in these mountains that you guys simply aren't prepared to travel through. If you try, you will die, and that path you're on right now will take you straight into one of those places."

"Yeah, well thanks for your concern, but I think we'll take our chances." Jax turned his horse to head back to the others.

Birdie called out after him. "I'm serious kid. Unless you've got someone on your team whose skilled in ice magic or perception techniques you won't make it past the Slime Pits. You need my help!"

Jax almost turned back again to argue more, but decided it wasn't worth his time. He returned to Kelva and the others and told them what Birdie had told him.

"We'll check it out," Kelva said, referring to the cave. "If there's anything suspicious we'll move on further. Otherwise we'll stay there for the night."

Half an hour later, the party located the cave, exactly where Birdie had said it would be. Everything seemed fine, so the group went to work setting up a fire with hot stones to cook the meat. With full stomachs and a safe place to spend the night, a guard schedule was set up. Once bedding was brought in from the outside, the group settled down for the night.

Birdie's warning about the slime pit bothered Jax, but not enough to keep him from sleeping. Even if she wasn't saying things just to scare him, whatever dangers lay ahead of them couldn't be as bad as what they'd already overcome. What was more concerning to Jax was Ev's behavior. Just like the night before, she'd made her bed on the side of the cave opposite him, and he was starting to think maybe Gare was right about needing to talk to her. It wasn't a conversation he wanted to have in front of the others, though, so he'd have to wait until tomorrow. Hopefully, something would come up that would give him the chance he needed.

Chapter 4

Morning came, and despite Birdie's warnings Jax was feeling much more relaxed than he had at anytime since this journey had begun. With no further midnight occurrences or signs of Dezeroth's forces, it seemed they were safe for the time being. The first few hours saw the terrain as essentially the same it had been the day before — green grass, forests scattered here and there along the road, and far too few monsters for Jax's taste. Most of the ones he did see were off the beaten path, and Kelva just had the group gallop past to avoid confrontation. Eventually, though, Jax got the encounter he was looking for.

While the party passed through a particularly dense grove of trees, a horde of shark-toothed furballs ambushed the party from all directions. The little monstrosities were no larger than cats, and despite the ferocious front they put forth they hesitated to get close to the stamping horses.

Still, it was all the excuse Jax needed to let loose with his light magic. He was pleasantly surprised to see a single blast was sufficient to fell one of the creatures. He fired again and again, and though his energy wained towards the end, he could also feel his skill slowly improving. Each blast was slightly stronger than the last, and by the time the surviving critters decided to flee, he was quite satisfied with his little workout. His left arm felt as if it had been shoved in a bag of icy needles, sure, but in every other way he felt great.

Once the road was clear again, Ev healed the few injuries that the horses had sustained and the group was back on their way again. After another hour or so of boring travel, the landscape started to change. Trees became scarce, and the ground became barren. The slopes of the valleys were much steeper and rockier, and patches of sticky yellow goo were splattered across the trail at irregular intervals. The wind that blew towards them was hot and wet and smelled strongly of sulfur, and Jax had a sinking feeling about where they were going.

Huxley waved his hand in front of his face. "Pew! We must be getting close to the Slime Pits."

That was what Jax was afraid of. "So, this slime place, you've traveled through it before, right?"

Huxley shook his head. "Oh, lords no. I've never traveled this deep into the mountains before. It's much safer to stick to the greener areas."

Not a comforting answer. "Are you saying it's dangerous to go in there."

Kelva answered for Huxley. "This entire mountain range is dangerous, but we are soldiers of Grandis. We are equipped to take on any obstacle we face."

As inspiring as Kelva may have meant to be, she wasn't making Jax feel any better about continuing forward. "So what obstacles will we face in these Slime Pits."

"Honestly, I only know the tales that have been told," Huxley answered, going into theatrical hands mode again. "Boiling lakes of yellow ooze, eruptions of scalding slime from cracks in the mountain, the dreaded snot wyrm...!"

"Snot wyrm?" chuckled Gare. "What? Is it supposed to climb up your nose or something?"

Huxley laughed. "Not a worm, my boy. A wyrm!"

Gare just stared.

Ev sighed and rolled her eyes. "He means a giant, wingless, snake-like dragon," she said as if it was common knowledge.

Gare harrumphed. "Big deal. It's still got 'snot' in its name. How bad can it be?"

"It is not a foe to be mocked, Mr. Hue," answered Huxley, his tone shifting to dark and ominous. "The snot wyrm may not have the most impressive moniker, but in the old days countless Divine were split by it. Only those who had ascended to Radiance could stand against it of their own power."

Jax stopped his horse, causing the others to stop as well. "Wait a minute. You're telling me there's a monster in there as strong as a Radiant, and we're just going to try and waltz right past it?"

"Of course not," said Huxley, waving his hand dismissively. "The snot wyrm is said to reside at the bottom of the deepest slime pool. As long as we avoid approaching any large bodies of goopy glop, we shouldn't have anything to worry about."

"I don't know," Jax responded. He didn't want to sound like a coward but... "I heard that one needed either ice magic or perception skills to travel through the Slime Pits."

That caught Kelva's attention. "And where did you hear that?"

Jax didn't really want to say. "Well, to be honest, it was that hunter who told me."

Kelva paused before responding. "I see. And you believe her?"

Jax shrugged. "I don't know."

"Well," said Huxley, "I can certainly see those abilities being very useful here."

"Wait, really?" Jax wasn't expecting anyone to agree with him.

"Of course," said Huxley. "I imagine most beasts in the area would be covered with slime and accustomed to high temperatures. Extreme cold would not only solidify the slime, but would likely also cause substantial damage to them."

"I suppose that makes sense," said Kelva, still sounding not completely convinced. "Any idea why perception skills would be any more useful here than elsewhere?"

Huxley crossed his arms and stared down at a slime puddle. "Well, they would help us avoid the snot wyrm. People with strong perception skills can sense nearby monsters even if they are out of sight, which I imagine the snot wyrm would be. Other than that, though, I have no idea."

"I see. So what do you recommend then? No one here has either of those skills."

Huxley hesitated briefly before answering. "Honestly, Captain, I don't feel I'm qualified to make that judgment."

"Then let me rephrase my question. Do you think we can safely travel through the Slime Pits?"

"Oh, yes," Huxley nodded emphatically before stopping. "Probably."

Kelva raised an eyebrow. "Just 'probably?'"

"Well, between Diana and myself we can keep a protective barrier up to protect against erupting slime. As long as we don't disturb the wyrm, I don't think we'd have any trouble with any other monsters in there."

"Then it's settled. You said the wyrm lives in the deepest pool, so we only go near the smaller ones. Jax, go get your sister. We're moving."

Jax hadn't even realized that Ev had wandered off during their conversation. He saw her hunched over a puddle of slime up against the stone walls of the valley, fiddling with lords knew what.

"Ev!" he shouted. "Come on, we're going!"

Ev didn't answer.

Jax huffed and steered his horse over to her. They didn't have time for whatever she was doing.

"Ev, we need to get moving," he said again when he got to her.

"I'm not done yet," she answered as she picked a wriggling creature out of the puddle.

"What in Doxla are you doing?"

"These lizards got covered in slime," she replied. "They've been half-cooked alive..."

Ev wiped the slime off of the little reptile and cast a healing spell on it. Jax watched as the tiny creature scurried off into a nearby crevice, where a few other tiny limbs were poking out.

"Seriously, Ev?"

"What? They were going to die if someone didn't help them!"

"Yeah," replied Jax, "and we're going to die if Dezeroth's forces catch up to us."

"Do you see any revenants around here?" she asked.

"Not yet, but that doesn't mean they aren't on their way."

"Well, if they aren't here yet, then we have time to help hurting creatures."

"No, we don't." Jax caught himself raising his voice. They didn't need to waste even more time arguing. "Look, your lizards are fine now, right?"

"Yes," answered Ev, climbing back onto her horse without looking at Jax. "So now we can go."

* * * *

The decision to journey through the Slime Pits soon proved to be a regrettable one. The outer valleys may have been cold, but these slime-filled chasms were sweltering. To make it worse, travel was extremely slow going. The horses had trouble walking through the puddles of yellow goo scattered about the path, as the substance was incredibly sticky, and unfortunately there were several occasions where the path was completely covered in it from wall to wall. Further compounding the discomfort was the pervasive stench of sulfur belching out from every crack and crevice around them, occasionally accompanied by eruptions of burning glop. The only upside was the quick realization that the hot stew was always preceded by a distinct gurgling sound, which gave Diana and Huxley ample time to put up their protective barrier around the group.

Deeper in, the chasm opened up into a large caldera filled with lakes of yellow slime separated by a network of stone pathways and ridges. Hot gas occasionally burbled up from beneath the lakes, creating large bubbles that dotted the surface. To their right, a single path followed the edge of the caldera for a good ways before jutting out towards the center. Everyone present agreed that having a boiling lake on just one side of the path was preferable to both sides, so that was the road they took.

There was no sign of monsters around, yet Jax couldn't help but be on edge. He kept scanning the surfaces of the slime for any hint of movement of gigantic paladin-eating monsters. The constant burbling and bubbling gave him plenty to concern himself with, though as they crept ever deeper into the hellhole, his worries appeared to be more and more just that.

A sudden jet of steam erupting behind him caused him to jerk around, where he spotted a large bubble rising up at the edge of the lake. It grew larger and larger, and just when Jax was sure it would burst it instead spilled over onto the path.

And then it started creeping after them.

"Um, guys?" he called. "We might have a problem." He pointed at the blob — twice the size of his horse — that now blocked half of the path to their rear.

Gare was the first to follow Jax's finger. "Lords, what the hell is that?"

"I don't know," answered Kelva, "but I'd rather not find out."

"Captain!" Huxley called out as another large mass emerged from the slime in front of them.

Kelva raised her sword and fired a beam into the creature, but to no effect. She fired two more. The huge blob continued towards them undeterred.

"Huxley!" she shouted. "Lightning, now!"

Huxley unleashed a blinding arc of electricity that caused the surface of the creature to pop and fizzle, but it did nothing to slow its advance.

Diana then raised her bow and fired an arrow into the beast. The arrow flew straight through it. Huxley cast an enchantment on her arrows and she fired another one to the same effect.

"Move!" shouted Kelva, and the group galloped around the large creature, Jax barely scraping by as he took up the rear.

More slime beasts rose up from the lakes as the party rode past. They steered their mounts around the wet puddles of glop on the road up until the point where the path broke away from the edge of the caldera. There, the path before them was completely covered in a sticky mess, forcing them to slow down.

Another monster climbed onto the stone not far behind them, and Kelva urged her horse forward through the glue-like substance. The strength of the adhesive made it impossible to rush through, however, and the horse stumbled and fell, landing Kelva right into the sticky muck.

"Captain!" Huxley shouted as he dismounted his horse to try and pull Kelva up.

More creatures climbed out of the ooze and surrounded them — two in front and three in back. There was no way they were getting around the beasts, horses or no.

Jax and Gare dismounted and drew their weapons, facing the blobs coming up from behind them. Diana pulled out her bow and fired several arrows at the ones in front, each of which disappeared into the slimy masses with no discernible effect. Ev, unequipped to fight, ran over to help Huxley and Kelva.

"Any idea how to fight these things?" asked Gare.

"My guess is don't let 'em touch you," answered Jax, though that was simpler said than done. The blobs had all but formed a wall that was steadily encroaching upon them.

"Alright, well let's see how they like the taste of ax, then!" Gare yelled as he charged the lead monster.

With a quick swipe he cut deep into the side of the creature, splashing slime onto the ground. The gash filled in as quickly as it had been made, and the monster opened up a giant mouth that Jax could swear hadn't been there before.

Gare instinctively backed away but couldn't escape the scalding mucus the creature sprayed from its maw out onto him. He screamed and fell backwards, the side of his head covered in steaming glop.

Jax rushed over as the monster bore down on Gare, and sliced deep into the monster, cutting through it like butter.

The blob retaliated by spraying hot goo at Jax as well, but he was prepared for it. He ducked out of the way and fired a blast of light into the slime's open mouth.

The blast exploded, and the slime shook and retreated a few feet.

"Hey!" panted Gare, pushing himself up for a second go. "I think you actually hurt it! Let's see if you can do it again!"

Gare charged in a second time and cleaved his ax through the slime beast's flesh, ready for the spray this time. The monster didn't open its mouth again, though. Instead, it lunged at Gare faster than a blob of slime ought to be able to move, knocking him to the ground and covering his legs.

Jax attacked the beast with light blasts, sending bits of goo flying with each attack, but nothing he did from the outside was having the same effect as before. As long as the thing wouldn't open its mouth it was practically invulnerable! Maybe...

He had a crazy idea. Running up to the slime beast, he slammed his fist straight into it. The pain was immediate, his hand screaming as the slime oozed into his armor. It felt as if he'd just thrust his arm into a pot of boiling water, but he pushed past the pain and unleashed a heavy blast of light straight into the monster.

The reaction was instantaneous. The blob retreated off of Gare and away from Jax, quivering violently.

Gare, covered up to his chest in slime, looked up at Jax, panting. "Lords, man, I owe you one." He then noticed Jax cradling his arm. "Damn, are you...?"

Jax held his burned hand close to his body; the pain he'd fought to ignore coursed up through his arm like a wave, but he wasn't going to let it show. "I'm fine," he grunted out, probably unconvincingly.

"You need to get to Ev," Gare said, pushing himself up once again. "I'll hold them off! I'm ready for them this time!"

"We don't have time to heal," Jax replied as the other two slime beasts behind them grew nearer. "We need to figure out how to kill these things before..."

Jax trailed off. A horse was galloping towards them.

"Who's that?" asked Gare, and Jax recognized the rider as that hunter, Birdie.

Birdie shot a single arrow into the slime monster Jax had driven back and the creature convulsed and exploded, leaving behind a small glowing sphere with the arrow wedged in it. She fired two more each at the others between her and Jax, and each of them splattered into steaming puddles as well. She rode up next to Jax and stopped.

"Well, well, well," she said, "it's almost as if you should have listened to me when I said you wouldn't make it through here without my help."

"Wha-? How?" stammered Gare, looking back and forth between Birdie and the now dead piles of goo.

"Forget that!" yelled Jax, pointing with his uninjured hand towards Kelva, Huxley, Ev, and Diana. "The others still need help!"

The remaining two blobs were still trying to get to their prey. Diana and Huxley were so far successfully repelling them with a repulsive shield spell, but they were clearly nearing the limits of their endurance.

The blobs were not.

"Oh, dear," said Birdie, "they look like they might be in trouble. Oh, well, you did say you could take care of yourselves, if I recall..."

"Help them!" Jax yelled.

"I suppose I could, but, what's in it for me?" she asked.

Jax pointed his sword at her, scowling. "If you don't save them, I'll kill you!"

"Oh-hoho, yes, that makes me so much more willing to help you."

"You can't just let them die!" shouted Jax.

"Well, technically, I think I can. But I won't," she added just as Jax was about to throw a blast at her.

She raised her bow again and downed the remaining two blobs, then cocked her head towards Jax with a smirk. "Happy?"

Jax and Gare rushed over to the others, Birdie following close behind.

When they arrived, Birdie addressed Kelva, who was nearly as covered in goo as Gare was. "So, it appears we meet again."

"Yes," responded Kelva, trying to wipe some of the glop off of her armor. Failing that, she focused her full attention on Birdie. "At the risk of sounding ungrateful, is there a reason you followed us all the way here?"

"What can I say?" shrugged Birdie. "I knew you wouldn't survive on your own through the Slime Pits. That, plus seeing how well you're outfitted, tells me there's good money to be made if I can get you safely to your destination."

"That's it?" said Kelva, narrowing her eyes. "You only saved us because you want money?"

"Oh, it's not just the money. Hunting monsters gets boring after a while, and this seems like it could be a good change of pace."

"Well, I hate to disappoint you," responded Kelva, "but this is a mission we must complete on our own."

"Well, that will certainly be a trick, won't it?" responded Birdie. "After all, you're only half a mile into the Slime Pits with another two to go, not to mention a second trip through them once you've reached the eastern side of the roc's nest."

Kelva paused to consider for a moment. She clearly didn't want Birdie going with her. Jax didn't either, but if he was honest with himself, he really didn't think they'd be able to make it without her. She did just single-handedly wipe out an entire group of monsters when the rest of them combined had failed to kill a single one.

"Captain," Jax offered, "as much as I hate to say this, I think we actually could use the assistance."

"...Perhaps some aid would be beneficial," Kelva managed, "but I'm afraid our... 'friend' is still out of luck. We don't have a single bit of gold between us."

"Mm, maybe not," said Birdie, "but I'm sure either wherever you're going or coming from has plenty. And just in case they don't, I can think of a few tiny little errands you can help me with along the way that should cover my price."

"We don't have time to go off on random adventures," Kelva responded, "but if all you care about is money, then I suppose we can arrange to have you paid once we arrive at our destination."

Birdie grinned. "Then it's a deal."

"Yes," said Kelva, frowning, "if you can get us through the rest of these mountains safely."

"As long as you listen to my advice from now on, I don't think that will be a problem."

Kelva eyed Birdie for a moment before turning to the rest of the party. "Help me get my horse out of this muck."

Gare, Diana, and Huxley all joined Kelva in pulling her mount out of the glue it had fallen in while Birdie went to collect the arrows she'd used. While they worked, Jax approached Ev to have his hand looked at.

"Hey, Ev," he began, "do you think you can—"

"Fine," Ev interrupted after glancing at his arm. "Just hold it steady."

Her response caught Jax off guard. "Is everything okay?"

"I don't know, you tell me," she responded as she started to work on his hand.

Well, something was certainly wrong, but Jax could only guess as to what. "Look, if this is about those lizards—"

"It's not."

Jax was not about to play this kind of game right now. "Well, if you don't want to tell me, then I'm not going to worry about it then."

Ev stopped healing Jax's hand. He was about to tell her off for stopping just because she was in a bad mood when he realized she'd actually finished.

"Thanks," he managed before turning away.

The others had managed to get Kelva's horse up again, so Jax mounted his as well, and they prepared to saddle off.

Shortly after they started moving, Gare addressed Birdie. "Alright, I can't figure it out. How the hell did you kill those things so easily?"

Birdie tapped her temple with her finger. "Very high perception skills. Bublobs have a small, very delicate core at their center. Though impossible to see with the naked eye, a few direct strikes from even the weakest attacks will bring them down."

"And you somehow knew where they were," Gare stated.

"I just said 'perception skills,'" Birdie replied. "Offensive and defensive abilities are all fine and dandy, but they're useless if you can't find your target."

Gare "harrumph"ed.

Jax wasn't sure what to think of their new companion, but he did know this. Someone who only cared about money was someone he didn't trust. Not one bit.

Chapter 5

The remainder of the journey through the Slime Pits was remarkably without incident. Any time one of those bublobs crawled out of the grime to block their path, Birdie popped them like bad tomatoes, always making sure to recollect her arrows after each kill. They never encountered the snot wyrm, thank the Masters, and after they'd passed through the last of the calderas, they found themselves at the opening of a magnificent valley. A shallow grassy slope stretched on for miles in each direction. Huge granite outcroppings jutted out from the ground at regular intervals, giving the slope the appearance of magnificent broken stairs. At the bottom of the slope was a cliff that dropped off into an immense black forest, and beyond the forest were more mountains. The mountains stretched far above the clouds, significantly higher than the peaks the group had thus far traveled through. The relief from the cool, clean breeze was most welcome after the sweltering stench of the Pits.

"Ahh, out of the muck at last," Birdie declared loudly as the group finally stepped onto green grass again. "Now tell me, aren't you glad you survived to see this view?"

"It's beautiful..." remarked Ev.

"It is, isn't it?" replied Birdie before brushing the hair from her face and turning to Kelva. "Now then, I assume you want to continue heading east?"

"Yes," answered Kelva, "our destination is on the far side of the Windy Mountains."

"In that case, our best route to take would actually be north from here," Birdie said, pointing along the slope to their left.

Kelva followed Birdie's finger with a frown. "I fail to see how traveling north will take us east."

"Oh, it won't take us east until we turn east, but at least we'll all get there eventually."

"Meaning?" asked Kelva.

Birdie pointed down to the dark forest below them. "Tell me, do you know what those woods are called?"

Nobody answered.

Birdie smirked. "I see. Well, in that case—"

"Shadowknot Forest," Ev answered.

Everyone stared at her.

"Yes," said Birdie with a smile. "So you've heard of it before."

"I'm pretty sure everyone's heard of it," replied Ev. "It's the place parents tell kids they'll be taken to if they don't mind their elders."

"Oh, come on," said Gare. "Those are just fairy tales. Everyone knows Shadowknot Forest isn't real."

"It looks pretty real to me," said Jax.

"Yeah, well, she says it's real," Gare pointed at Birdie, "but how do we know it isn't just a really dark forest?"

"What's the matter, Gare?" Jax taunted. "Don't tell me you're actually scared of a few ghost stories."

"What? No! But come on, if you expect me to believe stories of roots growing up under the beds of naughty children to drag them away in their sleep, you've got another thing coming!"

"You're right, Mr. Gare," said Birdie.

"See!" shouted Gare. "Wait, about what?"

"You're right that the tree roots don't go after naughty children." Birdie's smile faded. "They go after anyone and anything that disturbs them. So do the vines and the branches, and if they grab you, it's over. The trees are nearly indestructible, strong enough to crush steel, and grow back within minutes even if you do manage to harm them." Birdie turned back to Kelva. "The only way to get through that forest is to travel slowly and carefully, and we wouldn't be able to take the horses."

Kelva pondered this information for a moment. "If what you say is true, then I'm inclined to take your recommendation of heading north." She turned to Huxley. "What do you think? Do you know anything of this forest?"

"Only the stories, I'm afraid. Supposedly the Masters created the forest as an obstacle for Divine seeking ascension — part of the trial of taming the roc if

I recall. I'd bet my giblets we could make it through, but I don't doubt what Miss Birdie says about the horses."

Kelva turned back to Birdie. "About how far would we have to travel before we are past the forest?"

"The forest forms a circle around the roc's nest," Birdie said, pointing towards the peaks on the far side of the woods. "It's roughly ten miles straight from here to the far side of the Mountain Navel, so we'd have a little over fifty miles journey if we travel close to the forest's edge."

"That would take us two days, Captain," Huxley offered.

"I see," responded Kelva, clearly considering her options. "That's unfortunate, but if we have to give up our horses, we'd end up taking far longer if we cut across it." Kelva addressed Birdie once again. "Very well, we will travel around the forest. Lead the way."

* * * *

Several hours later, the party stopped for a break at a stream nestled tightly between the great stone outcroppings, halfway down the slope and several miles from where they'd exited the Slime Pits. The sun was already starting to go back down once again, leaving the side of the mountain they were on covered in shade.

Jax was busy working to remove bits of slime still embedded in his mail. Apparently the goo had been more than just hot, as it had eaten away a bit at the metal and nearly disintegrated the padding underneath. That arm he'd shoved into the bublob was not going to be comfortable to wear after this. The glop had hardened into a sticky snot that was safe to the touch by now, but it was still a huge pain to remove. He tossed aside the fifth twig he'd been through trying to dig it out and reached for a sixth when he caught sight of Birdie heading over to Ev, who'd settled down a short ways away from the rest of the group and was currently digging through some flowers.

"What do you think she's up to?" Jax asked Gare, who was washing out the inside of his plate armor in the stream.

Gare looked up for a second, then back down to what he was doing. "I dunno. Seems to me like she just wants money."

"No, not that. Why's she going over to Ev?"

"Ya know, bud, sometimes you worry too much." Gare tossed a piece of his left leg's armor into his "clean" pile and started to work on a boot. "She's a girl. She probably just likes flowers."

"I get the feeling this girl isn't into flowers," Jax muttered.

He kept scrubbing away at the slime in his mail's left sleeve, but he kept an eye on Birdie and Ev while he worked. He'd caught Birdie hanging around Ev during their last break as well.

"Mr. Ruthoree."

Jax jumped. He looked over his shoulder to see Kelva standing over him. She motioned for him to follow her, and he did.

The two of them walked over to where Huxley and Diana were waiting. Both of them were looking at him.

"What? Did something happen?" he asked.

"What happened is right over there," Kelva motioned with her eyes towards Birdie.

"Right," Jax said. "So you don't trust her, either, then."

"I haven't decided yet," answered Kelva. "I don't like having an opportunist with us, but for now it seems we have little choice."

"Why?" Jax asked. "We're more than capable of handling ourselves."

"No, we're not," Kelva stated, surprising Jax. He never expected to hear the captain say something so defeatist. "You were the one who said we needed her help, and you were right. We don't have a balanced group. We lack support classes, we have a single inexperienced cleric, and the only offensive forms of magic we have are light and lightning. We don't know what's ahead of us. Huxley is the only one of us who's traveled these mountains before, and even he's never seen this region of them. You might not like it, and I certainly don't, but we need this Birdie woman if we're going to make it to Roehelm."

Jax rubbed his arm. He knew Kelva had a point, but he didn't like how much time Birdie was spending around his sister. "So what did you bring me over here for, then?"

Diana answered. "A woman unknown might an enemy be."

"Now, now," chastised Huxley, "let's not forget she did come to our aid."

"And one who chases riches is easily bought," Diana replied.

Huxley crossed his arms. "Well, if she only cares about money, I reckon she's not doing a good job of it. Those bubble blobs, or whatever they're called, would have made short work of us, and our equipment is worth far more than what she'll likely get at the end of this."

"A fact she may not know," returned Diana, "and we know little facts of her. Such skill as hers is rare, and such an encounter out here is uncanny."

"Agreed," added Kelva, "and that's why I brought you over here, Jax."

"What do you mean?" he asked.

"I'm sure you've noticed our new friend seems rather fond of your sister," Kelva stated.

Jax bristled. "Oh, believe me I've noticed. I plan on putting a stop to it, too."

"Absolutely not," said Kelva.

"Excuse me? Why not? I don't want that woman near my sister."

Kelva glanced over at Ev and Birdie without moving her head. "If she has some sort of affinity for Miss Eveline, then that gives you an excuse to keep an eye on her."

Jax scowled.

"Do you understand what I want from you? Stay close to Eveline and observe Birdie. Keep us informed if she says or does anything that might hint to her being a danger."

"Well, if you're just going to use my sister as bait, why don't you ask her to report on Birdie?"

"No one is using anyone as bait. Your sister is still a child. She might start trusting our new guide more than she should and hide things from us. I know you won't do that."

Jax huffed. "Fine. If that's what you want, then I'll do it, but I don't know why you think I'd see anything you guys won't. It's not like she and Ev are wandering off together anywhere."

"Are you sure about that?" Kelva asked, motioning with her head behind him.

Jax turned around to see Ev and Birdie walking along the stream towards the edge of the granite block they were on.

Kelva continued. "Seems to me like they're hitting it off pretty well."

"Ugh, what the heck, Ev?" Jax shook his head. "I just don't get her. She's been acting weird all day. I'm going to talk to her."

Kelva called out softly after him. "Not a word about what we discussed, Jax."

Jax crossed over to where Ev and Birdie had taken a seat without acknowledging Kelva. When he got there he found them talking about streams and bugs, of all things. The topic wasn't really out of the ordinary for Ev, but she rarely talked to anyone about her interests. Maybe she really was opening up to this greedy hunter.

"Hey, um, Ev?" he prompted.

Ev and Birdie both looked up from their conversation.

"Can I talk to you about something?"

"I'm kind of in the middle of something," she answered. "I'm sure it can wait until later though, right?"

"No, er, maybe?" Jax hadn't expected that response.

"So which is it?" Ev asked. "'No' or 'maybe?'"

"It's..." Jax glanced between Ev and Birdie, "...I guess it's not important right now. Would you mind if I joined you?"

Ev didn't answer.

Birdie tilted her head wryly. "I didn't take you to be the sort who's interested in the correlation between water quality and the chirality of snail shells."

"He's not," said Ev. "What do you want Jax?"

"I just wanted to talk," Jax answered defensively, "is that a bad thing? We haven't had a chance to sit down together in a while."

"Sure we have," retorted Ev, "we just didn't. You spend every break with Gare and stay glued to Captain Kelva when we're moving. You haven't even tried to talk to me since...." Tears welled up in Ev's eyes. "It's like you don't even want me here!"

"Ev..." Jax lifted his hand to comfort his sister, but she pulled away.

"Ev, look, I just—"

"What the hell?" Birdie interrupted.

"Excuse me?" Jax started, turning on Birdie.

"Look!" she pointed up in the air behind them.

Ev's expression instantly changed to one of shock. Jax spun around just in time to see a skeletal soldier atop an ethereal flying beast retreat out of sight beyond the granite outcrop above them.

The blood drained from Jax's face. "Dezeroth!" he shouted, and he bolted back to warn the others. "Gare, put your armor on!"

"Why? What's going on?" Gare asked, but Jax didn't stop to answer.

He ran up to Kelva and told her what he'd seen. She seemed incredulous.

"You saw a flying beast," she stated plainly.

"Yes! And a revenant was riding on the back of it!"

Kelva considered for a moment before turning to Huxley. "I was under the impression that the only thing that could fly in these mountains was the roc."

"Well... I can't say I've heard of any other creature able to fly in these winds," Huxley responded, "but that doesn't mean there isn't one."

Kelva turned back to Jax. "Tell me exactly what you saw. What did this creature look like?"

"It was yellow and... you could kind of see through it. It looked like a big fish with wings, and had all of these sparkly bits inside of it that looked like stars."

"Huxley?" prompted Kelva.

"I can't say I've ever seen one myself," said Huxley, hand on his chin, "but it sounds like it could be a zodiac beast."

Jax had no idea what that was, and apparently he wasn't the only one.

"What exactly is a 'zodiac beast?'" Kelva pressed.

Huxley answered. "It's a creature that supposedly lives far to the north, beyond the Jesimine Peaks. I'm afraid I don't know much about them, but supposedly they are the embodiment of the wind and stars, which would explain how it wasn't blown away by the mountain winds."

"This isn't good," Jax exclaimed. "Once Dezeroth finds out where we are —"

"Calm yourself, Ruthoree," commanded Kelva. "Dezeroth's scouts are likely spread out thin across these mountains. It will take time for his forces to get to us, and we will be far away from here by the time they do. Put your armor back on and mount your steeds. We ride until we reach the far side of the Mountain Navel. We'll need to pass through the Slime Pits a second time, but once we are through we should be able to continue under the cover of forest until we are clear of these mountains."

* * * *

Jax and the others must have galloped for nearly two miles before letting their horses slow for a rest. To minimize the distance to their destination, Kelva had directed them to travel closer to Shadowknot Forest. The trees rose up over the side of the cliff that separated them from the forest floor, but the group dared not approach too closely, and Jax could understand why. Scattered about in the branches of the leafless ebon trees were mangled skeletons of unfortunate creatures that had ventured too close and fallen victim to the forest's bloodlust, and an unnatural shadow darkened the interior of the woods. Even before the sun had set, Jax couldn't see more than a few yards in, suggesting some sort of dark enchantment permeating the entire forest.

The forest was not at the forefront of Jax's mind, however. His thoughts kept switching back and forth between Ev and Dezeroth. At first, he was angry. Angry at Ev for not wanting to talk with him, and angry at Dezeroth for ruining their lives... but the more he thought the more Ev's words began to sink in.

He had been ignoring her. He might have claimed it was because he didn't think she wanted to talk about what had happened; however, deep down, he knew it was because he was the one who didn't want to. He didn't want to tell her how he'd failed to save their father. In his heart he knew there wasn't anything more he could have done, but his feeble attempt had been so pathetic Dezeroth hadn't even noticed he was there.

A sudden glint in the sky drew Jax's attention back to the reality at hand. They were being hunted, and their horses were tired. It would be difficult for them to be spotted from above where they were now — with a stone outcrop leaning up over them from the left and dark forest on their right — but it wouldn't be impossible.

Jax looked up towards where he'd noticed a faint gleam and spotted another zodiac beast, though against the night sky it appeared as little more than a group of shooting stars.

"Captain," he pointed up at the sky.

"I see it," Kelva said. "Let's hope it doesn't see us."

A few minutes passed and Jax spotted another zodiac beast. Then another. Soon, the valley was filled with shooting stars zooming about, each constellation searching for the Heart and those who carried it.

"Captain," Huxley said, "I think we might need to reconsider our plan of action."

"If you have any suggestions I'd be happy to hear them," Kelva replied.

"Well, it's just a thought, but, perhaps we could seek shelter in the forest until the scouts move on?"

Kelva examined the foreboding trees, clearly considering this option.

"Miss Birdie," she said at last, "do you know if it's possible to survive in those woods?"

"Of course it's possible," Birdie answered, "but if we go rushing in it's basically suicide. Only Radiant class beings and native monsters can survive attacks from the trees."

"How would we enter the forest?" Kelva asked.

"Hold on," interrupted Jax. "You don't really expect us to go in there do you?"

"Oh, nonono," remarked Garrison. "Please don't tell me that's what we're doing."

Kelva looked out at the sky. "It looks like we may have little choice."

"Not a chance!" said Garrison. "There is no way I'm going in Shadowknot Forest."

"Then you can fight off Dezeroth's soldiers while we seek cover," responded Kelva. "I'm sure your sacrifice will be remembered."

Garrison pouted. Jax wanted to protest as well, but he held back. It was hard to count the zodiac beasts against the night sky, but he was sure there were more than ten of them now. It was only a matter of time before one came in close to where they were, and then the rest would be upon them in moments.

Kelva turned back to Birdie. "So how do we enter the forest?"

"We just passed up an entrance about a mile back. I'm sure you noticed these big rocks don't go entirely around the forest. Every now and then there's a gap in them that stretches back to the hillside, and that's the best way in." She pointed at a fissure in the rock a short distance ahead of them. "Or if you're really feeling brave you could try climbing down one of those."

"How far until the next slope?" Kelva asked.

Birdie shrugged. "How should I know? And does it matter? You're aware that you can't take horses into the forest, right?"

"I know you said that," responded Kelva, "but you didn't say why."

"Because horses are big animals that will trigger the trees immediately. Just brushing up against a vine or branch will set them off, and you have to watch your step constantly. The roots are safe as long as you don't step in the circles, but they aren't always obvious. Bringing a horse is stupid, because it will inevitably get caught, and the trees will grab you too if you're too close when it happens."

"Captain," Jax offered, "maybe we can find a crevice to hide in instead?"

Kelva shook her head. "No, then we'd just be cornered if we're found. If we go in the forest, at least we'd be able to retreat further in."

That set Ev off. "So, what? Are we just going to leave our horses? They won't survive out here on their own!"

"And if we're caught by the revenants, we'll die with them," Kelva answered.

Ev's face turned red, but she didn't argue further. Jax almost joined her in her protest, as without horses it would take over a week to make it to Roehelm, but the number of zodiacs in the sky was still increasing, and every additional star in the sky was another reason such a sacrifice might be necessary.

"Well, then," said Birdie nonchalantly, "since it sounds like we're set on where we're going, maybe someone can clue me in as to why we're being hunted by zodiac-riding revenants?"

Kelva eyed Birdie for a moment before answering. "Let's just say we have something they're after, and if they get it, then all of Doxla will suffer."

Birdie actually smirked at that news. "You're kidding, right? All of Doxla? I think you might be exaggerating a bit on that."

"She's not kidding," Jax stated, "or exaggerating."

Birdie smirked again, but her expression wasn't as playful. "Well, if what you've got is so dangerous, why don't you just get rid of it? What's the point in even keeping something like that around?"

"We can't get rid of it," Kelva answered. "What we carry is indestructible and impossible to hide. Our only option is to take it somewhere where it can be protected until Supreme Lord Grandis brings judgment upon Dezeroth and his horde."

"Okay, sure, whatever," said Birdie. "So what exactly is this thing anyway?"

"Something dangerous," said Kelva. "That's all you need to know. Now we have to get to the next entrance to the forest before any of those scouts spot us."

The group barely made it fifty more feet before that goal shattered with a flash of crimson light off to their side. Jax looked out over the forest to see a robed revenant atop a starry boar staring right at them, sending blinding jets of fire high into the air and lighting up the entire valley.

A flash of light shot past Jax and knocked the revenant off of its mount and into the forest below, putting an end to the light show. The trees where the enemy soldier landed twisted and waved before returning to stillness once again.

Jax looked to his left to see Kelva sheathing her still glowing sword.

"That should buy us a few more seconds," she said. "Now ride! We must get to the forest before we're surrounded!"

The party galloped along the granite outcrop at top speed. Wherever the next entrance to the forest was, it was farther than Jax could see. What wasn't so far were the hundreds of shooting stars converging rapidly on their location.

Chapter 6

Brilliant flares lit up the valley as more revenants closed in on the party. In the light, Jax could make out another slope down to the forest in the distance.

"There!" he pointed.

"I see it," returned Kelva before looking back at the others. "Our escape is in sight. Protect Huxley at all costs!"

The group rearranged to surround Huxley and the Heart. Gare pulled back to take up the rear. Diana took up position to Huxley's right, ready with her shield. Ev stayed on his left, closest to the wall and furthest from danger. Jax remained up front with Kelva and Birdie.

That wasn't where Kelva wanted him, though. "Ruthoree, get back with Mr. Hue. Use those light bursts you're so fond of to keep the zodiacs at a distance."

Jax tugged on his horses reins and fell to the back. Being relegated to the rear wasn't ideal, but it made sense. He had been fighting almost exclusively with magic these past few days, so of course Kelva took that to be his specialty. Hopefully, all that practice would pay off, because if these revenants were like the ones he'd fought before, they weren't going to be easy to take down.

The first wave of riders swooped in from behind, illuminated by the blinding flare the undead sorcerers kept aglow in the sky.

Jax launched a blast of energy at the lead rider, knocking him off balance but not off his beast. The leader recovered and continued the charge.

Jax cursed, but he wasn't about to give up. He wasn't strong enough to knock them off, but that didn't mean he couldn't take them down another way.

Jax drew his sword and fired a beam at the head of the zodiac the lead rider was on. The creature flailed and fell well behind the others.

"Ha!" Jax shouted. "Looks like we can hurt those things," he smirked at Gare.

Gare grumbled, "With magic maybe. Fat chance my ax will do any good."

"Guess I'd better keep you safe then," Jax grinned as he concentrated and fired another beam at the next rider. This met with equal success, but another rider took his place, bringing along more than enough friends to make up the difference.

Gare was quick to notice. "Nice job, buddy. Now start shooting twice as fast and maybe I'll believe you."

Jax grin disappeared. He fired another beam, but the revenants had adapted to his attacks and were quick to avoid and recover from them.

Another flash of light surrounded the group. Huxley and Diana put up their barrier. Sparks exploded off of it as spells from sorcerers to the front were deflected. Birdie let her arrows fly at the sorcerers, and Jax thought he caught sight of her casting some sort of spell at them as well, but his attention was quickly drawn to one of the riders slamming her spear into the barrier. Whatever enchantment was on that weapon, it was a strong one, as the spear pierced right through, connecting with Diana's shield and temporarily bringing down their protection.

A pair of revenants at the rear seized on the opportunity and closed the distance to Jax and Gare. A single strike from Gare's ax downed the wolf-like zodiac of the first, prompting a shout of triumph. Jax had no time to join in the celebration, as the second approached from his side, twisted blade poised to strike.

Jax pointed his sword at the revenant's zodiac, but the enemy blade knocked it away. Jax missed his shot, and a second swing of the revenant's unholy sword connected with the mail on Jax's right arm, shattering the weakened metal but fortunately not cutting deep beyond that.

Jax fired a blast from his left hand straight into the revenant's face, blinding it for just long enough for Jax to strike its zodiac.

The beast pulled away, but Jax had little time for relief. Several more undead were waiting to take the place of the one he'd just driven away, and as they closed in Jax knew he and Gare wouldn't be able to handle them all.

Another soldier flew in with a spear towards Jax, ready to strike, when the light from the flares disappeared.

Jax barely had time to register what was happening when a massive figure slammed into the mountainside, shattering stone, toppling the horses, and sending out a blast of wind so powerful the zodiacs and their riders went careening into the rock face.

Jax found himself on the ground beside his horse. A huge, flailing shadow loomed over him. The light from the sorcerers' flares had disappeared, and for a moment Jax wasn't even sure what he was seeing.

Then it dawned on him.

It was a bird. A colossal, mountain-sized bird.

And it was panicking.

The roc had attacked them, but it had landed too close to the forest, which was now pulling it in. Each flap of its wings unleashed a hurricane. Branches and zodiacs went flying. The ground shook as it struggled to free itself from the grasp of bloodthirsty trees.

The roc slammed against the stone outcrop a second time, scrambling to climb out of the forest. A large segment of the outcrop beneath them gave way in front of Jax.

Diana managed to hold onto solid ground as the stone fell away, but Huxley and Ev toppled into the newly formed chasm along with three of the horses.

"Ev!" Jax shouted, darting to the edge.

The stone had collapsed into a crude slide that had funneled his sister towards the thrashing feet of the roc. She pulled herself out of the way of its talons, but Huxley wasn't so lucky. Jax winced as the massive claw came down, crushing one of the fallen horses and Huxley's legs before throwing the both of them back into the woods.

Jax looked down in horror. Both his sister and the Heart had fallen into Shadowknot Forest. If he stayed where he was he'd be abandoning both his father's wishes and his mission. With only a moment's hesitation, he picked up his sword and ran to the highest point of the collapsed slide and jumped down.

"Jax!" he heard Gare shout, but it was too late. Jax had made his choice. He slid down the granite towards the forest floor and jumped off the side before getting too close to the roc's deadly talons.

"Jax?" Ev was visibly shocked by his appearance.

Jax grabbed her by the arm. "Move!" he cried, pulling her away just as more of the outcrop came crashing down. The two of them didn't stop until they were a good fifty yards away from the roc, careful to keep far enough under the overhang to remain out of reach of the deadly trees.

Jax and Ev watched as the roc tried once more to pull itself free of the grasping branches. This time it succeeded, managing to grab a hold of a solid piece of stone as it pulled itself up onto the mountain. A group of trees were uprooted in a battle between their grip on the bird's feathers and the ground. The ground won, but only barely, and the trees toppled over into the gash in the mountain the roc had made, only a few bits of plumage as their prize.

From the safety of their alcove, neither Jax nor Ev could see what was going on above, but they could certainly hear and feel it. The roc may have narrowly escaped the forest, but it was far from defeated. The ground shook and hurricane winds blasted through the trees as the King of Land and Sky rampaged above, asserting its dominion as the one true lord of the mountains.

When at last the violence subsided, Jax and Ev stood huddled together for a few moments in silence, listening for any sign of life above.

"Do you think it's gone?" Ev asked.

"There's only one way to find out," Jax answered, and he let go of Ev as he started back towards where they'd dropped down into the forest.

The trees the roc had uprooted blocked their way back up. Jax had no idea if they were still dangerous or not, but he wasn't about to risk getting close to them to find out. He looked up at where they'd fallen from, not sure what to do next.

"Do you think the others are okay?" Ev asked quietly.

"I don't know," Jax answered, equally quiet. Birdie hadn't mentioned anything about monsters living in these woods, but if they existed, then attracting them with noisy banter would be the last thing Jax needed now. "If they are alive, I doubt they're still around here."

Ev looked around at the nearly black forest surrounding them. "What do we do now?"

"I... don't know," Jax began, but then he remembered the other reason he'd jumped down. "Wait a minute. Huxley fell down here too."

Jax looked around for any sign of him, but saw only his staff. Jax collected the staff and handed it to Ev, then ventured a few steps further into the unnatural darkness. Still no sign, he risked calling out.

"Hello?"

No answer. Jax took another step forward and thought he could make out a figure on the ground in front of him. He focused a weak light blast into his hand and held it there to act as a makeshift torch.

The scene he uncovered almost made him wish he hadn't. One of the horses, or what was left of it, lay flattened on the ground, essentially reduced to paste. Off to either side of him he could make out the other two fallen horses, or perhaps more accurately, he could make out bits of them protruding from huge knots of vines hanging from the trees.

Jax swallowed, then looked back at Ev, her face pale from the sight. "Stay here," he said.

"W-what?" Realization appeared on her face. "No! Jax, you can't go in there."

"I have to find Huxley. If there's even a chance he's alive, I have to look."

Jax stepped around the flattened horse, taking care not to touch any of the fallen branches, vines, or basically anything made of wood. Not an easy task when stepping into a forest.

"Wait," Ev called, hopping after him.

"Ev, I have to do this."

"I know," she answered, "but Father told me to make sure you don't do anything stupid, and going alone is stupid."

"Both of us going is stupid. What if something happens?"

"Exactly. Besides," Ev held up her hand, glowing with a soft light, "two lights are better than one."

"Ev, I'm not going to argue on this."

"Good. Then it's settled."

"Ev, I said 'no.' You don't even know what we'll find."

"Are you going to keep wasting time, or are we going to go?"

Lords, she was stubborn. "Fine. Just don't follow too closely, and remember what Birdie said. Don't touch anything and watch out for circles on the ground."

Jax cautiously led the way deeper into the forest. He held up his hand, already starting to get hot, and focused more light into it. The effort was hardly worth it. No matter how brightly he shined his light, the darkness of the forest swallowed it up.

"Jax!"

Jax turned around to see Ev pointing back the way they'd come. There, underneath one of the roc's feathers, he caught sight of a metallic glint. Hurrying over, he pushed the feather off of Huxley, prompting one of the forest's vines to instantly latch onto it and pull it into the treetops, crushing it. Jax nearly fell backward from shock but quickly recovered and turned his attention to Huxley.

"Is he...?" Ev whispered.

Jax knelt down beside Huxley. His legs were completely mangled. "He's breathing," Jax said, relieved, "but he's in pretty bad shape."

Ev ran forward and dropped the staff next to Huxley, healing hand at the ready.

"His armor's been crushed," Ev said, referring to Huxley's legs. "We need to get it off or I can't heal him properly."

"On it," Jax replied, setting to work on unstrapping the mutilated plates as Ev started on healing Huxley's upper half. He had to cease channeling magic into his hand to do it, but Ev's healing light kept them from being swallowed by the dark. Honestly, the break was a relief, as Jax's hand was on fire by that point. That was one thing nice about recovery magic, now that he thought about it; its wielder didn't have to worry about burning their hands off casting spells.

Jax removed the front plate from Huxley's left thigh, but when he saw what was beneath it he had to look away. "Oh, lords, Ev. I think you might have your work cut out for you."

"What's wrong?" she asked, but gasped the moment she looked over.

The back plate had split, the lower half embedded so deep into Huxley's leg it nearly poked out the other side, snapping the bone clean through. The leg below the split looked like ground meat wrapped in torn cloth.

"What... what should I do?" Jax asked, forcing himself to look at the wound.

Ev took a deep breath. "We need to get the metal and cloth out of him, and... let me see."

Ev crawled over and examined the wound. She ran her fingers over the metal and felt along the leg. Watching her work, Jax gained a new level of respect for his sister. He'd always thought of her as weak and naive, what with how she shied away from violence and spent her days playing in the garden, but here she was, in the middle of the most dangerous forest in the world, examining a wound Jax was squeamish about as if she'd done it a thousand times before.

At last Ev looked up, but she didn't look happy. "I don't think I can fix this."

"Why not?" Jax asked. "You can't just heal it?"

Ev shook her head. "I can heal the wound but, I think the leg has to come off."

"Come off? No! Just, make it better like you always do."

Ev shook her head. "That's not how healing works Jax. I can aid and accelerate the body's natural healing, but if I tried with something like this, his leg would at best be useless, and would probably die and rot off anyway."

"But... you can't just cut his leg off," Jax protested.

"Jax, it's barely even attached as it is."

"I know but, shouldn't he have a say in this?"

Ev reached for Jax's sword, which he reluctantly handed to her. "The leg's already gone, and the longer we wait, the more blood he loses."

Ev was right. The thought of blood loss hadn't even occurred to Jax. Actually, there was hardly any blood around, now that Jax thought about it. The forest floor was spotless, even beneath Huxley's leg, with every last drop pouring from the wound vanishing into the soil.

Ev placed the sword against Huxley's thigh. A part of Jax wanted to stop her, but he knew she knew better than him about this. Instead, he looked away. Something about watching his sister saw through someone's leg was just... it wasn't something he was comfortable seeing.

The operation only took a minute. "I'm done," Ev said. "Do me a favor and move the leg somewhere else. I'm going to start healing."

Jax reluctantly obliged, taking the limb and placing it out of sight as Ev focused on fixing up the tiny bit of Huxley's leg that remained.

"There," said Ev after a few minutes, sweating. "That's the best I can do."

The wound on Huxley's thigh was completely healed over. "That's... really impressive, Ev. You really are an amazing healer."

Ev gave just the faintest of smiles. "Help me get the plates on his other leg off. We've still got work to do."

Jax set back to work unstrapping more plates when he was interrupted by what sounded like someone calling from back the way they'd come.

"Did you hear that?" Jax asked, standing up.

Ev stood up as well. "I heard something."

The voice reached Jax's ears once again. There was no question this time — it belonged to Captain Kelva.

"Stay here," he told Ev, "I'm going check it out."

"Jax, wait! It could be the forest playing a trick on you!"

"I don't think the forest does that."

Ev still looked concerned.

"Look, I'm just going check it out."

Jax lit up his hand again and made his way back towards where the roc had torn apart the forest, not that it was that far. He looked up at the ledge above, but didn't see any sign of anyone there.

"Captain?" he called out.

"Jax!" Gare's head popped out over the crack in the rock the roc had made. "Lords, man! We all thought you were done for!"

Jax breathed a huge sigh of relief and smiled. Somehow that big goober had survived up there. "Why would I be 'done for?' Ev and I just felt like taking a walk in the woods, is all.

"Wait, so Ev's okay too?" Gare turned away and called to Kelva, who joined him. "Man, you guys are lucky—"

"Where's Huxley?" Kelva demanded. "Tell me he's still alive down there."

Jax's smile left him. "Huxley's hurt, bad, but Ev's taking care of him."

Even from this distance, Jax could see Kelva's body relax. "Stay there," she called. "We'll enter the forest further down and meet up with you as soon as we can."

Kelva turned, but didn't leave. Jax could hear Birdie talking, but couldn't make out what she was saying. After a moment, Kelva nodded and turned back to Jax again.

"Actually," she called, "step forward into the clearing a bit more. Birdie has an enchantment I want her to cast on you."

"An enchantment?" Jax asked. "What kind of enchantment?"

Birdie joined Gare and Kelva in looking over the ledge above. "It's a tracking enchantment. Perfect for making sure I don't lose speedy game, but it will also help us find you in case you need to relocate for some reason."

"And why would we need to relocate?" Jax called back. "It doesn't look like there's anything dangerous down here, aside from the trees."

Birdie pointed her hand towards Jax, a dark aura surrounding it. In the blink of an eye the aura transferred to Jax before disappearing. He looked himself over, not feeling any different.

"There you go," said Birdie. "Just remember not to let your guard down. The forest might seem quiet, but there are spectral beasts in there that can walk through the trees and appear without warning."

"What?" Jax shouted, his mind immediately returning to Ev.

"Yep!" replied Birdie, obnoxiously cheerful. "The good news is that you've got Ev with you, and they don't exactly like going near healing magic."

Well, he supposed that was something to take comfort in, but not much. "I need to get back to Ev."

"Jax!" shouted Kelva before he had the chance to retreat. "If you have to move, head north," she said, pointing. "That's where we'll be coming from."

Jax nodded, but before he could leave Kelva continued.

"One more thing," she said. "Remember our purpose. If you have to move before Huxley is able to, the mission comes first."

Jax looked up and met Kelva's eyes, nodded, then turned and hurried back to Ev, still working on Huxley. He told her what Kelva and Birdie had said. "As soon as you're finished with Huxley, we should take him back under the cliffs to wait. At least we'll be out of reach of these trees there."

Ev agreed, but Huxley began to stir before they reached that point.

"Easy there," she said softly. "You're still hurt. Stay still until I finish healing you."

Huxley raised his hand to his temple as Jax took over providing the light. "What... happened?" he grunted, then looked around. "Where is everyone?"

Ev answered. "I need you to stay calm. We were separated from the rest of the group, but they're on their way."

"Are we in the forest?" he asked, now staring out into the trees. "Is this the Shadowknot?"

Jax answered this time. "Yeah. We were attacked by the roc. It made the ledge we were on collapse. The only good news is I'm pretty sure it also chased all the revenants away."

"The roc? At night?" Huxley chuckled. "That must have been sight." Huxley tried to sit up, but Ev put a hand on his chest and coerced him back down.

"Mr. Huxley," Ev said, "before you get up, you need to know... you were really hurt in the attack."

Huxley stared blankly.

"I did the best I could, but there are some things I can't heal."

"Oh, dear. Is that why my leg hurts?" Huxley asked.

Ev glanced briefly at the ground before looking back up into Huxley's eyes. "Mr. Huxley, your leg is gone."

"Gone?" Huxley sat up. When he saw the stump where his leg had been, he froze.

"I'm sorry," said Ev, placing a hand on his shoulder.

Huxley didn't respond. Neither Ev nor Jax could think of anything to say to him. After a few moments of silence he pulled his gaze away from his missing leg and examined the forest again, his eyes stopping on the remains of one of the horses.

"Well, I suppose I'm still better off than him."

Jax nodded almost imperceptibly. "Are you going to be okay?"

Huxley looked down at his missing leg once again, taking a moment to respond. "I suppose I'll have to be."

Ev handed him his staff, which he used to push himself up into a standing position while Jax helped stabilize him. Jax had to admit, Huxley was taking the loss of his leg remarkably well, or at least was doing a great job of pretending to.

Jax pointed Huxley towards the outcrop they'd fallen from. "Come on, we'll probably be safer over there."

The journey back may have been short, but it wasn't easy. The area was littered with fallen vines and branches, and Jax didn't dare tempt fate by testing if they were still dangerous. They were simple enough obstacles for him and Ev, but Huxley was in no position to be nimble. Using his staff as a crutch, he allowed Jax to help him along a path around the carnage. When the group did make it back under the rocky overhang, Jax was more than ready to give his hand a rest. He was fairly certain he was slowly cooking his own hand, and made a mental note to learn some other spell he could use as a torch that wouldn't feel like sticking his arm in an oven once this journey was over.

Once nestled safely under the overhang, they waited for what must have been over an hour. Prior to falling, Jax had seen the slope down to the forest from up above. There was no way it should have been taking Kelva this long to reach them. No one had said anything yet, but the sinking feeling something bad had happened grew harder and harder to ignore.

Then, something else happened that they definitely couldn't ignore. In the darkness of the forest, ghostly green lights began to appear in the distance. The lights flickered about through the trees, but one thing was clear. They were getting closer.

Jax reached for his sword as Ev helped Huxley stand to face whatever was coming.

"What are those?" Ev asked.

"I don't know," said Jax, "but don't forget what Birdie said about the monsters here not liking healing magic."

"I didn't forget," replied Ev, holding a glowing hand towards the forest.

The lights grew closer, and a pack of ghostly skeletal hounds stepped right through the trees at the edge of the forest.

Ev's hand glowed brighter, and the hounds ceased their approach.

Jax raised his own hand, emitting a brilliant flash, but the hounds didn't react.

"I guess it's just healing magic they don't like," Jax said, putting his hand back down.

"Yeah, but what do we do about them?" asked Ev. "I can't fight with healing spells!"

"Maybe we don't need to," Jax said. "They aren't coming any closer."

"I can't keep this up all night," Ev said. "We need to do something before I run out of magic."

Huxley pointed his staff towards the creatures. "Perhaps a bit of lightning will scare them away."

"Good idea," said Jax, stepping forward. "Hey! Get out of here!" he yelled, launching a light blast at one of the hounds.

He barely had time to realize his mistake. As soon as the blast connected the rest of the hounds charged. Jax raised his sword as one of the beasts lunged at him. He deflected the hound's attack, but another latched onto his leg, fangs biting through his armor. Another jumped at him, this time knocking him to the ground. He tried to swing again, but a third hound grabbed his sword arm. The one that had knocked him down headed straight for his face, jaws agape.

The bite never came. With a thunderous crack and flash, the charging hound disappeared in a puff of smoke. Another flash, and as suddenly as it had been taken, his arm was free again. Jax took the opportunity to strike at the devil hound still gnawing at his leg, which knocked it loose but did little more. The hound lunged once again, but found its ribcage impaled on Jax's sword. Jax channeled his magic through his blade, and the monster vanished into dust.

The sound of Huxley shouting told Jax this wasn't over. Jumping to his feet, he prepared to fire at the hounds that had knocked Huxley to the ground, only to stop himself as he watched Ev throw herself on top of them. The moment her glowing hands touched them the monsters disappeared, ending the battle in an instant.

Jax withdrew his hand, thoroughly impressed and a little shocked by his sister's behavior. "Wow, Ev. Are you okay?"

Ev stood back up panting and looked at her hand. "Yeah. I never thought I'd use healing as a weapon."

Huxley grunted and Ev turned back to help him sit up again. He nodded in gratitude. "Thank you, Miss Ruthoree. You can really pack a wallop when you want to, can't you?"

Ev smiled. "I think they just were really weak to recovery spells, Sir Huxley."

Another thirty minutes passed, and finally Kelva arrived, along with Gare, Diana, and Birdie.

"My apologies for taking so long," Kelva said as Gare ran up to give Jax a big bear hug. "Apparently the traps in this forest form some kind of maze. It will take a while for us to get back out."

Kelva then noticed Huxley. "Oh..."

Huxley managed to push himself up with his staff and met her eyes. "Don't worry about me, Captain. I know the mission is what's most important. If you have to leave me behind—"

"No one is leaving anyone behind," Kelva interjected. She turned to Gare. "Mr. Hue, do you think you can carry Sir Farrow?"

"Who?" asked Gare.

Kelva sighed, but Huxley spoke up first. "Now, now, I'm hardly sure that's necessary. I can walk decently well with this staff of mine."

Kelva approached Huxley and put her hand on his shoulder. "That may be so, but if we need to move quickly that won't be an option." She turned back to Gare again. "Would you be able to carry him if we need you to?"

"Oh, him!" Gare exclaimed. "Yeah, sure, no problem. I'll have you know I carried Jax halfway across the city back when we were attacked."

"Good," replied Kelva. "In that case you and Diana can take turns carrying him. From now on I will carry the... item," she said, eyeing Birdie.

Diana joined Kelva next to Huxley, plopping her hand on his other shoulder. "Through dark and dim, together we will overcome all."

Back at the edge of the forest, Birdie cocked her head and chimed in.

"Well then, Miss Captain, if that's all sorted out we do have a long way to go before we meet up with our feathery friend."

Kelva took the bag with the Heart from Huxley and turned to face Birdie, who was gesturing with her thumb towards the forest.

Jax was confused. "What's she talking about? I thought we were heading to Roehelm."

Kelva looked back at Jax. "We are, but we lost all but four horses in the attack. We've been discussing alternative methods of reaching Roehelm because of that."

"Okay... like what?" Jax pried.

Gare gave a lopsided grin. "Hoo boy. Bud, you are not going to like this."

Chapter 7

High atop the southern-most peak of the Windy Mountains, overlooking a camp of dragons, revenants, brigands, and shades, the Undead King Dezeroth gazed to the north, where his band of scouts had just failed in their mission. All was not a loss, however, as at least they had succeeded in narrowing down the Heart's location — assuming the mortals who protected it hadn't fallen, that is. If they had, then all the better. The shades he had hidden in Marisol would seize it immediately should the Heart ever return there.

"My liege," gurgled one of his undead servants, "Exalted Lord Syrus has returned and requests your presence."

"Tell him to come to me," Dezeroth commanded. Being forced to ally himself with a disgraced Radiant was an indignity he had no choice but to bear. He was not about to further his self-abasement by giving the impression that he respected the Divine's wishes.

His servant grunted and bowed before wandering off to deliver his message. Dezeroth turned back towards the horizon, considering his options. The roc made aerial searches impossible by day and apparently by night as well. He would need a different approach. He needed soldiers who could move quickly through the Shadowknot Forest if that was where the mortals hid, and scouts who could observe the entirety of the Slime Pits should the mortals attempt to exit the Mountain Navel. Shades were the obvious choice for the forest. For the Slime Pits, he could use harpies, but getting them into position with those winds would be difficult, and he had too few of them he could rely on besides. No, onis were the better choice. They lacked the eyesight that harpies possessed, but they could travel quickly enough over land, and despite their low numbers in his army they would be strong enough to hold their own against warriors of Grandis. If he sent gremlins along with them to act as extended eyes and ears, that would be sufficient to ensure that the Heart did not escape his grasp again.

Approaching footsteps told Dezeroth that it was time to entertain his temporary ally, and so he deigned to turn and speak to his visitor face to face. Seeing Syrus again just reminded him of how much he hated everything about this dark-haired Divine, a so-called protector of Doxla who had chosen to take on the form of a diminutive scholar, forgoing armor and weapons in favor of a cloak and decorative rod. Of course, Dezeroth wouldn't let any of his disdain show when he actually addressed his audience.

"I take it by how long you were away that your assault on Roehelm was successful."

Syrus bowed exaggeratedly, then stunned Dezeroth as a pair of brilliant crystal wings emerged behind him. The Radiant looked up and smiled. "Not only was my attack on Roehelm successful, but so was the one I led against the Altar of Restoration. Now," Syrus continued as he stood up straight once again, "not only have I reclaimed my Heart, but I have regained my status as Radiant as well."

So, the fool had done it then, but Dezeroth was not one to be intimidated. "I hope your newfound power doesn't mislead you into thinking the balance of our relationship has changed."

Syrus's smile faded. "You know as well as I that only together do we stand a chance at restoring Eclipse's power and defeating Grandis and Escalor."

"Indeed I do," replied Dezeroth, "but what of after? We have a deal, you and I."

"And I will honor my word," answered Syrus. "Your only concern then will be what Eclipse decides to do. He is beyond the control of any of us."

"If he does not respect the efforts I am going through to restore his power, then I will spend the rest of eternity plaguing him with each and every one of my resurrections."

Syrus shrugged. "You did as I requested regarding Marisol, yes?"

Dezeroth scowled. He did not take kindly to being spoken to so flippantly. "We slaughtered all who fought under the banner of Grandis, but spared the rest, despite the foolishness of such mercy."

"In that case, I will do all I can to convince Eclipse to let you expand your domain and not send you back into slumber upon his restoration."

"Then let us hope you find Eclipse before Apollyon reawakens. My forces will have the Heart by this week's end, and I do not wish to see all of this effort prove meaningless because you preferred restoring your own power to locating Eclipse."

Syrus placed both hands atop his decorative little rod. "As I said before, Eclipse will be drawn to the Heart. His memories may have been lost when he was split, but he will certainly be near it wherever you find it, and he likely has been close to it for a long time."

Dezeroth sneered. "Assuming you are correct, I hope you have soldiers waiting at his place of resurrection, because I intend to kill every one of those fools who would dare serve in the name of Grandis."

"You go ahead and do that," Syrus replied, turning to go. "Now that my strength has been restored, I believe I'm ready to try and convince the Dragon King Tyranor that an alliance is no longer an option."

Dezeroth watched as Syrus marched back down the mountain towards the camp. Every second the Divine was in his sight reminded him of how his entire world had flipped on its head after the so-called Masters abandoned them all. For so long he'd striven to overcome the Divine, to expand his empire to cover all of Doxla, only to realize now, after the Divine had also disappeared, that he could not survive without the very beings who had for so long thwarted his ambitions.

He had only ever unwittingly danced to the Masters' machinations, but he would dance no more. This world belonged to him, and if an alliance with a traitorous Divine was the only route forward, then so be it. They may have abandoned the world to be consumed by Apollyon, the only force capable of granting even he, the immortal Dezeroth, a true death, but he would not sit idly by awaiting this destruction. With Eclipse by his side, not only would Apollyon be a neutered threat, but at last he would wring this world away from the few Divine who remained — the outsiders who asserted themselves as the rulers and protectors of Doxla. He would drive them out, and finally establish his empire as the greatest power in the world.

Syrus disappeared from sight, and Dezeroth was ready to enact his plans. Soon, the Heart would be his, and justice would quickly follow.

Chapter 8

Jax shuffled around what had to have been the hundredth root circle they passed that night... or was it day now? He wouldn't have been surprised if it was. They'd spent hours wandering through the forest, and despite every tree being completely bare of leaves, not a single speck of light entered from the sky above. No stars, no moon, and presumably not even the sun. Time seemed to stand still here. Not just because of the perpetual darkness, but because of the endless monotony of the forest. Everything looked the same. Walls of vines, circles of roots, the occasional band of roving ghost hounds and other specters — eventually it all lost its menace. Sure, it was creepy, and the knowledge that a single misstep could be his last kept Jax alert, but the monsters of the woods didn't pose much threat to the group now that they were together, which meant that a bit of caution was all that it took to stay alive here in this darkest of forests.

In fact, the last scary thing they'd seen was Ev's reaction when Kelva had told them they would be abandoning the remaining horses they'd left at the entrance to the forest. She'd practically thrown a fit at the thought of leaving the horses to die. To be fair, Jax wasn't exactly happy about the whole thing either, especially after Kelva had explained they'd be traveling clear through the forest just to try and tame the roc. So what if Divine had done so in the past? They were Divine! Jax and everyone else there were decidedly not, and that thing could crush any one of them with a single talon if it wanted to.

Still, he supposed, Kelva's reasoning was sound. Dezeroth likely had an idea as to where they were now, and with only three horses Kelva would either have to leave people behind or travel too slowly to escape the forces inevitably coming for them. And, as it turned out, this forest really wasn't as impassible as tales had led him to believe.

"I don't get it," Jax said at last. "This place was made to test the Divine, right?"

"According to legend," said Huxley. "Why do you ask?"

"I dunno," answered Jax as he skirted around an ominous hole in the ground. "I guess I just thought we'd have more trouble doing something that was supposed to challenge Divine."

Kelva spoke this time. "Prior to ascending to Radiance, most Divine were no more powerful than nepacs. I imagine the Masters would have accounted for that when they created this forest. Divine weren't exactly known for their patience or caution, either, so a challenge demanding both likely proved difficult for them."

Jax considered that for a moment. "Did you ever meet any? Divine, that is?"

"I saw them, but I never associated with them," answered Kelva. "Marisol was one of the last remaining Radiant Halls. Radiants and other Divine from around Doxla would gather there to trade and converse with one another, but they paid little attention to nepacs such as us. Of course, that was before the Dark Radiant attacked."

"But Lord Grandis expected that attack," Jax replied. "The Dark Radiant was split. Why did the Divine stop coming?"

Kelva shook her head. "I imagine for the same reason they've gone from the rest of the world, whatever that may be. They'd been disappearing for a long time, even before the traitor Syrus created the Dark Radiant. Supposedly, long ago, there were once millions of Divine and thousands of Radiants, but I myself never laid eyes on more than a few dozen, at best."

"Well," said Jax thoughtfully, "whatever the reason, we still have Supreme Lord Grandis and Esteemed Lady Escalor to protect us from Apollyon. If we can handle trials the Masters made for the Divine on our own, maybe that's all we need. Forget all those other Divine."

"If we had more Divine in the world, Marisol never would have fallen," Kelva said. "They protected us from fiends such as Dezeroth — monsters too powerful for ordinary nepacs to face on their own."

Jax fell silent. Kelva's words restoked the memory of his father's death, of his own inadequacy, of the failure of the entire Light Guard to perform the one duty they'd been given by Lord Grandis. They'd all tried and all folded against a single Radiant class entity, and Jax's recent successes all smalled in comparison to that moment of utter defeat. Still, the Heart was in their possession, not Dezeroth's. As long as he didn't falter again, he could accomplish something yet worthy of a paladin of Grandis.

A light up ahead announced that the party had very nearly reached the edge of the forest, and also confirmed Jax's suspicion that they'd walked through the night and into day. The trees parted, and Jax leaned his head back, looking up the mountain that stretched above the clouds. The path ahead was carved into dull gray stone and led straight up through large, open cavities in the mountain. At the top of that path, the roc waited for them. Jax had no idea how they were supposed to "tame" it, but if the feat was no more difficult than traversing Shadowknot, then perhaps the idea wasn't as crazy as it had at first sounded. Getting up there, on the other hand…

"Oh, boy," Gare sighed, "this is going to be a hike isn't it?"

Kelva turned to Birdie. "How long did you say it would take to reach the roc's nest?"

Birdie placed her hand on her hip cockily. "Well, I could reach it by sundown. Given our present company, though…" she looked in Huxley's direction, "we probably won't get there 'til noon tomorrow."

"And you know for sure where it is," Kelva stated.

"I already told you that. It's at the top of the highest peak, which is the one behind that one," Birdie pointed at the mountain right in front of them.

Kelva nodded, then turned to Huxley. "Do you need to take a break soon?"

"Let's see how I'm doing after we climb a few hills," Huxley replied.

Kelva turned back to Birdie. "Alright then. Lead the way."

* * * *

The climb up the roc's peak was remarkably unremarkable. The most interesting part was stumbling across a few worn rope bridges that had somehow survived years of neglect. Aside from the trouble of getting Huxley up some of the steeper slopes — a problem which Gare ultimately solved —

the only real obstacle they faced was an ambush by a group of invisible reptiles similar to the ones Jax had seen that first night after exiting the caves. Even Miss Cocky "Perception Skills" had trouble spotting them before they moved, but in the end they proved little more than a minor annoyance. Sure, the monsters got in a couple of cheap shots, but they were easy enough to kill, and Ev fixed up the few wounds the party received in a matter of minutes.

Then came nightfall, and with it a much needed opportunity to rest. The group found a nice little nook to settle into — one of the large cavities carved into the side of the mountain that in this case only had one way in or out. It was sheltered from the wind, and a large portion of it was completely hidden from view from the outside. Neither Jax nor Kelva put it past Dezeroth to send more zodiacs after them, so the secrecy was a major plus for the location. There was also just enough vegetation growing around to put together thin little mats for beds. They weren't exactly comfortable, but they helped fend off the cold of the ground a tiny bit.

Yet, despite the conditions and everything else that had happened, Jax slept the soundest sleep he'd had in a while that night. He barely registered having any dreams — maybe something about eating glowing moss, but it was gone the moment Gare shook him awake.

"Hey bud, your turn. Just a heads up, but Birdie's kind of taken over the watch."

Not really registering what Gare was saying, Jax sat up, rustling the grass and leaves beneath him as he did so. Only half awake, he pushed himself to his feet, picked up his sword, and shambled over to the mouth of the cave where Birdie was already waiting.

She spoke just above a whisper. "You sure you're up for this? I can stand watch on my own ya know."

That snapped Jax awake a bit more. Not completely, but enough to get defensive. "I'm fine. I've stood watch every night so far, and I'm not about to stop now, and weren't you supposed to have the first shift? Diana's supposed to be sharing my watch."

Birdie shrugged. "I'm not going to be able to sleep. Might as well let someone else get some rest. You can sleep, too, you know. I guarantee it's going to be boring."

"It always is," Jax answered, though as he said that he remembered how the first night's watch was anything but.

Tonight, however, boring was the only term to describe it. The only sound to be heard was the wind, the only movement a few shrubs waving in the moonlight. There wasn't even a good view where they were. Another mountain face rose up directly across the small chasm that ran alongside the path they'd been following, preventing Jax from looking out over the surrounding landscape and instead providing him only with the sight of gray rock.

"Hey," said Birdie after a while. "Just what is it that's so important that you keep safe anyway?"

Jax really didn't feel like talking to Birdie. "You aren't part of the Light Guard, so you aren't supposed to know."

"Right, and not telling me accomplishes what, exactly?"

"It accomplishes following orders," Jax replied.

"Mmhm. Okay. Tell me this, then. What are you going to do after you've finished taking your little whatever to Roehelm? Abandon your sister and run off to fight this Dezeroth?"

Jax's face grew hot. This woman was way overstepping her bounds. "First off, I would never abandon Ev. Our grandmother's in Roehelm — she can take care of her. And second—"

"So you are planning to abandon her."

"What? No! I'm not doing anything until I've made sure she's safe and taken care of."

"And then you're going to leave her," Birdie accused.

"I'm going to avenge our father," Jax corrected, "and I don't think what happens with me and Ev is any of your business."

"You know, I suppose it's not," said Birdie.

Jax expected her to say more, but she didn't. She just turned towards the entrance to their little shelter and watched the wind whip the leaves about outside.

Jax walked over to the other side of the entrance, not wanting to stand guard close to her. He was wide awake now, his mind going over all the ways he'd love to tell her off. Just who the hell did she think she was, anyway? The trip to Roehelm couldn't be over soon enough. The sooner they delivered the Heart, the sooner he'd be done with Birdie once and for all.

An hour must have passed before either of them moved from their spots. Eventually though, Birdie stepped out from under the cover of the stone cavity, hand on her dagger. Jax wondered what she was up to, but didn't exactly feel like engaging with her either.

Out on the path, Birdie stood completely still, staring back down the way they'd come. Whatever she was doing, it was making Jax nervous. Suddenly, she turned and walked briskly over to Jax.

"Wake everyone up, we need to go," she said.

"What are you talking about?" Jax asked, peeking out down the road and seeing nothing.

"We're being followed," Birdie answered. "I can sense them."

"Oh really?" Jax responded. "You mean like how you 'sensed' those furry lizards earlier?"

"Camodo dragons don't have any magic to sense. What's coming up that path definitely does."

"Uh-huh. And just what's coming up the path, then?"

"Look, you don't believe me? Fine. I'll wake everyone up then."

Birdie hurried over to Diana and shook her awake. She clearly thought something was coming, and as much as he didn't like her he couldn't help but start to believe that she might be right. As she moved on to Kelva, Jax hurried over to wake up Gare and Ev. Once everyone was up, Kelva demanded an explanation.

Birdie looked Kelva in the eye. "Shades."

Kelva's eyes opened wide. "Shades? You saw them?"

"I sensed them."

"You sensed them," Kelva repeated, somewhat dubiously.

"One of my earliest memories was a horrible experience involving shades," Birdie stated. "I'd never mistake the feeling of their presence."

"Captain," Jax offered, "maybe one of us should go take a look before we jump to conclusions."

"No," Kelva answered. "If there is even a chance that shades are approaching we can't wait here. A battle against them in the dark is not one we would likely win. Here," she said, handing the Heart to Jax.

Jax was completely taken aback. "What are you doing?"

"If we are attacked, Diana and I are the ones best suited to holding them off. It will be up to you to continue on to Roehelm." Kelva then turned to Huxley. "I'm sorry, but Garrison's going to have to carry you."

Huxley nodded, and the group started back up the path once again. They moved quickly, but didn't run. Jax repeatedly made certain the bag was secure on his back. He never expected he'd be the one to carry the Heart, but now that he was he was absolutely not going to mess it up.

"Keep your eyes open for moving shadows," Kelva told the group. "If you see anything suspicious, let me know immediately."

Five minutes later, and with no sign of any shades, Jax had all but dismissed Birdie's suspicions. He supposed there was no harm in moving early, but the inconvenience was still annoying. Eventually, though, Birdie gave an update on the situation.

"They're getting closer," she said.

"How close?" asked Kelva.

"It's hard to tell," Birdie answered, "I just feel they're magic getting stronger." She looked back down the path.

Jax and a few others looked to. That was when he saw it. An inky black puddle sliding quickly up the mountain towards them.

"What the heck is that?" he asked.

"Shade!" Kelva shouted, and suddenly a whole slew of the dark puddles appeared around them, gliding across both the ground and the side of the mountain, heading to cut the party off.

Kelva held up her sword and unleashed a blinding light from it. The puddles immediately reshaped into humanoid figures, the ones on the wall falling to the ground. Most of them stood up completely unfazed, but a couple of them that landed close by disappeared when they hit the stone pathway. The remaining white-eyed shadows formed smoking black blades seemingly out of nothing and charged forward.

"Run!" Kelva shouted.

They ran. Jax led the pack, with Ev and Birdie close behind. Kelva and Diana held back until everyone else had passed before following.

Jax looked back to see Kelva running with her sword outstretched behind her. It was hard to make out the dark figures following them through the intense light emitted from her blade, but Jax was sure he counted over a dozen shades chasing after them.

Around the corner, the path ended at an old bridge spanning a large chasm, perhaps a hundred feet in length and supported by six ropes attached to two posts on each side. Jax sped towards it when a pair of dark puddles shot out from his and Ev's shadows in front of them. The puddles stopped at the bridge and took shape, blades at the ready.

One of them turned towards the bridge and cut through one of the ropes holding it up.

"No!" Jax shouted, firing a blast at the saboteur.

The second shade jumped in front of the blast, blocking it with its blade as the first raised its own sword to cut into the bridge once again.

Suddenly, Birdie appeared out of nowhere between the shades. She slashed at the bridge shade with her dagger and spun around, nicking the defending one as well.

Both turned on her. They swung their swords, but she ducked low and slammed her shoulder into the bridge shade, knocking it back. The bridge shade wrapped its arms around her neck, and the second plunged its sword straight into... the other shade?

The image of Birdie faded away as the injured shade stumbled backwards. Jax couldn't make out facial expressions on either of them, but he was sure they were both just as confused as he was.

He looked back to where he'd thought Birdie had been following behind him and saw her panting, arm outstretched with faint wisps of dark magic still leaving her fingertips.

"Wh—"

"Don't ask, just attack!" yelled Birdie.

The urgency of the situation came back to Jax, and he fired another blast at the uninjured shade. This time his attack hit. He knew it wouldn't be enough to down it, but he didn't need to. He fired again and again, keeping the shade off balance until Gare appeared with Huxley, who fired a bolt of lighting at the two shades.

The lightning blasted a hole in the closest shade, but didn't kill it. The two fiends dropped back into their puddle form, but Kelva and Diana rounded the corner before they could escape, the light from Kelva's sword forcing them to take solid form once again. Jax charged forward and struck before the nearest one was able to recompose itself. His sword cleaved clean through the half-formed figure, and the two halves of its body fell to the ground in a puddle of smoking ink. The second shade slipped over the side of the cliff and disappeared.

"Keep going!" Kelva yelled. "Get across the bridge!"

Jax didn't need to be told twice. He paused only long enough for Ev to run on ahead of him before following her across the shaky planks. Gare was right on his heels, and Jax could here Huxley yelling for Gare to stop and put him down. Gare obliged, but not until he'd made it safely to the far side of the chasm.

Just as Huxley was placed on the ground, the light from the other side disappeared. Jax looked across the ravine to see Diana running for her life across the bridge, shades right behind her. Kelva was lying motionless on the ground.

Jax drew his sword and yelled to Gare. "Get ready to cut the bridge!"

Birdie rushed towards the bridge with her dagger. "We have to cut it now!" she yelled.

"No! We have to wait for Diana," Jax yelled back, jumping in her way.

"That's not Diana!" Birdie shouted, grabbing Jax and throwing him behind her.

She started cut through one of the ropes, but Gare leapt forward and stopped her before she got further.

"Let go of me!" she yelled.

Gare threw her back the same as she'd done to Jax. "I don't know how you do things in the wild, but we don't leave people behind."

Gare turned towards the bridge, ax at the ready, and the moment Diana reached their side he slammed it into one of the posts holding up the bridge, cutting one of the ropes. Jax joined in, cutting the ropes on the other post. A second swing from Gare and the bridge sagged violently, knocking the shades off balance. They formed into their little puddles and started sliding along the tilted planks.

With a final swing Jax cut the last remaining support. The bridge fell, slamming into the far side of the chasm. The shades started sliding back up, but Jax had an idea. He wasn't sure it would work, but if the shades wanted to go up, then he wanted them to go down. He raised his sword and, focusing his magic into it the way he'd done with his hand in the forest, succeeded in emitting the same blinding light that Kelva had earlier. It lit up the far side of the canyon, and the shades popped out of their little puddles before falling to the ground far below. Jax stepped to the edge of the cliff, sword raised high, and watched to his satisfaction as the shades disappeared into splats of ink and clouds of smoke. Once the smoke cleared, he let his sword dim once again. He was far away yet from avenging his father, but at least he'd been able to exact justice for Captain Kelva.

A shout from Ev cut his victory short. Jax spun about to see Birdie's dagger plunged deep into a struggling Diana's neck, dark smoke spraying from the wound. Jax pointed his sword at Birdie when a scream from Huxley drew his attention to his left.

To his horror he saw a smoking blade protruding from Huxley's chest, another shade standing in is shadow. Before Jax or Gare had a chance to react the shade swung its sword to the left, tossing Huxley from it and over the side of the chasm. With a roar Gare raised his ax and charged the fiend. The next thing Jax knew Gare was on the ground with the shade standing over him, blade raised for the killing blow. Jax swung his sword around and fired a beam straight into the shade's chest, knocking it back a step.

The shade recovered and swung its blade down, but Gare had managed to block the blow with his ax. Jax closed the distance between him and the shade and swung with all his might. The shade avoided the attack and returned a strike that sent Jax reeling. Before he could recover, the shade lunged forward with a thrust that cracked through the mail on Jax's chest.

Jax staggered backwards as the shade raised its smoking blade for a followup strike. Just as the fiend swung it was interrupted by an arrow piercing straight into the side of its face.

The shade turned to face where the arrow had come from when Gare took a swipe at its legs, knocking it to the ground. The shadowy fiend melted into a puddle and sped away from the group, but Jax wasn't about to let it escape. He lit his sword up once again, forcing the injured shade to take form once more. Ignoring the pain in his chest, he fired a blast from his hand at the foe, nearly knocking it to the ground a second time. The shade stood to face Jax, but a barrage of arrows brought it to its knees. Jax pointed his sword at its chest and fired a beam of light straight through it, felling the fiend for good.

Gare stood back up next to Jax as the shade melted away, the arrows in its body dropping to the ground. Jax looked around the area for any sign of more danger, but the mountain was quiet. Satisfied there were no more shades, he turned his attention to Birdie and pointed his sword at her.

"You. What the hell just happened?"

Gare placed a hand on his shoulder. "Bud, chill, she just saved you."

Jax didn't relent. He jerked away from Gare, his eyes darting to where he'd seen Birdie attack Diana. All he saw now was a smoking puddle. Inside, he knew the answer, but he couldn't bring himself to believe it. "Where's Diana?" he demanded.

Birdie said nothing.

Ev stepped forward to Birdie's defense. "Jax, there was no Diana. The Diana that crossed the bridge was really a shade."

Jax glanced at the inky stain on the ground, and after a moment's pause lowered his sword. He swallowed. Diana was gone. Kelva was gone. Huxley... was gone. All in a single attack. If they hadn't had any warning, if they'd been caught sleeping in their camp, they would have all been dead. The realization was sour, but as much as Jax hated to admit it, the only reason any of them were alive at all was because of Birdie.

Ev approached Jax and placed her hand over where the shade had injured him. Without a word she began healing him.

After a moment Gare asked, "So now what do we do?"

Jax hesitated before answering. "I don't think we have a choice. We have to tame that roc somehow."

Birdie abruptly turned and started walking away from them. "Yeah, well, good luck with that," she called back over her shoulder.

Jax frowned. "What are you on about? You're coming, too."

Birdie wheeled on him. "Why should I? You clearly don't trust me. You won't even tell me what it is you're trying so hard to protect."

Jax went straight back on the defensive. "Of course we won't, and why do you care so much about it, anyway?"

"Jax, just tell her," Ev said, surprising him.

"I can't," Jax returned, taking Ev's hand off his chest. "We can't. She isn't part of the Light Guard!"

"Who cares?" said Gare. "Dezeroth already knows what we have, and she's obviously not working for him, so what does it matter?"

Jax looked back and forth between Gare and Ev. Gare had a point, but still...

"We took an oath, Gare. I'm not going to break it."

"Well if you won't then I will," said Ev, challenging Jax with her eyes.

Jax met Ev's gaze, but when she didn't back down he relented. "Fine. You both want her to know? Then fine." He turned towards Birdie. "The thing we're keeping away from Dezeroth is a Heart. A Heart that belongs to the Dark Radiant, Eclipse."

The look of absolute shock that appeared on Birdie's face filled Jax with more satisfaction than he expected it would. For the first time, she wasn't acting like she knew everything.

"W-what...?" she began, but Jax continued.

"You heard me, but you probably haven't heard of him, because unlike other Radiants, he never worked to gather followers. He didn't protect the people like Lord Grandis. He appeared out of nowhere, a servant of the Fallen Radiant and traitor Lord Syrus, the monster who sought to purge the world of Divine and bring about the apocalypse with the next awakening of

Apollyon."

"Now hold on," Birdie interrupted, her composure somewhat regained. "No one can kill a Divine. Not even the Masters could do more than temporarily banish them."

"Maybe so," Jax said, "but Syrus and his followers split countless Divine, destroying all of their worldly possessions and hounding them relentlessly until they fled from Doxla. The Dark Radiant was the worst of all of them, even more powerful than Syrus himself."

Birdie seemed unconvinced. "If all that is true, then what does Dezeroth want with the Heart?"

"To destroy the world?" Jax offered. "To defeat Lord Grandis and Lady Escalor?" What does it matter? The Dark Radiant brought nothing but suffering to Doxla. It was only through the sacrifice of dozens of Radiants that Lord Grandis was able to stop them before. If the Dark Radiant returns, there won't be anyone who can stop him."

Birdie looked at the faces around her. "Alright, I get it. This Dark Radiant is bad. But Radiants can't be killed. They can be split, but they can be restored. You said that Radiants were sacrificed, but how? Where did they go? All of the Radiants who fought with this Grandis should still be here, right?"

"No one knows why the Divine have been disappearing," Ev said sadly, "but before Syrus and the Dark Radiant, there were still hundreds of Radiants and tens of thousands of Divine. They drove so many of them from our world. You've seen the effects. Monsters destroy towns and villages and lay waste to countrysides. Warlords and brigands kill thousands every year in areas not protected by Lord Grandis or Lady Escalor. If the Dark Radiant returns and splits both of them, then we won't have anyone left to defend us when Apollyon awakens again."

Birdie stared at the ground, processing everything she'd been told.

"Do you get it now?" Jax asked. "This is why it's so important we keep the Heart out of Dezeroth's hands. We can't destroy it, and we can't hide it, so we protect it. If it's too much—"

"It's not," Birdie answered, looking Jax in the eye.

"Good," Jax replied before looking towards the path ahead of them.

"I'll say 'good,'" Gare said. "We kind of need her at this point."

Honestly, Jax wasn't sure they could do it with her. Kelva, Huxley, and Diana were gone. He, Gare, and Ev were just cadets, and Birdie was just some random hunter. Sure, the roc could fly them most of the rest of the way, but... that required them first to tame the roc.

"Well," he said, looking back at where the others had fallen, "I guess we'd better keep moving. We still have a long way to go."

Chapter 9

The light of morning illuminated the mountainside. Rows of poofy sedges opened up into a sea of tiny flowers along the path leading ever upwards. The violent winds that the mountains were known for were but a gentle breeze here — the eye of the storm at the center of the Mountain Navel. The vegetation swayed ever so softly under its caress. Tucked away in the hollows of the mountain where the wind failed to blow were feathers the size of trees, reminders of who this peak truly belonged to. Far to the southeast, a sea of clouds had formed against the horizon, promising a storm in the future.

No one had talked much since the attack by the shades. Even Birdie had kept unusually quiet. When Jax had asked her about how they were supposed to tame a bird the size of a cathedral, her response was to the point and unenthusiastic.

"We need to slay a septipede, then bring it to the roc's nest."

"And after that?" Jax pressed.

"That's it," answered Birdie, not even looking back at him as she spoke.

"That's it," Jax repeated. "Just kill a monster and give it to the giant bird."

"You want it to be harder?" Birdie asked, finally giving Jax a sideways glance.

"Well, no... I guess I just expected a trial for Divine to be more than something anyone could do," Jax replied.

"Divine aren't any stronger than nepacs until they ascend," said Birdie, looking forward again. "Of course anyone can complete pre-lord trials."

"Pre-lord?" asked Jax. "What the heck is pre-lord?"

Birdie just looked the other way, clearly not wanting to continue the conversation. Ev, on the other hand, was more than willing to chime in.

"I think I've heard that term before. It refers to trials Divine face before becoming Radiants. After ascension, they have further trials that allow them to earn prestige among their peers. If I remember right, they call those the lord trials, because all Divine are given the title of Lord when they ascend. By conquering the lord trials they can gain the titles of High Lord, Esteemed Lord, Exalted Lord, and eventually Supreme Lord."

"Where the heck did you hear all that?" asked Gare.

"It's called a library," responded Ev, "something both of you could stand to visit more often."

Jax heard Birdie chuckle under her breath. "And where did you learn about pre-lord trials?" he asked her. "I never would have taken a hunter to be a scholar."

Birdie gave Jax the same sideways glance she'd given him earlier. "Just because I prefer the outdoors doesn't mean I don't have an intellect."

"I didn't say it did," Jax said.

"Yeah," cut in Ev, "you kind of did."

"No, I just don't see why a hunter would need to know about Divine trials," he shot back, gesturing towards Birdie.

"Everyone should want to know as much about the Divine as possible," Ev answered. "Maybe if more people did, someone would have figured out why they're disappearing and found a way to stop it."

"That..." Jax began, but he relented. It wasn't like it mattered anyway. Why should he care what Birdie's interest in the Divine was? "You know what, forget that," he said after a pause. "Just tell us more about this... what's-a-pede thing."

"Septipede," Birdie corrected. "It's a giant armored worm with seven legs and deadly venom."

"Uh-huh," pressed Jax, "and? What do we have to do to kill it?"

"The same thing you do to kill any other monster," Birdie replied annoyedly. "Stab it with your sword until it's dead."

"Gee, what excellent advice, I'm glad you were here to tell us," Jax spat.

"Jax, please be nice," Ev interceded. "She's obviously still upset about last night."

"She's upset?" Jax practically yelled. He gestured back down the way they'd come. "What about me? What about you? Those were our comrades who died last night, not hers!" Jax pointed right at Birdie. "You don't get to be upset!"

Birdie narrowed her eyes into an icy stare. Behind those light blue eyes was a forcefulness that warned him not to press himself any further.

"Jax, calm down!" Ev yelled, stepping between him and Birdie.

"Yeah bud, chill," added Gare.

Jax looked between Gare and Ev, then turned away from all of them and continued up the mountain on his own. He heard Ev address Birdie behind him.

"Sorry about Jax....," she said quietly, probably hoping he wouldn't hear.

Jax didn't care, and he didn't want to hear, either. After climbing on his own for a bit, he turned back to see how far behind the others were following. It turned out they were a good fifty yards away. Ev, Birdie, and Gare were walking side by side, chatting about who knew what. Probably him.

Not wanting them to catch him looking at them, he turned back to the path ahead and continued on, focusing on his own thoughts. He was getting rather irritated with how chummy Birdie was getting with Ev, and now Gare was also acting like she was one of them. The woman was an outsider. They weren't supposed to trust her the way they were, and frankly, Jax was sick of her condescending attitude. Now that they'd told her what they were carrying, though, they didn't have any choice but to take her with them. If they tried to ditch her, Jax in no way would put it past her to hand over that information to Dezeroth for profit.

After another few minutes of climbing he heard Gare call out to him. When he looked back he saw no sign of Birdie or Ev. Gare waved him over, then pointed down a side trail after Jax had joined him.

"We need to go this way, bud."

"Why would we go that way?" Jax asked. "That path heads down."

"Yeah, well it also leads to the septipedes, which you kinda would know if you hadn't run off ahead of us."

Jax felt his face heating up. "Well excuse me for not wanting to listen to you pal around with someone we don't know anything about and who's only helping us because we promised her money."

"Bud, who cares why she's helping us? Do you honestly think after everything we've been through she's going to stab us in the back?"

"I think it's a risk we can't afford," answered Jax.

"Are you serious right now, Jax?"

"Of course I'm serious!" Jax exploded. "I know we need her help, but that doesn't mean we can trust her. We let her do her job, but we watch her, and we don't let our guards down."

Gare frowned and shook his head. "No, bud. I don't know what your hangup is, but you need to get over it. She's one of us now whether you like it or not."

"No, she isn't," Jax got right up in Gare's face. "She's a mercenary, not a soldier."

"Yeah, well guess which one of us isn't acting like a soldier right now," Gare responded.

Jax's face turned red. "You know what, you want to trust her, fine, but I don't want to have anything to do with her." He stormed past Gare but was stopped when Gare latched onto his arm.

"Let go of me!" Jax pulled away, but Gare held on tight.

"No way. We're dealing with this right now."

Jax tried again to break free of Gare's grip. "There's nothing to deal with. If you want to put your life in danger by trusting her, then fine, but I'm smarter than that."

Gare finally let go. "Yeah, Jax, you're real smart. Us not trusting her about that fake Diana's the reason Huxley got killed, so still not trusting her sounds like an absolutely great plan!"

Jax rubbed his wrist as he avoided eye contact with Gare.

"Look, I get it. I really do. You like doing things on your own, and you don't trust strangers, but right now it's not about you. It's about doing whatever it takes to get the Heart to Roehelm. You think I want to be out here in these mountains? Because I don't. All I want is to go home and see if my family's okay, but this is more important. If we fail, then nothing else matters, so I'm not going to let my worries about my family distract me, and you can't let your worries distract you."

Jax didn't answer as he continued to avoid looking at Gare. A gentle hand on his shoulder finally got him to glance back at his friend.

"Come on, bud. After this roc ride we'll only have a few days left to go and we won't have to worry about it anymore. You can get along with her for that long, can't you?"

Jax softly nodded. "Yeah. I can do that."

Gare smiled widely and slapped Jax on the back. "There we go! Now let's go kill this septipede thing so we can get out of these stupid mountains."

Jax and Gare made their way down the trail, which led them into a rather wet region of the mountain with puddles and streams trickling down all along the side of the path. Ev and Birdie were out of sight by now, but the path was straightforward, and somehow Jax doubted that even Birdie would have left them behind if there was a chance they could get lost. They pressed onward, ready to take on the giant bug that was their key to succeeding in their mission.

* * * *

Wedged between neighboring peaks, the home of the septipede turned out to be a large hollow in the mountainside covered in a thick layer of ivy. Water was pooled into little pits all around the area, each of them also filled with ivy. Jax and Gare both took the opportunity to take a drink before approaching Ev and Birdie, who were looking at some frogs in one of the pools while Ev munched on some sort of fruit growing from the ivy. Jax picked a few of the berries for himself and gave one a try. The flavor wasn't the best — mostly sour and bitter with just a hint of sweet — but it was the first food he'd had in over two days, so he wasn't feeling too picky. The four of them ate silently, the awkwardness of their earlier exchange still fresh.

"Alright," he said after he'd downed as much as he felt he could handle, "so where is this septipede?"

Birdie stood up, brushed off some vegetation that had clung to her and pointed to a pockmarked wall at the back of the hollow. "Over there. They live in those big holes. We'll have to be careful not to draw out more than one."

"And how exactly are we going to do that?"

"You just leave that to me," Birdie replied. "Once I lure it out, it'll be up to you and Gare to kill it."

"Right," said Jax, his hand on the hilt of his sword. "I don't suppose you're going to tell us how to do that before we head in there?"

Birdie gave him a tired look. "I already told you, just stab it. Aim for the eyes and joints in its armor. Gare won't even have to bother with aiming, an ax is more than capable of cracking its carapace."

"So that's it, then," returned Jax. "You don't have any more advice on how to fight this thing."

"Look, you clearly think this is going to be hard, but it's not. Septipedes are mindless beasts that can only focus on one thing at a time. Once I have its attention it will be wide open to attacks from you. The only thing you'll have to worry about are the babies."

Gare waved his hands in front of him. "Whoa, whoa, whoa, hold on a second. What do you mean, 'babies'?"

Birdie spoke as if she were reading straight from a book. "Septipedes are one of the few monster species that reproduce. The young make their nest in the ivy, and though they never mature, their venom is just as deadly as an adult's, and their pincers will pierce plate armor."

Jax stepped up to the edge of the ivy patch, which went up to his shins. He didn't see any sign of the baby septipedes, but assumed that they must be hiding beneath the leaves. "So how will we be able to know where the babies are in all of this?"

Birdie tapped her temple, but her usual smirk was absent. "I can sense them. Just follow me and I'll find us a safe spot to fight the big one."

Jax took a deep breath and looked over at Gare. "Alright. You're the monster hunter. You ready, Gare?"

"Not really," Gare answered, but he pulled out his ax nonetheless. "You sure there isn't some way we can do this without wandering into a pit of poisonous crawly things?"

"Come on Gare. Don't you trust her perception skills?" he jabbed.

Gare frowned, then without a word took a step into the ivy. "Let's just get this over with."

Jax crossed over into the vegetation as well, followed by Birdie. The three of them made their way — their very indirect way — through the ivy, while Ev stayed back by the pool with the frogs. Jax couldn't see any of the miniature septipedes they were supposedly avoiding, but Birdie was adamant about the path they took, so either she did or she was purposefully dragging out the venture. Eventually, though, they stopped, and when they did Birdie ordered Jax and Gare to take up positions on either side of her.

Reluctantly, Jax complied, as did Gare, though he seemed ready to do just about anything if it meant getting out of there sooner.

Then, Birdie took a few steps back, faced one of the holes in the mountain, and held out her hand, a dark aura surrounding it. Out of nowhere, a second Birdie — partially transparent — appeared in front of the hole. Almost immediately, a huge centipede-like worm shot out from the darkness. It was as thick around as Gare's shoulders were broad and had six long, needly legs and an equally long "stinger" that looked just like an extra leg. Fierce mandibles protruded from its jaw beneath its beady black eyes. The fake Birdie vanished as quickly as the septipede had appeared, then reappeared closer to the group. The septipede chased after it. The illusion disappeared and returned once again, this time standing between Jax and Gare. The septipede rocketed towards the fake Birdie, and Jax couldn't help but take a stumble backwards. The monster struck, smashing its head down on the illusion.

"Now!" shouted Birdie as her doppelganger disappeared.

Jax hadn't been prepared for the quick attack, but Gare was, and he slammed his ax into the back of the creature's head. The septipede lurched upwards, throwing Gare to the ground as he struggled to hold onto his ax. The septipede reared back to strike at Gare, but Birdie recaptured its attention by shooting an arrow at its face. She then conjured up another fake immediately in front of herself, which promptly ran towards Jax.

The septipede whipped its stinger around and impaled the fake Birdie, which fell with a slight delay from when the stinger hit it. The septipede clearly didn't notice anything off, though, and it bit down on the fallen clone.

This time Jax was ready, and he plunged his sword deep into one of the cracks separating the segments of the monster's armor. The great beast jerked away, pulling Jax's sword with it as it reared back again. Its movements were much more sluggish now, and it wobbled unsteadily as if it were having trouble remaining upright. Birdie, panting, held out her arm as if she were creating another illusion, but no new Birdies appeared. Instead, the worm toppled over towards Gare, flailing about on the ground. Gare seemed surprised by this, but reacted quickly enough, bringing his ax down one final time. The septipede jerked as the blade cracked through its armored head, then lay still.

After waiting a moment to make sure that the thing really was dead, Jax retrieved his sword from the septipede's carcass. He looked over at Birdie, not sure if he should be impressed or concerned that she had that kind of magical ability.

"Alright," he said, "so the thing is dead. Now what? How are we supposed to get it up to the roc?"

"We carry it," Birdie responded.

"Are you kidding me? That thing is huge!"

"Which is why we'd better get started," replied Birdie. "It's a long way to the peak, and I'd rather not spend another night on this mountain."

That was a good point. Jax sighed. "I don't suppose you know any strength enchantments, do you?"

Birdie shook her head, then cocked it to the side. "Best I can do is give you the illusion of strength. You won't feel tired while you carry it, but you'll probably end up hurting yourself if we do that."

"About that," Jax prompted. "Where did you learn illusion magic, anyway?"

"I learned it on my own to survive. Like I said before, knowledge wins most battles. Perception gives me knowledge, and illusions take it away from whatever I'm fighting."

Jax looked down at the big dead worm. He was starting to see where she was coming from. "Well, it definitely made killing that thing easier. I guess carrying it's going to be the hard part."

"No worries!" shouted Gare, pounding his chest. "With me here, we'll get that big bug up to the big bird in no time."

"Alright, Gare," said Jax, sheathing his sword, "prove it."

"I will! Let's go!"

Gare jammed his arm under the upper portion of the beast and lifted up with all his might. Jax moved to help stabilize him as he lifted, and eventually he succeeded in propping up the neck of the thing on Gare's shoulder, probably supporting a third of its body weight.

"See?" Gare said, straining. "No problem."

Jax and Birdie worked together to lift up the middle of the septipede. Its bulk was immense, but somehow the two of them were able to get it up off the ground. Its back end was still laying in the ivy, but together the three of them had about two thirds of it up in the air. They trudged back the way they'd come, dragging the back third of the septipede behind them.

As soon as they were clear of the ivy, Ev ran over to greet them while they dropped the beast for a quick rest. After a few minutes, they picked it back up again, Gare in front, Jax and Birdie in the middle, and now Ev as well at the back. As small as Ev was, the extra help was noticeable, which was good, because they still had to drag a thousand-pound monster up half a mountain by nightfall.

Several hours later the nest of the roc was at last in sight — an enormous crater at the top of the mountain peak surrounded by dead trees and branches piled high along the sides. A few of the enormous feathers they'd seen in the valley lined the pathway up to the nest's entrance, along with numerous smaller feathers that were fluffy and white. At the center of the nest was the roc itself. This was the first Jax had gotten to see it clearly. The night it had attacked he couldn't make out much more than its massive figure. Now, he could see it in the light, in all of its glory.

For all intents and purposes, it was just an eagle, if an eagle was as tall as a four story building. Its feathers were the same color as the stone on the mountain, and it was certainly large enough to be mistaken for a part of it. Its talons could easily wrap around tree trunks, and its beak looked like it could swallow the entire septipede they'd brought with hardly an effort.

The roc didn't seem to notice their approach, instead gazing out over the surrounding mountains far away. The group took advantage of its distraction and stopped short of the nest for another break before the final push to the finish. They dropped the septipede unceremoniously in a spot well out of sight of the roc in case it decide to look in their direction, and sat against a large stone beside it. Every part of Jax hurt. Ev had been doing her best to keep them in good shape, and while it kept Jax feeling strong, her magic couldn't stop him from getting stiff and sore.

"Ya know," said Gare, panting. "I'm starting to see why this is one of the Divine trials."

Jax nodded in agreement. He'd be hurting for days after this for sure.

During the break, Birdie took the opportunity to gather up several of the smallest feathers and stuff them into the same bag she'd shoved the other monster parts she'd collected.

"You want more weight to carry?" Jax asked. Those "smallest" feathers were still over a foot long, and likely weighed nearly a pound each.

Birdie looked over at Jax as she shoved another feather into her bag. "Roc down is a very valuable material for armor synthesis. I'm not passing up this opportunity."

Jax had heard of alchemists being able to extract magical properties from monster parts and imbue them into other objects, such as armor, but he'd never heard of them using feathers for armor. He decided he'd just take Birdie's word for it, as she did hunt monsters for a living.

Break over, and with Birdie's bag stuffed to bursting with feathers, they hoisted the septipede up on their shoulders one last time and made their way to the nest.

As they approached the threshold, Gare was understandably nervous. "So, um, we're absolutely sure this is going to work, right? Cause I'd really hate it if it turned out I brought this bird its dinner just to be dessert."

The roc must have heard Gare, because they didn't manage to get a step further before it snapped its gaze upon them. Moving far more quickly than anything that size had a right to move, it closed the distance in a single bound, nearly knocking the party over from the blast of wind it unleashed with its motion.

"Well," said Jax, swallowing, "I guess we're about to find out."

Chapter 10

The roc towered over everyone, tilting its head inquisitively at the intruders that had dared step into its home and eyeing the septipede hungrily.

Trying not to make any sudden movement, Jax hissed under his breath. "Birdie, what do we do?"

Birdie responded just as quietly. "I think we just drop it."

"You think?" Great. So they were playing this by ear.

"Do you have a better idea?" she retorted.

Jax didn't, and the roc hadn't shifted its gaze in the slightest.

"Alright then, on three," he said. "One, two... three!"

He, Birdie, Ev, and Gare let go of the septipede and darted away from it. The offering barely hit the ground before the roc swung its head down and snatched it away, devouring the thousand-pound carcass in a single motion. The septipede gone, the roc turned its attention to the humans still in its nest.

When its gaze fell on Jax, he instinctively reached for his sword, not that it would do him any good. He quickly realized he had no need of it, however, as the roc took two steps back from the group and, leaving Jax absolutely dumbstruck, lay itself down on the ground in front of them.

Gare and Jax exchanged glances, not daring to take their eyes off of the big bird for long.

"Is... did it work?" Jax asked.

Birdie answered with a smirk, walking past Jax as she did so. "Considering it didn't eat us, I'd venture to say 'yes.'"

Jax steeled his nerves and followed her, motioning for Gare and Ev to do the same. Sidling up alongside the roc, Jax truly appreciated the sheer scale of the thing. The roc's head was taller than he was, even with it laying against the ground. The nostrils on its beak were almost large enough for him to have fit into one of them if he'd tried. Even the "tiny" feathers running down its neck were easily longer than Jax's arm.

"So how are we supposed to ride this thing?" he asked, still admiring their new companion.

Birdie looked back with a hint of a smile. "Climb on and hold on."

"Really? Just... anywhere?" Jax was not at all comfortable with this.

Birdie shrugged. "One of us will need to be near its head to tell it where to go, but I guess other than that we can ride anywhere. I'd recommend not trying to hold onto the wings, though."

"So, wait." Jax was confused. "This thing can understand us?"

Birdie rolled her eyes. "Of course not. You just steer it, like a horse. Pull its feathers the way you want it to go."

Jax looked at the massive thing in front of him. "You want me to steer this thing like a horse."

"I don't remember us agreeing you'd be the one steering," Birdie stated.

"We didn't," Jax replied, "but you don't know where we're going."

"Roehelm," replied Birdie. "We've even talked about it."

Jax blinked. He'd honestly forgotten that conversation.

"Not that it matters," Birdie continued. "The roc won't fly much further than the edge of the Windy Mountains."

"Alright, but just how do you know so much about this thing anyway?" Jax asked, gesturing at the wall of feathers to his left.

"That's not really that much to know," Birdie answered, crossing her arms.

Jax frowned. He looked at the roc and considered their options. If it couldn't fly all the way to Roehelm, then that meant they wouldn't have protection from Dezeroth's forces when they landed. There was no way they'd be able to fly out of here without enemy scouts spotting them. Jax turned away from the roc and examined the sky. The storm clouds were getting closer, and that gave him an idea.

Turning back to Birdie, he told her his thoughts. "What do you think? Sound good?"

"Bud, you are a genius," Gare commented before Birdie had a chance to answer.

Birdie ignored this, tapping her finger against her arm while looking at the ground. "You know, I have to admit that's good thinking. They'll probably figure out where we're going regardless, but even if they do it would at least buy us a little bit of time."

"So you agree we should do it, then?" Jax asked.

"I said it's a good idea," Birdie replied. "Just try not to fall off while you're steering, okay?"

Jax was taken aback. "Wait, you want me to steer it now?"

Birdie shrugged. "I don't think it really matters who does. It's your idea, anyway, so you might as well."

Jax examined the roc once again. In all honesty, he wasn't that comfortable with the idea of riding on its head, or of trying to control something this big.

He turned back to Birdie. "Actually, maybe you should be the one to control it."

Now Birdie was the one who looked surprised. "Me?"

"Yeah," said Jax. "You know more about this thing than anyone else here, and you've got more experience with monsters than the rest of us put together. I don't like the idea of riding it with someone else in control but, you're probably the one least likely to mess it up."

A slight smile tugged on Birdie's lip. "Alright then. Leave it to me. Once we throw Dezeroth off our scent, we'll head as far into the Myco Fields as this thing will take us."

Jax watched as Birdie pulled herself up onto the back of the roc's neck, then headed over to climb up as well. Before hopping on, he helped Ev up, and Gare climbed up after that. Once they were on, Gare helped Jax on as well, giving his friend a pat on the shoulder once they were secure. After double checking to make certain that the Heart was secured in its pouch on his back, Jax wrapped his hands around the quills of two large feathers, hoping it would be a stable enough hold to keep him from falling during the flight.

"Everyone ready?" he asked the others, who were lined up behind him. After receiving the affirmative, he relayed that up to Birdie.

A big grin broke out on Birdie's face, and she pulled back on the roc's neck feathers. Immediately the colossal bird lifted up. Jax held on to the feathers with all his might as the roc turned toward the south, his muscles still aching from carrying the septipede up the mountain. The roc took a few steps forward and hopped up onto the edge of its nest. It stood up tall, leaving Jax and the others almost vertical as it opened its wings. A sudden jerk and, the next thing he knew, he was horizontal once again, now being pressed into the roc's fluff as it lifted rapidly up into the sky. The roc gave a single flap of its wings, and suddenly the wind blowing past reversed, pushing upwards and in the direction they were flying.

So that was how the big thing flew, Jax realized. Just like the zodiacs, it held some sort of elemental control over the wind.

The roc held out its wings as it rose higher and faster, soaring towards the south. It settled into a steady glide, and with the wind moving with them Jax realized there was little concern of falling off after all. He let himself relax a bit — a huge relief to his arms — and looked back to check on the others behind him. Gare and Ev both appeared to be doing well. In fact, once Gare noticed Jax looking back at him his eyes lit up.

"Bud, can you believe what we're doing? We're freaking flying! On the back of a bird that's bigger than my house!"

Jax forced a smile and a nod in response, but he didn't quite feel the same degree of excitement. He'd never thought himself afraid of heights, but... even if the roc was as steady as a rock in flight, he couldn't convince himself to get comfortable. The view was absolutely amazing, though. The ground directly below him was hidden by the roc's bulk, but he could see off into the horizon for miles upon miles.

To the west was Marisol. He couldn't quite make it out as it was hidden behind mountains, but if they hadn't been there he knew he'd be able to see it. To the east, a stretch of purple fields extended beyond the edge of the Windy Mountains, disappearing beneath the darkness of the approaching storm. To the south, the Sea of Rezin, and beyond that Grandis's citadel, also hidden by the storm clouds they were rapidly approaching.

Once they'd reached the storm and were completely over the sea of clouds, the roc banked hard to the left, nearly doubling back on itself as it now flew to the northeast, hidden from the ground by the storm beneath it.

Jax smiled to himself. If Dezeroth's forces suspected they were flying on the roc, they'd now think they were heading towards Grandis's citadel. Birdie was probably right that they'd eventually realize they'd been duped, but by the time they did the Heart would be on Roehelm's doorstep.

After soaring for some time, the roc began to flutter, coming quickly to a halt and nearly shaking Jax loose from the sudden change in motion. The next thing he knew the roc was diving down through the clouds, soaking his face with the cold mist blowing past. The roc burst through the bottom of the clouds, then hovered for a moment, giving Jax time to get his bearings.

The ground below them was mostly various shades of purple, with a few large patches of teal and long streaks of pink and blue stretching across the land like monstrous veins. For the most part the landscape consisted of mildly sloping hills, with a few distinct protrusions and gullies here and there.

The roc continued its descent, angled slightly towards the north now, and as it lowered Jax caught sight of a group of people on horseback not far from where they were landing. Curious, but probably not a concern. To the northeast were a cluster of lights that likely belonged to a small town. It was tempting to head there to gather supplies, but the fastest route to Roehelm was straight east.

Touching down onto the purple surface, the roc lowered itself to the ground once again, allowing its passengers to disembark. Jax slid off of his feathery perch and was surprised by the spongy consistency of the purple growth beneath him. The others hopped off as well, and as soon as the last of them had disembarked the roc stood up and opened its wings. Two mighty flaps later and it was up in the air once again, racing back into the sky.

Jax looked around at the bizarre landscape. Instead of soil there was the strange purple mesh. Instead of plants, huge speckled lumps and fields of mushrooms. The sky was dark with clouds, but for now kept the rain to itself. There weren't even any rumbles of thunder, but the dark clouds in the distance assured Jax that a storm was indeed on its way.

"Come on," said Birdie, taking the lead. "We'll want to find somewhere to wait out the storm. These plains aren't safe out in the open when it rains."

Jax didn't argue. Birdie had proved time and again her knowledge of the dangers they'd faced. If she said they needed to find shelter, they probably needed to find shelter.

Their trip across the plains was soon interrupted, however, as Jax spotted the riders he'd seen earlier galloping towards them.

He sighed audibly. He was tired and still very much aching from the rest of the day. Whoever these people were, he didn't want to deal with them.

Deal with them it appeared he would have to, though, as they galloped right up to them — four in total, all wearing odd grins. They wore expensive looking outfits and had eccentric hair styles, each wilder than the last. The horses they rode were equally odd — their legs bare and hooves jagged.

"Hey there!" the one in front shouted, pushing his spiky black hair out of his face. "You guys the ones who rode the roc?"

A woman with long pink hair leaned over so far she nearly fell off as she swiped playfully at Spike Hair. "Obviously! No one would walk all the way out here."

"No one would come out here without a hyphorse anyway," the third commented while patting his mount. This one had a blue cowlick. He turned his attention to Jax. "I mean seriously, did you guys forget how to fly a roc or what? I get reliving your glory days, but you should at least have gotten a refresher first."

Jax's gaze cycled through each of the three who'd spoken in turn, not quite sure what to make of them. He didn't have time to think of a response before the fourth, another woman with blond hair shooting out like a bug's antennae, coughed out a laugh.

"Are you kidding?" she remarked to Blue. "Look at these guys, they've got horrible equipment. My guess is they never had glory days, they just heard the world's about to end so they're trying to make Radiant before it happens."

Jax looked back at his companions to see if any of them had any idea what these weirdos were talking about. Gare appeared just as confused as he did, while Ev and Birdie seemed agitated.

Jax returned his attention to the riders. "Look, I don't know what you guys are talking about, but we're kind of busy."

"Busy?" Spike Hair almost shouted. "You flew the roc into the middle of the Myco Fields. The only thing out here worth a visit are these psyshrooms."

He pulled out a luminescent green mushroom from his pocket. "If you've got time for shrooming you're not busy."

"We're not here for mushrooms," Jax replied, trying not to raise his voice.

"Right..." Blue said, "you just felt like wasting the last few weeks we've got here wandering around this dump."

"Okay, seriously, what the heck are you guys talking about?" Jax asked, losing his patience. "Last weeks of what?"

The group of riders chuckled, angering Jax even further. Pink took notice and stopped laughing.

"Oh, you really don't know?" she asked.

"Know what?" Jax replied, scowling.

Spike Hair spoke up again. "Dude, how can you not know? This place is done for. In twenty days Apollyon's gonna wake up, and no one's gonna stop it. Game over."

Jax felt that familiar heat in his face once again. He didn't know who these fools were, but clearly they had no faith in or respect for Lord Grandis.

"You're wrong," he told them flatly. "Supreme Lord Grandis watches over us. He'll stop Apollyon, just as he always has."

The riders burst out laughing. That wasn't the response Jax expected.

"How dare you!" he shouted, clenching his fists. "If it wasn't for Lord Grandis none of you would even be here right now!"

The riders stopped laughing, but their response still wasn't what Jax expected. They looked down at him curiously.

This time Blondie spoke up. "Wow. Are you like, for real?"

Jax was about to yell again, but Pink snapped her fingers in a bid to get Spike Hair's attention.

"Hey," she hissed. Spike Hair looked over and Pink continued. "You don't think these guys are nepacs, do you?"

The look of surprise on Spike Hair's face matched Jax's own, but Jax hid his shock as quickly as it appeared.

There was no way. There was no way that these people were Divine.

Spike Hair looked back at Jax and his friends with a puzzled look, but he quickly shook his head and that stupid grin he'd had when he first arrived returned.

"Nah," he said. "They rode the roc. At least one of them's legit."

"Unless they changed the rules again," offered Blue.

"Yeah," said Pink, "like what they did with Apollyon."

"No way," said Spike Hair, but he didn't seem convinced. He addressed Jax once again. "Alright you. Out with it. Which one of you is Divine?"

"None of us," Jax replied resolutely, staring Spike Hair in the eye.

Spike Hair looked each of them in the face one at a time, as if expecting one of them to say something to the contrary.

"See," said Pink, leaning obnoxiously over again. "They made all sorts of changes back when they left. Who knows how things work these days?"

"Huh," Spike Hair said, turning his steed away from Jax. "Too bad, but I guess it is a bit early for people to start showing up for the show."

"Come on," said Blue. "No point in wasting time with nepacs."

"Yeah," said Blondie, "let's finish getting our psyshrooms so we can get going to Ars Summis."

The riders kicked their hyphorses and galloped away. Jax wasn't about to stop them. Whether they were Divine or delusional from the mushrooms, he didn't care, but he didn't want to ever see them again.

He took a deep breath before addressing Birdie, who wasn't doing a much better job of hiding her disgust with those creeps. "So, we need to find shelter, right?"

Birdie snapped her head up as if she'd just remembered what they were doing here. "Oh, yeah, that's right. I was just thinking I would have loved to have taken their rides from them."

Jax was a little shocked at her comment, but after thinking about it, he realized he completely agreed with her.

* * * *

The Myco Fields didn't exactly offer much in terms of shelter. It wasn't until nearly an hour after landing that they spotted a nice protrusion jutting out from the spongy ground with a significant enough overhang to protect them from whatever rain might come their way.

Upon reaching the protrusion they discovered it to be some sort of massive fungus, like the kind sometimes seen growing out the sides of trees. Of course, everything around here seemed to be some sort of fungus, but unlike the purple mesh surrounding them, which was odorless, this big mushroom stunk something fierce.

"Ugh," retched Gare. "Are we sure we want to stop here? What's the harm in a little rain?"

Birdie plopped her bag down against the base of the huge mushroom and walked over to a small pool of water that had collected in a dip in the landscape nearby. She dipped her fingers into it and held them up in front of her, made a face, then turned away.

"Don't drink that," she said. "Once it rains, it should get flushed clean. We can drink then."

Jax headed over to drop his bag down by Birdie's, but caught himself before it hit the ground, silently cursing himself that he'd almost caused the Heart to return to the Citadel. He wasn't used to carrying it yet, and only just now realized he'd just have to sleep with the bag on until they reached Roehelm. Re-securing his pack, he stepped away from the mushroom for a bit. It wasn't raining yet, after all, and he didn't want to smell that thing any more than he had to.

The storm was definitely getting closer though. The sky was nearly as dark as night, though admittedly the setting sun contributed to that somewhat. A cold breeze had been blowing steadily for the last half hour or so, picking up in intensity as time passed. A big patch of "trees" a short distance away swayed in the wind, releasing clouds of spores into the air. There was still no sign of thunder or lightning, but it was surely on its way.

After a few minutes of watching the clouds move in, Jax headed back under the shelter of the mushroom. As long as he didn't get too close to its base the stench wasn't too bad, considering that most of it was carried away on the wind. Ev and Birdie were sitting together beside the pool, chatting. Gare had relocated further away, staring back towards the Windy Mountains. Jax joined him, but didn't say anything. The two of them stood in silence, just letting the wind blow over them as they looked back at the way they'd come.

Gare broke the silence. "Ya know, I've been thinking."

"That's dangerous," Jax replied with a sly smirk.

Gare continued. "It's about those Divine we ran into…"

"They weren't Divine," Jax cut in. "There haven't been any Divine other than Lord Grandis and Lady Escalor for years."

"Do we know that, though?" Gare asked, looking at Jax earnestly. "Just because we haven't seen any doesn't mean they all disappeared."

Jax shook his head. "Did those sound like Divine to you? They were clearly just a bunch of morons messed up from the mushrooms."

"They called us 'nepacs' and said they were headed to Ars Summis," Gare replied.

"So?"

"Ars Summis was the home of the Masters. Only Divine can go there. Even I know that."

Jax frowned. He had to admit it was a possibility, but he preferred to think they were just crazy.

"Divine wouldn't turn their back on the world the way those people did," he said after a pause.

"Sure they would," Gare responded, surprising Jax. "That's like the one thing the Guard made sure all of us learned, right? The whole reason the Dark Radiant was even a thing? The Divine started a war with each other when the Masters left because some wanted to abandon us while others wanted to protect us. What if those guys we met were from the group that fought against Lord Grandis?"

Jax shivered at the thought. If Gare was right then the only reason they'd walked away was because the riders didn't know Jax had the Heart. Sure, whatever they were they weren't Radiants, probably, but the thought of having to fight against Divine wasn't one he was comfortable with.

"I guess I'd always assumed Lord Grandis had split all of the traitors, you know?" Jax replied. "Put guards around their Hearts, locked up their reincarnations…"

"Well, that is what they tell us," Gare said, "but I bet they're only talking about the dangerous ones. I doubt even Lord Grandis has the resources to build a citadel where every bad Divine was split."

"Yeah," Jax conceded, "and those guys we met didn't seem very impressive."

"I'll say!" agreed Gare. "I bet we could have taken them on."

Jax smiled at that, and the two of them stood in silence until night was truly upon them. The sun had long since dipped behind the mountains to the west, and the cloud cover blocked out whatever light would have been reflected off of the sky.

"Come on," Jax said. "We need to pick shifts for the night."

"Seriously?" asked Gare. "We left Dezeroth's guys in the dust."

Jax frowned at Gare. "If those goons really were traitorous Divine, they might come back for us. We can't take a chance on them sneaking up on us."

Gare shrugged. "Yeah, I guess that's a good point."

Jax headed back to the others. He hated to ask Ev to stand watch, but there were only four of them now. Before he had the chance, though, his thoughts about standing guard disappeared as Ev suddenly retched into the pool under the mushroom.

He hurried over to her side as Birdie helped her back up. "What happened?" he asked. "Are you okay?"

Ev wiped her mouth with the back of her hand and moaned. "I'm fine," she gritted out. "I think the smell here is making me sick."

Jax heard an "Mm-hmph" of agreement behind him. He turned back to see Gare looking away with his hand over his mouth.

"Maybe you should sleep over there," he said to Ev, pointing to the edge of the mushroom's base that was most upwind. "The breeze should keep the worst of it away."

Ev nodded, and the four of them made their way over to where Jax was pleased to see that his intuition was correct. The cold wind from the storm may have been chilling, but it was at least more welcome than the stench of the fungus. If it started raining they'd move further under shelter, but for now they'd breath much easier out by the edge of the mushroom's cover.

Jax explained to them his thoughts on setting up a watch and the others agreed. To his surprise, Ev was enthusiastic about helping, despite her still not looking well, and she offered to take first shift. Birdie would go second, then Jax, and finally Gare. With the shift schedule decided, the group began to settle in for the night.

As Jax worked to find a comfortable position to sleep in without removing his bag, Gare sidled up next to him. "You know, if you want, I can sleep with that thing on instead."

"I'm fine," said Jax as he flipped over onto his side.

"You sure?"

"I said I've got it."

Gare shrugged and plopped down on the ground himself. "Alright, suit yourself. But ya know we could probably take a look at it now that you're the one carrying it."

That got Jax sitting up again. "Are you serious?"

"Well, I..."

"No, Gare."

"Oh, come on, you have to be curious," Gare prodded.

"I said 'no.' End of discussion."

Gare frowned, and after a few seconds of staring he laid down and rolled to face the other way. Jax did the same, leaving his back facing Gare's. This was not the kind of thing he needed to deal with right now. They weren't out of danger yet, and they were stuck sleeping out in the open because the only alternative was sleeping in an unbearable stench. Laying on the ground, though, he realized that, if nothing else, at least the spongy mesh made for a surprisingly decent bed. It was soft, and nowhere near as cold as the rock and dirt they'd been sleeping on before. Even without a pile of leaves beneath them, it was probably the most comfortable "bed" they'd had since leaving Marisol. If only they had some protection from the wind, spending the night out here might not be so bad.

That realization gave Jax another reason to want to get to Roehelm as soon as possible — a reward worthy of making it through this whole ordeal. A full night's sleep indoors, in a bed, with a blanket, not wearing his smelly armor.

Chapter 11

Birdie jostled Jax awake for his shift early in the morning. He reluctantly pushed himself up, stretching the kinks out of his body. He still hurt from moving that giant bug-worm up the mountain, and from how much he hurt he expected he still had a few days left of it before he was fully recovered.

Looking around, Jax realized just how absolutely dark it was. The clouds completely blocked the light from the moon and stars in the sky. The only light around came from a few glowing fungi scattered here and there and the occasional flash in the sky off in the distance. The far-off lightning brought the realization that, amazingly, they still hadn't gotten even a drop of rain.

This was his first time standing guard without a partner, and it was a bit unnerving. He wasn't sure if the total darkness made things better or worse.

He started to wish Birdie "goodnight," but before he could, she said she needed to attend to some business in the "bushes" a short ways away, saying she might be a while. Jax just shrugged and took up position a short ways out from where the others were sleeping. He was a little curious as to why she went up and around to the other side of the big fungus they were sleeping under rather than into the patch of nearby "trees," but he figured it wasn't any of his business where she did hers.

Then, time passed. First five minutes, then ten, then twenty.... After half an hour, his concern got the better of him. Illuminating the area with a faint light from his hand, he made his way over to Gare.

"Hey, wake up," he said, shaking Gare's shoulder. "I need you to take over for me."

Gare moaned as he sat up. "Is it my shift already?" he asked.

"Birdie's missing," Jax responded. "I need you to keep watch while I go look for her."

Gare took a moment to process what Jax had said. "Wait, what do you mean 'missing'? Where'd she go?"

"That's what I'm going to find out," Jax answered. "I'll be back soon."

Gare didn't argue, so Jax took off in the direction he'd seen Birdie go. He climbed up the backside of the fungal outcrop to see if he could spot any sign of where she'd gone. A small distance away, he spotted a faint light in a large patch of mushrooms similar to the ones near their camp.

He doused his own light, not wanting to be seen as he made his way to the other light's source. As he drew near, the light disappeared. Jax quietly unsheathed his sword and pushed into the forest of mushrooms, each one towering above him. He stopped when he felt that he was close to where the light had originated from. He strained his ears to pick up any sound that might alert him to danger. Hearing nothing, he continued deeper into mushroom patch until he stepped into a small clearing where he spotted a dark figure sitting in its center.

"Hello, Jax," Birdie said to him before he realized it was her.

"Birdie? What are you doing out here?" Jax lit up his hand again to make certain it really was her. It was definitely her face, but he wasn't ready to sheath his sword just yet, not after their experience with the shades the previous night.

Birdie held up her hand and surprised Jax by emitting a light of her own — an ability he had no idea she possessed. "I wouldn't be able to sleep if I tried, so I figured I might as well practice some spells."

"All the way out here? I was worried about you!" Jax lowered his sword but still wasn't quite ready to put it away.

Birdie gazed at him with one eyebrow raised. "You're kidding, right? You were worried about me?"

"Of course I was!" Jax responded. "I mean, you are kind of part of the team now."

Birdie didn't respond, instead turning away from him and staring into the forest.

Jax approached her, finally returning his blade to its scabbard. He wanted to tell her to come back to camp, but something was clearly bothering her. Whatever Birdie's faults, she'd been there for Ev when he hadn't. The least he could do was try better now.

"So... what's keeping you from sleeping?" he asked her.

Birdie rubbed her shoulder, still not looking at him. "I just have a lot on my mind, is all."

"Yeah," replied Jax, "me too."

Birdie finally looked back at him, but now Jax was staring off into the distance.

"After I saw Dezeroth kill my father, I could only think of revenge, of getting stronger, of making sure his sacrifice wasn't for nothing. That's still what I think about, but... I don't know anymore." Jax met Birdie's eyes. "You were right that I was going to abandon Ev when we got to Roehelm, but I don't know if I can do that. Father told me to watch over her. I can't let Dezeroth get away with what he's done, but I also can't leave Ev. I... just can't figure out what to do."

Birdie's eyes held genuine concern in them. "You said you saw your father die?"

Jax clenched his fist as he recalled the memory. "I tried to save him, but my magic was so weak it never even reached. Dezeroth never even noticed me."

"And you think if you'd been stronger you could have saved him?" she asked.

"...No," Jax finally admitted, fighting to keep his tears from showing, "but I could have at least done something."

Birdie sat quietly for a moment before speaking again. "I also want to get stronger, but for a very different reason than you."

"What's your reason?" Jax asked, curious, and eager to change the subject.

"Freedom," Birdie answered, now looking up at the sky.

"I'm not sure I understand."

Birdie sat quietly for a moment, then sighed and turned her attention back to Jax. "There are people out there who want to hurt me."

"Hurt you? Why? What did you do?"

Birdie glared at Jax, and he realized that probably wasn't the right response, but to his surprise Birdie continued anyway.

"Honestly," she said, "I don't know. I'd never seen the people who came to my village, but apparently I'd upset their leader at some point, and he'd figured out where I lived."

Jax found it hard to buy Birdie's claim that she was clueless but tried his best not to show it. "How do you know they were after you if you'd never seen them before?"

Birdie frowned as she answered. "They knew my name. They demanded my village turn me over to them, and they would have, but I've always been cautious around people I sense are stronger than me, especially back then. I stayed well away from anyone I knew I couldn't take in a fight, so when those people came into town, I hid. When I heard they were after me, I ran. I knew the nearby forests well, so I was able to lose them and the townsfolk who helped them."

"And you still don't know who they were?" Jax asked.

Birdie shook her head. "That was a few years ago. I think I might have figured out who they were, but I haven't confirmed it, and I still don't know exactly what I did."

"Well, whoever they are, you don't have to worry about it," Jax said confidently.

Birdie raised an eyebrow.

Jax sat down on the ground next to her. "You're part of the Light Guard now. We never would have made it this far without you. When we get to Roehelm, I guarantee you'll have a home with Lord Grandis's soldiers. No one will mess with you after that."

Birdie let a small smile slip. "Thanks," she said. "I'm not sure how comfortable I'd be being a soldier, but I appreciate the offer."

"Well, if you change your mind, you can count on me to put in a good word for you," Jax offered.

"I'll... keep that in mind," Birdie replied, looking at him suspiciously. He didn't really blame her. Up until then he hadn't exactly been the nicest to her.

They sat in silence for a few moments before Birdie finally asked, "So what made you want to be a soldier anyway?"

Jax was surprised by the question. "Oh, uh, probably my father, I guess. And my mother."

"Both of your parents were soldiers?" Birdie asked.

"Yeah," Jax replied. "Father was a knight like Diana. Mother was a Ranger."

Birdie looked at Jax sympathetically, something he wasn't used to from her. "So, they both…?"

Jax shook his head. "Mother died a long time ago. There was an accident at sea. Ev never even got to know her."

"I'm sorry," Birdie said, and Jax could tell she meant it.

"Thanks, but it's alright. Like I said, it was a long time ago. Father raised Ev and me to be soldiers like he and Mother were. He wanted us to be strong, to do our part to help the Divine protect the world." Jax smiled faintly. "Ev didn't want to have anything to do with fighting, so she and Father compromised and she became a cleric."

"I guess I can see that. She doesn't seem to mind fighting monsters, though."

Jax rubbed the back of his head. "Yeah, she's a little weird about that. I think she hates monsters more than she hates hurting things."

Birdie cocked her head. "Well, I can't say I blame her. Monsters are basically mindless destruction machines. They do a lot of damage without the Divine keeping them in check, especially to the natural world. Normal animals don't get revived on the new moon, you know."

"Yeah," Jax said with a slight smile, "Ev's told me that more than once. That's why I really don't get why she didn't want to be a ranger or something."

"Because being part of the Light Guard meant she still wouldn't use her skills to fight monsters?" Birdie offered.

Jax shrugged. "I guess so. Father was pretty adamant that whatever we did, we had to support the Guard."

Birdie nodded. Jax guessed Ev must have already told her that much on her own.

"Anyway," said Jax, "you ready to head back to camp?"

"Sure," replied Birdie. "I suppose it wouldn't hurt to try and get some shuteye."

The two of them made their way back to find Gare waiting for them. "It's about time," he said way too loudly. "Can I go back to sleep now?"

"Sure," said Jax. "Thanks for keeping watch. I'll take your shift for you too."

This seemed to appease Gare somewhat. "Alright, well... good. Goodnight, then, I guess."

Gare curled back up near Ev as Jax found a spot to make himself comfortable. Birdie sat down nearby him.

"I thought you were going to try to sleep," Jax whispered.

"Eh, it was my fault you gave up your shift", she replied. "The least I can do is keep you company."

"Thanks, but you don't have to do that. You didn't sleep last night, either, right?"

Birdie chuckled. "Yeah, I don't think I've slept since the night before I saved you all from those bublobs." She paused as she realized what she'd said. "Wow, I guess it has been a while."

"You really should try and get some rest, then," Jax insisted. "It can't be good for you to go that long without sleep."

"No, it probably isn't," Birdie answered.

Jax frowned. "You really should go to bed. We need everyone as rested as possible in case anything else happens."

Birdie stood up and sighed. "Yeah, I guess you have a point. I'll try and rest, but I'm not making any promises."

She headed over to the others and nestled into a crevice in the mushroom out of sight. How she was able to tolerate the smell Jax had no idea, but he bet it was warmer in there away from the wind.

He settled in for a long night but was looking forward to the morning. They were well over halfway to Roehelm now. Even without horses, they'd be there within the week, and at last he'd have accomplished his mission of keeping the Heart out of Dezeroth's hands.

* * * *

Morning came, but the sky was so dark with clouds one would hardly be able to tell. There was enough light to be able to see, however, so Jax assumed the sun had to be up at that point.

Thunder had finally begun rumbling around them, with streaks of lightning striking the ground off to the east. Eager to get back on the road before the storm hit, he made his way over to where the others were sleeping. As soon as he approached, Birdie popped out of her little crevice with a grin.

"You better not have been awake all night," Jax told her.

She stretched her arms out above her and swung them back down. "Don't worry, worry-wart. I got some sleep. I just heard you walking over and decided I might as well get up."

"There's thunder all around us. How...?" Jax stopped himself, realizing it wasn't worth it. "Never mind. Help me get everyone up. We need to keep moving in case those riders come back."

"I kind of hope they do," said Birdie, leaning against one of the big mushroom's folds with a smile. "It would give us an excuse to take their hyphorses."

Jax shook his head, but allowed a small smirk to sneak out, then shook Gare awake.

Gare groaned. "Bud, I swear if you're tagging with me again..."

"It's morning," Jax stated flatly.

Gare looked around at the dark sky. "Are you sure about that?"

"Positive," Jax answered, grinning.

While Jax helped Gare to his feet, Birdie went over to Ev and tapped on her forehead without gaining a response. Birdie switched to shaking Ev gently as she told her it was time to get up. Still nothing.

Jax's smile disappeared. Something wasn't right. He joined Birdie in jostling his sister, whose face was deathly pale. "Ev, come on, wake up," he said, concern just starting to creep into his voice.

Birdie placed her hand on Ev's forehead and looked at Jax. "She's burning up."

Jax touched his sister's face for confirmation, then started tapping her cheek as he called to her. "Ev, come on, wake up!"

Still no response.

"Let me try," Gare said, and he shook her violently.

"Gare, stop!" Jax pushed him away.

Ev groaned, but didn't open her eyes.

Now Jax was worried. "What's wrong with her? Did the mushroom do this?" he asked, eyeing the smelly fungus.

Birdie shook her head. "The only thing in this field that could cause symptoms like this are the whitecap mushrooms, and she'd have had to eat them."

"Ev wouldn't just eat some random mushroom," Jax insisted.

"I know," said Birdie, "but I don't know what else could be wrong. I never learned to sense afflictions."

Jax looked to the northeast and tried not to sound panicked. "We have to get her to a doctor. I saw a town or something in that direction back when we landed. Maybe we can find one there."

"To the northeast?" Birdie paused to think for a second. "That would likely be a gobbol village. They won't be friendly."

"We don't have a choice," Jax replied, raising his voice.

"No, you're right," Birdie agreed, "and we'll need to get there as soon as we can."

Jax looked down at Ev for a moment. He and likely everyone else were still sore from yesterday, but they didn't have any other options. "Gare," he began, looking up again, "do you think you can carry Ev?"

"You can count on me," he replied confidently.

Jax nodded, then helped lift Ev onto Gare's shoulders. "Okay, let's get going. That rain looks like it will be here soon."

"It basically already is," added Birdie. "There's no way we'll make it there before it hits."

"All the more reason to get moving," responded Jax.

"It's not that simple," returned Birdie. "When it rains, most of the ground here becomes very slippery and huge holes open up everywhere. The underground is filled with monsters, and if one of us falls in we might not be able to make it back out."

"Then we'd better not fall," Jax replied. He didn't care what was in his way to the village, he was going to get Ev to a doctor. He got the feeling Birdie felt the same way, but while he understood her desire to make sure they all knew what they were heading into he didn't see how standing around here would help.

Birdie didn't say anymore after that, and the four of them set out across the Myco Fields. Cresting the top of the first hill, Jax strained his eyes to see if he could spot the lights he'd seen before in the distance, but a wall of rain and lightning was between him and his destination, making it impossible to see.

Perhaps an hour later, the storm struck, and it struck hard. Sheets of rain battered against the the group as they pushed ever forward. Lightning flashed all around them but had yet to strike anywhere close. As Birdie had warned, most of the soft mesh that was the ground had become as slippery as ice. Fortunately, not everywhere was affected that way. The ground that was tinted more pink than purple stayed rough and provided solid footholds, allowing them to make steady progress. The pink areas seemed to form long ribbons, which was convenient when they stretched in the direction of the village, but less so when they were horizontal to it.

Not long after the storm struck, Birdie's other warning came to fruition as well. The ground began to split along the large blue veins that cut across the land, leaving deep dark fissures where water poured in. The first fissure appeared right in front of them, but they hopped over it before it spread too wide. They were lucky enough that most of the later gaps ran either parallel or diagonal to the path towards their destination, requiring only minor adjustments to their course.

Their luck ran out, however, after they climbed one particularly large hill. In the distance, Jax could at last make out faint lights flickering through the haze of the rain, but at the bottom of the hill, stretching as far as he could see in both directions, was a great chasm opened up by the storm.

"Lords," shouted Gare over the storm. "Should we look for a way around?"

"There might not be a way around," Jax answered, though with the rain as thick as it was it was difficult to tell. Unfortunately, they didn't have much choice. He couldn't see any way back up if they went in, so he turned north to see if maybe there was an end to the chasm that way. There wasn't, and looking back to the south he saw no end that way, either, but he did spot a giant mushroom similar to the one they'd spent the night under in that direction as well.

"You guys wait over there," he told Gare and Birdie. "Take shelter with Ev while I look for a way across."

"Not a chance, bud," Gare responded. "I'm not risking losing you in this."

"I'll be fine," Jax insisted. "Take a break and get Ev out of the rain."

"Or," began Gare, "maybe we let the person who's used to living out here go take a look instead of the person carrying the Heart."

Birdie picked up on the cue. "That might be for the best. I doubt Ev would want to wake up to find her brother had died trying to help her."

"I'm not going to sit around while Ev is dying," Jax returned, pulling out his sword and holding it aloft, glowing. "If something happens I can at least send out a signal. Neither of you can do that."

Neither Birdie nor Gare could argue with that. "Fine," said Gare, "but if you're gonna insist on being stupid at least leave the Heart with us."

Jax sheathed his sword, took off his bag and handed it to Birdie. "Here. Don't put it down for anything."

Birdie opened her mouth, staring at the bag in her hands. "I... you're... giving this to me?"

"Gare's carrying Ev," Jax replied, turning away from them. "I'll be back in twenty minutes. Don't let Gare talk you into opening that while I'm gone."

Birdie gave a barely perceptible nod while Gare frowned, and Jax left them to set out into the storm.

The path to the north lacked any of the non-slippery pink patches, so he kept well away from the chasm and stayed on flat ground wherever he could. One bad slip and he'd find himself careening into the fungal underworld. His search for a way across proved more fruitless with each cautious step he took, unfortunately. The further he wandered, the further the chasm seemed to stretch, and the further he went away from the lights of the village. Not wanting to tempt Gare to wander off by prolonging his absence, Jax decided to call this direction a failure. He'd check in with Gare and Birdie before trying the other direction. If that failed, he didn't know what they'd do.

Before he made it back to the big mushroom, though, he spotted something he hadn't noticed on his way out. On the far side of the chasm was a thin strip of land, or whatever the ground was made of, sloping up and out of the ravine. If that slope was pink, then all he needed was to find a way down and they'd have their way across.

Deciding it worth a closer look he approached the edge of the chasm, taking care with every step not to slip on the slick purple ground. He underestimated the slickness, however, and with one tiny misstep he fell hard on his chest, sliding quickly towards the edge.

He grabbed desperately at the ground, trying to gain a hold of the purple mesh. The fibers snapped under his weight, slowing but not stopping him as his legs shot out over the edge of the cliff.

At the last second his fingers managed to poke through the ground at the lip of the canyon, tearing a large chunk of the purple mass loose, but not completely. A thick strip of mesh held the mass in place, leaving him dangling over the edge.

Jax tried to pull himself back up, but he couldn't get a grip on any other part of the ground, and there was no wall he could push off against with his legs. The edge of the cliff fell away beneath him, revealing massive caverns on both sides of the ravine with the ground about twenty feet below.

The chunk of mesh he held onto began to stretch and tear, peeling down the side like skin and providing a slow descent to the bottom of the ravine. Water poured in from all around him, but it flowed away into the caverns as quickly as it came from above.

At the bottom, Jax surveyed the area around him. He couldn't make out anything in the dark caves, but he had a very bad feeling about them. Turning his attention to the slope on the far side of the cavern, he discovered much to his relief that it was indeed pink. The rough surface allowed him to climb quickly back out of the ravine. Now he just needed to figure out how to get Gare and Ev over to his side.

Heading back in the direction of the mushroom he'd left them at he kept his eyes peeled for another slope on the far side for them to travel down. The presence of a pink strip running alongside his edge of the chasm was a welcome discovery and made his trip back much easier.

After a few minutes Jax passed the place he'd left the others. From this distance he could just barely make out the mushroom's figure in the rain. He still hadn't found another slope down from their side, so he continued a little further. Then, he spotted it. It was too difficult to make out its color from his side, but that didn't matter. They could climb up on this side, and that was the important thing.

Jax headed back towards the giant mushroom and fired a beam of light to get Gare and Birdie's attention. After seeing what looked like movement, he fired another, and slowly their silhouettes took shape.

Jax couldn't make out their faces, but he couldn't help but smile at the looks of shock he knew must have been on them.

"Bud, what the hell?" Gare yelled, his voice just barely making it across the ravine. "Why didn't you come get us before crossing?"

"I slipped and fell in!" Jax shouted back. "There's a way up that way," he pointed to his right, "and I found a way down over there," he pointed back to his left.

Gare just shook his head. "You're crazy, you know that? Where's this way down?"

Jax led the way to the slope he'd seen, where Gare carried Ev down it with Birdie following. The mere fact they remained upright the entire way down proved that the slope must have been pink. Jax then directed Gare and Birdie to follow him to the path up the other side. He wasn't at all comfortable with Ev being down in that creepy place, but with both Gare and Birdie with her he convinced himself they would be fine.

They'd made it about halfway to the up slope when Gare called up to Jax. "Uh, Jax, I think there's something down here!"

Jax cursed. He stuck his sword into the ground to stabilize himself as he stepped off his pink path to get closer to the edge and look in. He didn't see anything himself, but he didn't doubt there were creatures down there that were dangerous.

"Keep going!" Jax yelled in. "You're almost to the way out. Don't slow down!"

Birdie had already pushed Gare into running before the words had left Jax's mouth. Gare moved as fast as he was able with Ev on his back, and Jax followed up above.

A moment later, a horrid screech echoed up from the crevice. Jax cursed again. Whatever that was, it was bad.

He approached the edge in time to see a disgusting figure floating through the air towards Birdie, who'd spun around to face it while Gare kept running. The monster appeared vaguely humanoid, like someone covered in a cloak of drooping tentacles and fungus. A second creature appeared out from the caverns on the far side, this one homing in on Gare. Jax knew Gare wouldn't be able to fight while carrying Ev, so while Birdie danced around the first creature Jax fired blasts at the second. His attacks connected beautifully, and his target whipped its head towards Jax, revealing a rotting face that let out a howl comparable to a thousand hounds baying in the night. He then fired a blast at the one Birdie was fighting with similar results.

"Run!" he yelled at Birdie, "I'll hold them off!"

Birdie ran past where Jax was overhead, quickly catching up with Gare. A third monster had now crawled out from the depths ahead of them, so Jax launched more attacks at it. This one didn't break off its pursuit as the first ones had, however, so Jax raised his sword and fired a beam at it. The attack connected, and this time he succeeded in pulling the monster's attention away from the others.

Using his sword to get himself back to the pink ribbon, he hurried to catch up to others in case any more of the creatures showed up. He made it to the slope just as Gare did, when yet another rotting figure appeared as Gare started up the climb. It managed to grab Ev's leg, but lost its grip just as quickly when Birdie slammed her dagger into its head. The creature turned on Birdie, blocking her way to the slope as more figures approached her from behind.

Knowing his magic wasn't powerful enough to take any of those things down, Jax charged down the slope and leapt over Gare, driving his blade straight into the monster's back.

The creature howled as Jax kicked it from his sword with all his might, throwing it just far enough from the path out for Birdie to scrape past its clutches. Jax followed up with a powerful blast to its head for good measure, then retreated as well. The creature followed a few feet up the slope before stopping, staring with its dead eyes as it held its worm-filled mouth agape. After a brief pause it turned and sulked back into the darkness of the caverns below, along with its fellow monstrosities.

"You okay?" Jax asked Gare once they reached the top.

"Yeah," panted Gare, "but I am never going down in one of those places again."

After checking Ev to make sure she hadn't been injured by the creature that had grabbed her, Jax turned his attention to Birdie. "How about you? You okay?"

Birdie placed her hand on her hip cockily. "Of course," she paused, "but, thanks for the help down there, anyway."

Jax nodded and took the Heart back from Birdie, then faced the lights flickering in the distance. They couldn't have been more than a few hundred yards further, and there was no sign of any more crevices in the way.

"Finally, it looks like we made it."

"Yeah, we made it," said Gare, "but what do we do if they won't let us in?"

"Oh, they'll let us in," Jax replied. "One way or another, we're getting Ev to a doctor, even if that doctor is a gobbol."

Chapter 12

Jax and the others arrived at a large wooden gate leading into a village of short little huts. Large, almost white fires burned at the top of each post on the gate and in torches surrounding the town, completely oblivious to the torrential rain. At the foot of the gate was a squat little imp with a frog-like mouth and a scowl, staring them down. What it was doing guarding a gate that opened up into the middle of nowhere, Jax had no idea, but there it was all the same.

Not expecting to be allowed to just wander in, Jax approached the gobbol. "We need to get into the village. My sister is very sick."

The gobbol blinked, then held out his hand. "Outsider wants in? Outsider pays toll," it croaked.

"Are you kidding me?" cried Gare. "Didn't you hear him? We have someone sick here!" He shifted to show Ev on his back.

The gobbol eyed Ev momentarily, then twiddled his fingers greedily. "Four outsiders, four tolls."

"Why you little..." Gare started.

Jax took a step towards the gobbol but was stopped by Birdie's hand on his shoulder.

"Easy there, slayer. I've got this."

Jax blinked as Birdie walked past him and opened up her bag, fishing out the bugboar tusks.

"Here," she told the gatekeeper, offering him four of the trophies. "This should be more than enough."

The gobbol snatched away the tusks and sniffed them, then returned his attention to Jax. "Outsiders wait here. Orf must ask trader first."

The tiny guard knocked on a slat in the wall, which slid open to reveal another gobbol, who in turn took the bugboar tusks and disappeared.

Gare stepped towards the gate impatiently. "Well? We gave you the toll. Let us in, already!"

"Outsider waits!" the gobbol growled. "Trader must say items are good before entry."

"What the hell's he talking about?" Gare asked, turning to Jax.

"Just wait, Gare," Jax replied. "It sounds like they're seeing how valuable what we gave them is."

Gare growled, but held his tongue. He couldn't help but fidget as they waited, and Jax was having his patience stretched thin as well. They needed to be on these gobbols' good sides if they wanted to get Ev treated here, so he didn't want to start a fight, but boy, was it tempting.

The slat on the gate opened again, and the inner gobbol said something to the gatekeeper, who in turn turned back to the waiting travelers.

"Okay. Outsiders can go in."

"Finally!" said Gare, and the four of them entered into the gobbol village.

There weren't many inhabitants out and about, though considering the torrential rain, that wasn't surprising. The squat little buildings all looked the same. Even if there was a doctor here, he had no idea where it would be. Biting his pride, he turned back to the gate of the village.

"Excuse me," he said to the gatekeeper. "We really need to find a doctor. Do you have one in this village? Or a healer?"

The gatekeeper snorted. "Doctor is in skull hut in back of village."

Jax turned back towards the village and scanned it for a hut that had skulls on it. Even though he was as tall as most of the buildings, he couldn't get a good view of the ones further away. He led the way towards the far side of the village, and eventually spotted a single hut decorated on the outside with various monster skulls. Fairly confident he'd found the place they were looking for, he pushed aside a cloth curtain and stepped inside, ducking down to fit in the room that only went up to his shoulders. Gare had an even harder time, needing to bend himself nearly halfway over to fit with Ev on his back.

The inside of the hut was well lit, with a large fire in the center under a big cauldron. The smoke rose up out of a hole in the ceiling, which had a metal cover above it that kept the rain from sneaking in. All over the walls were monster skulls and a few curtains that appeared to serve as doors to other sections of the building.

"Hello?" called Jax, not seeing anyone in the main room.

One of the curtains swung aside, revealing a gobbol decorated in a similar fashion as the hut itself, with tiny animal skulls hanging from its ears, around its neck and across its waist.

The gobbol stared for a second with eyes as wide as saucers at the strange sight of a group of humans in its hut, but quickly composed itself and approached the group.

"Outsiders in Groochsog," the gobbol croaked. "Morf hasn't seen such in many years."

"Are you the village doctor?" Jax asked.

"Morf is doctor," was his reply.

"Well, where's this Morf?" asked Gare, still cradling Ev on his back.

"Morf is Morf!" exclaimed the gobbol, clearly referring to himself. "What do outsiders want with doctor?"

"It's my sister," Jax explained as Gare lowered her gently to the floor. "We don't know what's wrong. She just got sick when we were out in those mushrooms last night."

Morf stepped over to Ev and examined her with his eyes. "Young one is not sick," he said, looking back up at Jax. "Young one is poisoned."

"Poisoned? How?" Jax asked.

"Young one has sepsis venom in blood. Only few monsters have such venom. Young one must have contacted such monster."

Jax heard Birdie mutter the word "septipede," but before he could ask what she knew Gare interrupted.

"Do you really think we'll just believe that?" Gare asked, stepping towards Morf. "You didn't even check her over!"

"Gare!" Jax scolded. Gare stepped back again, scowling. Jax turned back to Morf. He supposed it didn't really matter what Birdie knew. There was only one thing that mattered. "Can you make her better?" he asked.

Morf tapped his little fingers together, grinning up at Jax. "Outsiders pay, Morf heals."

Jax looked back at Birdie, who'd already pulled the bag of monster parts out again. "Name your price," Jax stated.

Morf eyed Birdie's bag with clear interest. "Price is not cheap. Deadly poison cure price is five thousand grokens. Health recovery is two hundred grokens per session. Outsider also must bring eye of blood squid for cure."

Jax had no idea what a groken or blood squid was, but he had the feeling he was being given the runaround. "We have a lot of rare monster parts. Will that do?"

Morf's grin faded into a serious expression. "Outsiders must see trader first. Monster parts are useless to Morf except in potions."

"And where is this trader?" Jax asked.

"Trader is in green hut, in center of village."

"And this blood squid eye... can I get that from the trader?"

Morf snorted. "Trader has not had good ingredients in years. No Divine to bring them, so no eyes. Outsider must go to Red-Black Swamp to find such."

Jax erupted. "We don't have time to go to a swamp! My sister is dying!"

"Morf will keep young one alive, so long as outsider pays for healing."

"You greedy—"

"Jax!" Birdie interrupted, shaking her head. "There's nothing more he can do without an eye." She put her hand on his shoulder. "Ev will be okay. The Red-Black Swamp in only a few hours away from here. Let's go trade in what we have to pay for a healing potion and then go kill ourselves a squid."

Jax clenched his fists but held off on laying into the gobbol for the time being. Birdie had a point. They didn't really have any other options to keep Ev alive.

"Stay here with Ev," he told Gare. "We'll be back as soon as we see this trader."

"Bud, are you sure about this?" Gare asked.

"What else are we gonna do, Gare?"

Gare didn't have an answer.

"Alright then," said Jax, turning to the door. "We won't be long."

"Be careful," Gare cautioned. "Don't let them rip you off."

Jax nodded as he and Birdie headed back out into the storm, searching for the so called "green hut." After trudging through the mud and rain for far too long without spotting anything green, they decided to just start peaking into the various buildings until they found what they was looking for.

After several failed attempts and multiple angry gobbols shouting at them, they finally found their destination as Jax pushed aside the curtain leading into a hut with a green interior. From the outside it looked no different from any of the other buildings around, save for a pair of tiny flags above the entrance. Jax couldn't help but wonder why Morf hadn't just told him that instead.

Inside, Jax looked around. The curtains were all green, the carpet was green, there was a big table on the far side of the main room, and there was an odd smell pervading the building. Just as with the doctor's hut, the ceiling was so low he had to remain hunched over. Also like the doctor's hut, there wasn't any immediate sign of anyone home, so Jax called out as he'd done before.

A gobbol with a green cap, orange tunic, and ridiculously large eyelashes immediately appeared from behind the curtain behind the large table. "Outsiders!" the gobbol squeaked. "Ogg had said outsiders were in village. Outsiders have more bugboar tusks for Nard?"

Jax and Birdie strolled up to the table, where she pulled out her bag. Jax had no idea what was in there or what anything was worth, so he figured it was best to let Birdie take the lead on this.

"I do have a few, but more importantly I have this," she said, pulling out a single roc feather and presenting it to Nard.

Nard's eyes widened at the sight, but an odd expression followed, almost one of disappointment.

"Roc down," she stated plainly. "Nard has not seen such in years."

Birdie placed the feather onto the table. "Probably not since the Divine disappeared, right?"

"Outsider is correct," answered Nard, crossing her arms. "In old days, roc down was in much demand. Divine would buy and sell for high price."

"Perfect!" Jax interjected, though a look from Birdie told him he wasn't helping.

Birdie cleared her throat. "I can't imagine you'll see much more of it either. It's not like the Divine are coming back. What do you say to a thousand grokens per feather?"

Nard visibly scoffed. "Outsider asks far too much. Price has not been one thousand for many years. Roc down is rare, but demand for such is rarer. Valuable for Divine, yes, but not for nepacs."

Jax didn't like where this was going. "What are you talking about? I know you can use it for synthesis to make armor, which means alchemists will find it valuable."

"How many alchemists make armor in these days?" Nard retorted. "In Groochsog there are none. Nard would have to travel far to make profit. How many feathers is outsider selling?"

"Eleven," Birdie responded, pulling out the feathers for Nard to see.

Once the trader had counted to confirm Birdie's claim, she presented her offer. "Nard will offer three thousand grokens."

Birdie frowned, clearly not happy with the trade, but she pushed the feathers towards Nard nonetheless. Nard reached for the roc down, but Jax slammed his hand down on them before she could take them. Both Birdie and Nard expressed shock at his behavior, but he didn't care.

"Look," he said, "I get that you would have to travel far to sell these, but it's not like they're heavy. Just think about how much you'd be able to trade them for. Five thousand I think would be a good offer for them."

"Jax—" Birdie started, but Nard cut her off.

"Nard knows how much feathers are worth," she stated, placing her hands squarely on the table. "Two fifty grokens per feather. Nard gives good deal at three thousand."

This gobbol was worse than Morf, but Jax had one more tactic to employ, not that he had much hope that it would work.

"Listen, we need five thousand grokens. My sister is sick, and five thousand is the cost of the cure. She'll die if I can't get it."

Nard just snorted. "Nard has made final offer. Three thousand is plenty. Nard is not charity. Outsider wants grokens, outsider must hunt like Divine."

Jax clenched his fists as he glared at the heartless trader. Before he could say any more, however, Birdie plopped a pair of bugboar tusks down onto the table and proceeded to extract a plethora of other monster parts from her bag as well. A large number of claws, eyeballs, and other bits he couldn't recognize were all placed before Nard.

"How much for all of this, then?" she demanded, and Jax could hear in her voice that she shared his frustration, though she was clearly trying to hide it. He didn't expect what she'd presented would fetch them much more, but they needed every little bit they could get.

While the trader was sifting through Birdie's stock, a small thought occurred to Jax that made him feel just a slight bit better about the current situation. If Nard wasn't stocking what Morf needed for medicine, maybe he could work out a deal for the cure by bringing back a load full of those squid eyes.

Once Nard had finished, she presented a final offer of thirty-seven hundred. Honestly, that was better than Jax had expected, and the thought briefly crossed his mind that perhaps they were being given a fair deal for the feathers after all.

Regardless, Birdie accepted the offer, and Nard brought out a bag full of odd coins that Jax assumed were grokens. As soon as they were out of the shop, he shared his thoughts with Birdie, who he was happy to see agreed with his idea, though she was quick to point out that even killing a single squid was going to be extremely dangerous. The two of them made their way back to the skull hut and explained the situation to Gare, who was equally outraged, but also agreed that a little extra hunting was their best bet to saving Ev. In the meantime, Jax handed over two hundred grokens to Morf, who promptly brought out a glowing green potion and staff from the back room.

Morf sprinkled the potion on Ev's face and waved his staff over her, causing the potion to glow even brighter before disappearing. Jax was still angry about the situation as a whole, but he was happy that at least something was being done to take care of Ev.

"So what exactly did that do?" he asked.

"Potion heals toxin's damage to body," Morf replied, putting a stopper on the potion's flask. "Potion cannot fix all damage until toxin is removed, but young one will live longer with medicine."

"How long?" Jax demanded.

Morf peeled back Ev's eyelid and pressed two fingers against her neck.

"Morf predicts five days, if outsider pays for twice daily treatments."

"You…" Jax caught himself, and noticed that Gare also had a hard time holding his tongue. Taking a deep breath, he switched what he was saying to something more productive. "You said if we bring back a blood squid eye you can make the cure, right?"

"That is correct. Outsider will go to swamp?"

"If it's the only way to save Ev, then yes," Jax answered, dropping his bag of grokens and handing the Heart over to Gare.

"You want me to hold onto this?" asked Gare.

"Birdie said the swamp is dangerous. If we aren't back by tomorrow night, assume the worst, and do whatever you can to get Ev and this to Roehelm as fast as possible."

Gare didn't seem comfortable with this. "Well, maybe I should go with you then? We'd have the best chance of success if we all went together."

Jax shook his head. "One of us needs to stay with Ev. I'm the one who was supposed to keep her safe, so I'm going, and Birdie's better at hunting monsters than any of us."

Gare still didn't look sure about the situation, but he acquiesced. "Well, alright, man. Just be careful okay?"

Jax nodded. "I will," he replied before pointing straight into Gare's face. "Don't open that bag."

"Oh, come on," returned Gare. "Do you really think I'd do something like that?"

"Yes," Jax responded. "So don't."

Gare raised his hands in mock indignation. "Alright, geez. I will use all of my willpower to not open the bag. Just go on and get those eyes before my horrible impulses overcome me."

Jax took a step toward the door, but before leaving addressed Morf once again. "If we bring you back more eyes than what we need to make the cure, will you heal her for less than five thousand grokens?"

Morf perked up at that proposition. "Morf will agree to this."

"Good," Jax said, and he and Birdie stepped out into the rain.

* * * *

The trek to the Red-Black Swamp was shorter than Jax had expected, but still took more than enough time for him to talk to Birdie about the possibility of a septipede being responsible for Ev's condition. By the time they'd arrived at there destination, the storm had finally somewhat abated. There was still a hint of thunder in the distance and a light sprinkle all around them, but nothing like the torrential downpour they'd experienced earlier. The effects of the storm were more than evident in the swamp, however, as the Red-Black Swamp appeared more like a Red-Black Lake — a solid body of water broken up into transparent red and opaque black patches, with far more black than red.

"So, how do we find this blood squid?" Jax asked Birdie, who'd earlier made it clear that she knew about the creatures.

Birdie answered as if she were reading from a book. "The swamp is divided into red and black pools, as you can see despite the flooding. Blood squids live in the red pools further in, so we'll have to head in pretty deep to get to them. The red waters are corrosive, so we can't go in them ourselves without protection, which we don't have, so we'll need to draw the squids out to get to them."

"Okay, and how exactly are we supposed to draw them out if we can't go in the water?" Jax asked, gesturing towards the swamp. "I don't exactly see a path we can follow."

Birdie answered in the same monotone as before. "There's normally land separating the black and red ponds, but the rain made them overflow. Wherever the two colors touch should be shallow enough for us to walk, though. The black water is safe to walk in, and the two colors don't mix. We can also just walk straight through the black water if we see two red-black trees growing near one another. There's always a path between them. Just don't bump into them because they sometimes move around when things touch them."

"I see," Jax said. "In that case, lead the way. I'll trust you know what you're doing."

Birdie walked down to the edge of the swamp at a spot where red and black water were touching. The red water, or whatever it was, truly was very clear, as Jax could see right to the bottom of a deep pool with several monsters he didn't recognize swimming around in it. At the border between red and black there was definitely a path in the shallows. Birdie stepped onto the path in the black water, which was so murky Jax couldn't even see her boots.

"Stay close," Birdie said, looking back, her voice somewhat more lively now that they were stepping into danger. "I sense a few monsters in the dark water. You'll definitely want to be near me in case they attack."

"No worries. You can count on me to protect you," Jax teased with a smirk.

Birdie returned an odd expression that Jax wasn't sure how to take — some mixture of annoyance and approval at his comment.

He followed her deeper into the swamp, the water up to just past his knees. Wading through the dark water, unable to see the ground or anything else, was not a pleasant experience. Having Birdie go first made him much more confident in his steps, but the thought of large beasts lurking out of sight beneath the ripples sent shivers up his spine.

"So, how bad is it to touch the red?" Jax asked, hoping he'd be able to put a few more inches between him and the unseen horrors of the deep.

"It will corrode most armors and eat away at your flesh," Birdie stated matter-of-factly, but she let slip a playful smile as she added, "Feel free to dip your finger in it if you want to test it."

"I... think I'll pass," Jax replied, though he wished he'd brought something along he could dip in just to see how bad it really was.

Deeper in, the red pools became more rare. Eventually, they had no choice but to try and cross some shallows with black water on both sides, making the path impossible to see. As Birdie had said they should, they looked for two trees that grew relatively near one another. The trees in question were a mix of red and black segments just like the ponds. All of the trees' leaves were black, but the branches and trunk seemed to alternate in coloration, seemingly following some pattern but not one Jax could readily make out.

"Just walk straight from one to the other, and don't touch them," Birdie told him.

"Or else they move or something, right?" Jax asked, not seeing what the big deal was since the other would still be in place. He was much more worried about having to walk on a path that was completely obscured by the dark water instead of just half.

"They could, and they'll be more than happy to toss you into deep water if they do," Birdie added, clearing the "why don't" up for him.

Eventually, the rain stopped completely, and Birdie stopped at the edge of a red pool that was deeper than the ones they'd passed earlier. Pointing into it at a large tentacled figure at the bottom, she declared triumphantly, "There's our blood squid."

Jax didn't feel much like getting too close, but he knew they had no choice but to face the beast if they were going to save Ev. Even worse, they'd have to face more than one so they could get that greedy doctor to prepare the cure after they brought him the ingredients.

Jax steeled his nerves and took a deep breath. "So how do we do this?" he asked, not taking his eyes off the squid.

"Well first," Birdie began, and she dipped herself down into the black water before hopping up again, wiping her hair back out of her eyes, "you'll want to be covered in black water to protect you from red splashes."

"Wait, the black water protects us from the red?" Jax asked, miffed he hadn't known this sooner.

"Only slightly," Birdie replied. "It will wash off quickly if a lot of red gets on you, but it's good enough if we can draw the blood squid into the black."

"And how are we supposed to do that?"

Birdie grinned a full grin for the first time in a while, striking that cocky pose again. "Well, Mr. Paladin, that's where you come in."

Not a good start to that answer. "What's that supposed to mean," Jax asked, dreading the rest of it.

"Just take your sword," Birdie lifted her dagger and pointed it at the squid, "and fire a beam at it." She flicked the blade upward for some reason.

"And then what?" Jax asked. If he was fighting a giant squid in the water, he wanted to know the full plan.

"Then back up into the black and get ready for a fight. I'll distract it with an illusion, you blind it with your light blasts, then work on cutting off its tentacles. Don't worry about harming the eyes a little. As long as you don't blow them up they'll still be good." Birdie pointed to the murky water to his left and right. "Just be careful not to fall into either of the black pools. There are other monsters in there and we won't want to give them any more reason to come after us than we already will be."

Jax took another deep breath and drew his sword. This was for Ev, he reminded himself. He waded to the edge of the black against the red, then pointed the tip of his blade at the sleeping blood squid and fired a beam.

The squid's response was immediate. It flailed its arms and jetted towards Jax, who retreated deeper into the black shallows just as a transparent image of himself appeared where he had been standing. The blood squid burst from the surface, swiping wildly at the dancing image of Jax and spraying red and black liquid everywhere as it thrashed about.

Jax took aim, and the moment he saw an opening he fired a blast at the squid's left eye. He didn't like the idea of damaging what they were here for, but he'd leave one intact just in case Birdie was wrong about Morf accepting damaged goods.

The moment the blast connected with the eye, the squid spun around, swinging its tentacles savagely in Jax's direction. The tentacles connected, and Jax was thrown into the black pool.

Under the water, he could hear wild sloshing, and quickly sought to orient himself to climb back out and rejoin the fray. He breached the surface but was immediately pulled back under by something he couldn't see. Panicking, he stabbed with his sword in the dark around his leg. His blade connected with something soft and the grip around his leg loosened. Pushing himself to the surface once again, he arrived in time to see Birdie dipping in and out of the water to avoid the blood squid's attacks.

Jax made a move to attack the squid from its rear but was nearly pulled back under as his leg was yanked out from beneath him. Fed up with whatever was interrupting his fight, he plunged his blade down into the water in the direction he was being pulled.

Once again he struck something soft, and once again the grip around his leg loosened.

Jax swung his sword upwards, tearing through the unseen monster's flesh and hopefully guaranteeing it wouldn't be a problem any longer.

He turned his attention back to the blood squid, which had at this point chased Birdie a fair way across one of the shallow paths.

Jax chased after it, and remembering the plan, fired a blast at its backside in an attempt to get it to turn around again. One blast wasn't enough, but after the third one hit he'd finally managed to capture the beast's attention.

The blood squid spun around, and Jax swung his sword in tandem, severing one of the beast's larger tentacles.

The squid swiped with its other large tentacle in a move that would have launched him straight into the red pool it had emerged from, but Jax half-dodged the attack, being knocked only partway into the red. He pulled himself out of it as quickly as he could, the red water not seeming to have hurt him.

The squid spun back around again towards Birdie, and as it did so Jax noticed several large gashes on its mantle. The creature was moving more slowly now, but as was typical of monsters it hadn't yet given up. Jax pointed his sword at the squid and fired another beam into one of its wounds.

The squid turned back to Jax once again, but was clearly growing tired. When it swung its tentacle Jax had no trouble keeping up with it, slicing neatly through it and leaving the squid nearly helpless. He charged in and plowed his sword right between its eyes, channeling his magic through his blade to finish off the creature.

The squid fell limp, and Birdie made her way around it to his side. Jax panted heavily. He wasn't sure if that battle had gone better or worse than he'd expected, but either way it was over.

Birdie started to work on removing the blood squid's eyes when Jax realized there was a burning sensation on the back of his neck.

He put his hand up to touch it and winced at the pain. He pulled his hand away to see blood on it.

"Uh, Birdie?" he called, somewhat panicked and showing her the back of his neck.

Birdie looked up and rushed over the moment she spotted the blood. Before Jax knew what was happening she'd pulled him down backwards and was splashing black water on the wound.

"Hey!" Jax shouted, the water providing cool relief while at the same time stinging as it hit his wound.

Birdie stopped and examined the spot on his neck once again.

"You could have warned me before you did that, you know," Jax scolded.

"I could have," Birdie acknowledged, stepping away from Jax, apparently satisfied, "but then the red water would have had longer to burn through you."

Jax placed his hand back on his still burning wound. Blood was still leaking out of it, but after Birdie's surprise treatment and calm response, he was a tad less concerned. Standing back up, he surveyed the huge beast they'd just killed. He hadn't slain many monsters prior to this journey, but this squid was easily the largest one he'd ever taken down — about the size of a large carriage.

Birdie shoved the squid's eyes into her bag and turned back to Jax. "This should be enough. That old coot should take off a thousand from his price for two of these."

"We don't have much over three thousand right now," Jax reminded her. "We'll need at least one more squid to cover the cost, and even then I doubt he'll take off that much."

"You want to battle another one of these after almost dying?" Birdie asked.

"I know what to expect now," replied Jax confidently. "The next one won't stand a chance, and neither will the one after that."

Birdie placed her hand on her hip, seemingly unconvinced, but she agreed. "Alright, we'll hunt one more, but if it goes poorly we're done with squids. We'll find easier monsters to hunt to get materials for the trader. We can pay off the bill that way."

Jax nodded. "Thanks. I really appreciate you doing this. You have no idea how much it means to me."

Birdie cocked her head. "You know I'm doing this for your sister and not for you, right?"

Jax nodded. "That's fine. So am I."

Birdie gave back a small smile, and the two of them continued even deeper into the swamp.

Chapter 13

The silhouette of a massive dragon flew towards the camp at the top of the mountain, only visible in the storm against the bursts of lightning across the sky. No doubt existed regarding the identity of the great lizard. It was the Dragon King Tyranor, and his appearance here meant that Syrus had managed to tame him.

Dezeroth watched from atop his perch on the mountain peak as Syrus brought his new mount into the camp below. It stood twice as tall as any of the other dragons under Dezeroth's command and would make an excellent addition to his forces.

"Harell," Dezeroth growled to his attendant, "send for Lord Syrus."

"At once, Your Excellency," his servant gurgled before shambling away.

Dezeroth went back to watching the rain blow across the mountains. That accursed roc had twice prevented him from obtaining the Heart, and now but two weeks remained until Apollyon reawakened.

Minutes passed as he contemplated how best to lay claim to the Altar of Restoration and locate the fools who had somehow escaped him. Grandis would certainly have gone to protect the Altar himself after Syrus's earlier assault on it, though after the attacks against Marisol and Roehelm, this situation would have been a certainty nonetheless.

The sound of boots scraping against stone alerted Dezeroth to Syrus's arrival. The Undead King didn't bother turning to face his guest. "I see you were successful in your efforts with Tyranor."

"The Dragon King was rather obstinate, but I eventually convinced him to see things my way," Syrus replied.

"Good," returned Dezeroth, looking over his shoulder. "With his power it will be easier to draw those servants of Grandis out of hiding."

Syrus placed his hands atop his pretty little rod. "Yes, I noticed you still seem to be short one Heart."

Dezeroth glared at the disrespectful Divine and turned to face him fully. "The servants of Grandis escaped on the roc. They flew directly above our camp towards the Sea of Rezin."

Syrus appeared shocked by this, but he quickly regained his composure and chuckled. "Well, that is interesting, isn't it? But it sounds like an easy situation to remedy. Grandis will have taken his forces to the Altar of Restoration by now, so our little heroes will find nothing but us and an abandoned citadel once they've made their crossing."

"They will not be making a crossing at all," Dezeroth growled, taking two steps towards Syrus. "The roc flew out towards the Sea of Rezin, but it returned..." he pointed to the east, "...from there."

Syrus brought a hand to his chin and frowned. "So they are headed to Roehelm. Clever, but I would have expected better."

Dezeroth scoffed. Of course mortals would make such a foolish mistake. "I have sent half of my dragon riders to meet them there, and a company of harpies to scout for them along the road. I shall obtain the Heart well before the awakening, and Tyranor's flames will assist me in this. Let us just hope that you do not fail in your quest to locate Eclipse."

"Funny you should mention that," Syrus grinned, flipping his rod to his side, "because I think I just have."

Dezeroth narrowed his eyes. "Explain."

Syrus tapped the side of his head. "The roc will only permit itself to be ridden in the presence of a Divine. I told you Eclipse would have been drawn to his Heart long ago. He is with those who have the Heart, unknowingly aiding them against his own interests. When we find the Heart, we will find Eclipse."

"You can't be sure of that," Dezeroth scowled. "My scouts have spotted several groups of Divine. They are returning to aid Grandis. One of them could be helping the mortals."

"Unlikely," replied Syrus. "Grandis's obsession with defeating Eclipse drove away all but his most loyal ally. The Divine that have returned are only interested in witnessing the destruction of the world. They have no idea of our efforts."

Dezeroth snorted. "Regardless, I want you searching for Eclipse anywhere else he might be. If he is with the mortals, I will slay him, and he will resurrect where your soldiers are waiting for him."

"No," Syrus said flatly.

"You dare defy me?" Dezeroth scowled, taking another step towards Syrus, towering over him.

Syrus merely tilted his head. "We have two weeks until Apollyon revives. Eclipse has clearly regained much of his strength even without his Heart. He will need that if he is to survive our battle with Grandis. If he is slain, that strength will be lost."

"And if he is not slain, he will continue to believe Grandis's lies!" Dezeroth shouted. "I would rather a weak ally than a powerful hindrance! His memories must be reset once again, since you say that is what happens if he is killed."

Syrus tapped his finger against his rod in thought. He looked to the east and frowned. "You're right," he conceded, then turned back to Dezeroth, "but Eclipse is smart. Even if he hasn't figured out who he is yet on his own, it shouldn't be hard to convince him of it. If he still refuses to aid us after that revelation, I will kill him personally, then collect him once he has revived."

Dezeroth narrowed his eyes. Syrus's habit of choosing his own course of action was growing tiresome, but this plan was admittedly acceptable. "Very well. I will grant you authority to lead the hunt for the Heart, but in return, you will give me control of your armies, and I will prepare for the final assault against the Altar."

"As long as you leave my soldiers in Nox Lumos where they are in case I have to kill Eclipse, you have a deal."

"Do not take me for a fool," sneered Dezeroth, and he stepped past Syrus towards the camp. When he noticed Syrus wasn't following him, he stopped and looked back over his shoulder.

"Go," he commanded, "take Tyranos and find Eclipse. Turn Doxla to ash if you must, but do not disappoint me."

Dezeroth continued down the path to the camp, not knowing nor caring if Syrus was following. When he arrived at his tent, a great roar rolled across the mountaintops. Glancing to the side, he caught sight of Syrus taking off into the storm on Tyranor. Dezeroth ignored that and stepped out of the rain and into his tent.

In the center was a rough model of the Altar of Restoration and its surrounding terrain. Located atop a tall mountain with sharp peaks on all but the southern side, there was only one path that the majority of his forces would be able to assail. Grandis would have that path blocked by his own armies, while he himself would undoubtedly guard the Altar directly. Onis and shades would be able to climb the cliffs to flank whatever forces were directly guarding the Altar, but all of that was merely a distraction. The only battle that would truly matter was the one he, Dezeroth, would engage in — the battle against Grandis and that other Radiant Escalor. Every other soldier existed purely to prevent Grandis's forces from interrupting the battle at the Altar. Everyone was expendable — his soldiers, the dragons, Syrus, even Dezeroth himself. No matter the cost, it was time to end the farce that the Masters had transformed the world into. They had made the Divine its caretakers, the Radiants its rulers, and individuals like Dezeroth, fodder. The power they had given him wasn't so that he could rule his kingdom or the world, it was so that the Divine would have an enemy to busy themselves against — an enemy that would never truly die so they would never grow bored. Now, that "gift" they had given him, what they had intended would serve only to entertain the Divine, would instead be their undoing. Dezeroth had nothing to lose. If he died, he would return, so long as Eclipse was restored to power. Grandis was far beyond all others in strength, a fact Dezeroth was loath to admit, but Grandis couldn't afford to fall and would have to fight cautiously.

All Dezeroth had to do was sap Grandis of his strength while Syrus dealt with Escalor — keep him busy, keep him distracted, and when Eclipse returned to usher in a new age, Dezeroth would once again truly be king.

Chapter 14

Before they departed the swamp, Jax and Birdie managed to collect a second pair of blood squid eyes. The battle against the second squid went much better than the first, but Jax knew they were pressing their luck fighting them around those red pools — one wrong move and everything would be over. For that reason, he and Birdie decided it might be better to take a short detour through a nearby forest on the way back and hunt other monsters in a safer local, even though the materials they would get from them wouldn't be nearly as valuable. By the time they were through, Birdie's backpack was filled to bursting with various pieces of different monsters, as well as the fruit of a rare plant Birdie had spotted that she claimed should be worth a decent bit of cash. They still weren't sure if they would be able to afford Ev's cure, but they both agreed they had to be close.

By the time they made it back to the village, the sun had gone down once again. They stopped by the trader's hut and presented their spoils, sans the eyes, and claimed over five hundred grokens, putting them up to four thousand and fifteen total. Before leaving, Birdie had the trader appraise the eyes as well, revealing that they would sell for two hundred each.

Before making their way back to the skull hut, they made one more stop by the local inn to find out that it would cost fifty grokens per room. With that bit of information under their belts, they tucked away two hundred and fifteen grokens into Birdie's bag and headed to Morfs.

Jax pushed aside the curtain at the entrance and stepped in. Ev had been moved to the side of the room and given a bundle of cloth for use as a pillow, with Gare sitting close by. Ev's complexion was visibly worse now — pale and tinted green, and she seemed to be having trouble breathing.

Gare jumped up at the sight of Jax and nearly tackled him. "You're back! Did you get the eye?"

Jax grinned as Birdie showed Gare the contents of her bag. "Even better, we got four."

Gare slapped Jax on the back. "Hell yeah! Hey, doctor guy, we got your eyes right over here!"

Morf appeared from behind one of the other curtains in the hut and made his way over. Jax handed over one of the eyes.

"Hmm," he mused as he looked it over, "Morf is impressed. Outsiders are more resourceful than Morf expected."

"And we have three more," Jax told him, "plus three thousand and eight hundred grokens. I think that should be enough to cover the price."

Morf frowned and clutched the eye tight to him. "Deadly poison cure is five thousand grokens. No less!"

"You said we could trade the eyes for a reduced price," Jax reminded him.

"Yes," Morf agreed, still clutching the eye. "Morf give one hundred off per eye. Outsiders must pay rest."

"Funny," said Jax, casting a sideways glance at a smirking Birdie, "because we just checked with the trader and she says the eyes are worth two hundred each. Maybe we should just go sell them to her instead."

Morf looked down at the eye and growled. "Morf will check with trader. If outsider speaks truth, Morf will lower price two hundred each."

"Not so fast," said Birdie, blocking Morf's exit. "The buy price is two hundred, which means you'd have to pay much more than that to get them from her. I think twelve hundred off for four eyes is a good deal, wouldn't you say?"

Morf looked between Jax and Birdie with a frown, then ducked his head down and simply muttered "Morf will check with trader" before heading out the door.

Birdie grinned triumphantly. Jax didn't quite match her confidence, but he was feeling much better than he had thirty minutes ago.

Gare wasn't quite so certain. "So what do we do if he doesn't give us the deal?" he asked.

"Don't worry," replied Birdie. "He will."

"Yeah, but what if he doesn't?" Gare pressed, agitated.

"Relax Gare," said Jax, holding up his hand. "We've got a couple hundred extra groken if we need it and I can sell my sword if we need to get more."

"Sell your…!" Gare began, but he caught himself and spoke more calmly. "You can't sell your sword. What if we get attacked again?"

Jax held up his hand and emitted a glow.

"You can't…." Gare sighed. "Bud, listen, I know you've been practicing, but you can't fight off Dezeroth's soldiers with just light blasts."

"Maybe not," returned Jax, "but I'm the only one of us with offensive magic, and we all need armor. It's the only thing we have I'm willing to give up."

Gare didn't seem comfortable with that idea. "Well, I guess I can't stop you if that's what you want to do, but maybe we could go hunt some more monsters instead before we resort to that?"

Jax frowned. "Yes, we could, but that would take time. I'm not going to let Ev get any worse."

"I'm with Gare on this," said Birdie, surprising Jax. "If we hunted all night we'd have the money we need by morning, but," she said loudly, cutting off Jax before he could protest, "it's a moot point. There's no way that gobbol is going to turn down our deal."

Jax nodded in agreement, and Gare also seemed appeased.

"Well, alright then," he said. "So what do we do after Ev gets her medicine?"

Jax jabbed his thumb at Birdie's backpack. "Those extra grokens we kept can pay for a room or two at the inn, and some supplies in the morning. We'll stay here for the night to give Ev a chance to recover, but then we're back on the road in the morning."

Gare nodded in approval. "Sounds good to me. I can't wait to get out of this place. Those little guys give me the creeps."

A few minutes later, Morf returned with the eye he'd taken with them.

"Well?" Jax asked him, but he took the eye into the back room without so much as a glance.

Gare narrowed his eyes as he watched the curtain Morf had disappeared behind. "Should we go after him?"

"Not yet," answered Jax. He doubted the gobbol doctor would run off with the eye when he had money to be made. Deal or no, there was no way the cure cost him anywhere near his asking price to produce.

Sure enough, a few minutes later Morf returned with a box of supplies and ingredients, the eye sitting neatly on top. He set the box down in front of the cauldron in the center of the room and returned to the group.

"Morf will make cure, but outsiders must pay first."

Birdie put the remaining eyes in the bag of grokens Jax had and he handed it over. Morf took the bag, plus the other bag from their first visit to the trader, into the back room, and a minute later returned once again with his staff and a second smaller pot. He went to work tossing ingredients into the cauldron, occasionally stopping to wave his staff and mumble incantations. At the end, he tapped the staff against the cauldron and the mixture flickered with a red glow. He scooped out enough of the liquid to fill the smaller pot, then performed a second ritual that concluded with a large puff of smoke and light billowing from the pot, leaving behind just enough of a new reddish brown potion to fill a tiny flask, which he brought over to Ev. Morf sprinkled the potion on Ev's face and waved his staff, causing the potion to glow and disappear.

Ev's complexion immediately improved, the green disappearing entirely and a bit of natural color returning to her skin. Her breathing improved as well, but she remained unconscious.

"Treatment is done," said Morf. "Sepsis venom has been removed. Morf suggests another potion for health recovery."

"Thanks," said Jax, checking Ev over, "but I think we're good."

"Hmph," snorted Morf. "If outsiders have no further business with Morf, then outsiders get out."

Jax was more than happy to oblige and led the way back to the inn he and Birdie had scouted out earlier. Halfway there Ev opened her eyes, but she was understandably disoriented.

"Where... are we?" she asked, and Gare slipped her down off his back, though Birdie and Jax needed to catch her to keep her from falling over.

"Easy Ev," Jax said, "you still haven't recovered all the way."

Ev placed her hand to her head, wincing. "What happened? Were we attacked?"

Jax shook his head. "No. You were poisoned. Birdie thinks it was by a septipede."

Ev opened her eyes a bit wider, but still was clearly not completely with them yet. "What? No, I... I thought... I healed that."

Jax shook his head and sighed. "Why didn't you tell us you were bitten? We would have tried to get you here sooner if we'd known."

Ev stared blankly ahead. Jax wasn't sure how well she was processing what he was saying.

"Look, don't worry about it," he said. "You're better now, and that's what matters. You can thank Birdie for that. I doubt we could have done it without her."

Ev looked at Birdie, who gave a comforting smile, then turned her attention back to Jax. "I'm sorry. I messed up everything."

"What? No!" Jax responded. "Why would you even say that? It's not your fault you got bit!"

Ev just stared at Jax. He couldn't tell if she was listening to him or not.

Birdie put her hand on Ev's shoulder. "Hey, it's alright. The poison's out of you now. Do you think you can heal yourself the rest of the way? I know you'd feel a lot better if you did."

Ev shifted her attention to Birdie, and after a brief pause nodded. She placed both hands together and closed her eyes, as if praying. After a moment a soft glow surrounded her hands and made its way up her arms and around her body. The action seemed to put a good bit of strain on her, but after a few moments her muscles began to relax and the glow brightened. Another minute after that and the glow faded as she opened her eyes and released her hands.

"Feel better?" Jax asked, placing his hand on her shoulder now.

Ev nodded. "Much. I'm just a little tired."

"You and me both," chimed Gare. "No offense, but you get pretty heavy after a while."

"Shut up Gare," Jax quipped, "at least you didn't have to fight a giant squid monster."

Gare rolled his eyes, and Ev responded with surprise.

"A squid? Where...?"

Jax just shook his head. "It's a long story. We can tell you about it once we get to the inn."

Ev nodded, and the four of them made their way to the hut where they'd be staying the night. Unlike every other building Jax had been to, this one had a ceiling that was high enough for him to stand up straight. The main room was still empty upon arrival, save for the table on the far end of it, but Jax was used to this by now. He gave a quick shout and out came the same gobbol who'd given him the room price earlier.

The frog-faced proprietor was a tad more amicable than the trader and doctor had been, but Jax suspected the friendly demeanor was all for the sake of convincing them to stay. He doubted the inn received much traffic and figured the guy was desperate for business.

"Welcome back, outsiders! Hepp is happy to provide accommodations," he exclaimed. "Outsiders require four rooms, yes?"

"Actually," Jax said, placing his hands on Hepp's table, "we'll just take two. We can share them."

Hepp looked up with an uncertain expression, but managed to maintain his smile. "If outsiders desire such, Hepp will provide, but rooms have one bed only. Hepp greatly recommends four rooms for outsiders."

"That will be fine," Birdie chimed in before Jax could object, taking the grokens out of her bag.

"Uh, no, it won't be," Jax protested, leaning in front of her to prevent her from putting the coins down. "We need the money for supplies, remember?"

"And what supplies would that include, other than food?" she responded.

"Yo," Gare joined in, "I'll share a room if it means we get food. I haven't eaten anything in days."

"We'll have money left over for food even if we get four rooms," Birdie stated. "If we need more for anything else we can go out and hunt something." Birdie stepped around Jax to Hepp. "Besides, it's my money. We got most of it from selling my loot, remember?"

"Fine," Jax responded. "You want your own room, you can have it, but Gare and I will share one."

"Actually," Gare started, "now that I think about it, I wouldn't mind a room to myself either."

Jax stared at Gare.

"What? As long as we get some food tonight I'm good with spending extra if it means sleeping in an actual bed."

Jax sighed. "Fine. I guess I wouldn't mind my own room either." Jax turned to Ev. "Would you be okay sleeping by yourself?"

Ev lifted an eyebrow at Jax. "I don't know. It will be hard going to sleep without the sound of constant snoring all night."

Jax rolled his eyes and addressed Hepp. "Alright then, looks like four rooms it is."

Birdie plopped the coins on the table, which Hepp quickly counted. "Very good choice. Please follow Hepp, many rooms are open."

Hepp led the group down a small hallway off the left side of the room. Exactly four small rooms branched off of the hallway, a curtain hanging in the doorway of each of them. The rooms themselves were tiny, consisting of little more than a mattress on the floor and a pile of blankets, though there was just enough space for all of them to fit into one if they'd wanted to.

"Chamber pots are out back by bath house," Hepp chirped. "Outsiders feel free to use such as needed. Leaving time is noon tomorrow, unless outsiders want to stay longer...."

"Thanks," said Jax, "but one night will be enough."

"Very well. If outsiders change mind, Hepp is here." Hepp bowed and hopped away.

"Did you here that?" asked Gare. "They have a bath house! I've been needing a wash since we left Marisol!"

"Yeah, Gare, we noticed," Jax quipped, well aware that he wasn't exactly a bed of roses either. "Well, if you guys want to take advantage of that, I plan on going out to find us some food."

"Let me do that," Birdie said. "If you want, I can head out to bring us back some monster parts for the trader and we could eat well tonight."

"Aw, man, mind if I go with you?" Gare offered.

"Why do you want to go?" Jax asked him.

"Because if I help pick out the food, I get to eat it first, too," Gare grinned.

Birdie shrugged. "Sure, if everyone else is okay with that."

Jax didn't like the idea of any of them wandering off on their own around here, but if Gare and Birdie were together, he was sure they'd be fine. "I'm good with that. Ev?"

Ev nodded in agreement.

"Great! We'll be back before you know it," Gare announced, running off ahead of Birdie.

"Hold it!" called Jax, motioning to the bag on Gare's back.

"Oh, right," Gare said as he handed it over to Jax. "Guess I shouldn't take that with me, huh?"

Jax shook his head as Gare and Birdie left, then turned back to Ev. "Well, I guess we have to wait a bit before dinner. You want to go wash up?"

Ev shook her head. "I'd rather wait until Birdie comes back, actually. I think I'll lie down for a bit until then."

"You aren't feeling sick again, are you?" Jax asked.

Ev shook her head again. "No, I'm just tired is all. It's nice to see you and Birdie getting along better, though."

Jax rubbed the back of his head. He didn't want to tell Ev about what happened with the blood squid just yet. "Yeah. She really came through for us. I guess I was wrong to be so suspicious."

Ev smiled up at Jax, but the smile faded quickly. "I'm still sorry for all of this. I was so stupid getting myself bit."

"Nobody's blaming you for getting bitten, Ev."

"But they should, though! I saw one of the babies and thought I could kill it by stepping on it. Then it bit me when I tried and ran away.... I didn't even hurt it."

Jax failed to hide the look of surprise on his face. "Seriously? Why would you do that?"

"Because monsters are horrible and the world would be better off without them. You and Gare and Birdie kill monsters all the time, but the only ones I can hurt are those ghosts in that stupid forest."

Jax sighed. He didn't want to be angry at her, but he was frustrated that she'd let her passion get the better of her. "Ev, if you really hate monsters so much then why didn't you become a ranger like Father wanted you to?"

Ev looked at the ground. "A ranger in the Light Guard still wouldn't hunt monsters. They just train on targets all day. At least as a cleric I could spend my time reading instead of standing in a field."

Jax nodded almost imperceptibly. Ev did have a valid point. The Light Guard existed purely to guard the Heart. She would have had to have joined the Standard Guard to be tasked with killing monsters, and their father never would have stood for that. "Well, if you aren't going to bathe, would you mind holding the Heart while I do?"

Ev nodded and took the Heart back to her room as Jax made his way to the bath house. He didn't have any change of clothes on him, but even if his armor still stunk afterward it would be refreshing to clean up a bit.

A little while later Birdie and Gare returned with a sack of skewered meat, fruit, and mushrooms, as well as a few canteens of water. Jax and Gare joined Ev in her room, with Jax taking back the Heart. Birdie needed to take a break behind the inn, and took a stick of meat with her when she went. The gobbol dish had a pungent odor, but tasted good enough — a combination of sweet and savory. Birdie didn't seem to find it so appetizing, however, as she didn't eat another bite after returning from the back.

"So," began Gare, talking with his mouth full, "how much farther is it to Roehelm from here?"

"We should be pretty close," answered Jax. "Ev and I used to take the south road to visit our Gram. It was only a couple of days' ride after passing the mountains going that way, so we're probably not much farther than that right now."

"Well, that's good," said Gare before pointing behind Jax. "I'm more than ready to get rid of that stupid thing already."

"Yeah," said Jax, "me too, honestly. Not being able to put it down gets old real fast."

Gare took another big bite, finishing the last of his meat skewers. "Well, if you want, I can hold onto it again."

Jax shook his head. "Nah, I got it. I've figured out how to sleep without it bothering me too much."

Gare shrugged and fiddled with his skewer, seemingly unsure what to do with it now that he was done eating. "Well, if that's what you want, I sure won't complain."

Jax gave a quick smile and finished his meal as well. Birdie and Ev went to wash up once they were done, and Gare did the same when they were done. When he got back, they all retired to their rooms for the night.

Jax wasn't exactly comfortable with his door consisting of nothing more than a sheet of cloth, but the comfort of an actual bed with a blanket quickly won him over.

He snuffed out the candle in the corner of the room and tucked himself in to sleep. He closed his eyes, but as he was drifting off he started to worry about Ev. He knew any intruder would have to sneak past his and Birdie's room, and Gare's was right across from Ev's, but the thought that anyone could just wander right in off the streets made him reconsider going to sleep just yet. He opened his eyes and listened for the sound of anyone who might be sneaking around.

There was nothing, of course, and there stayed nothing for a while. He was about to close his eyes again when a strange light began flickering into his room from under the door's curtain.

Curious, he got up and crept to the door, his feet silent on the dirt floor of the hut. As he cautiously pushed aside the curtain, he noticed the light was coming from Birdie's room. He'd seen that light before, back when she'd gone off on her own in the Myco Fields. Now even more curious, he snuck to the curtain that was her door. The moment his fingers touched the fabric, the light dimmed drastically.

"Can I help you?" he heard Birdie ask from the other side.

Knowing he'd been caught, he went ahead and pushed aside the curtain anyway, revealing himself to a frowning Birdie.

"Do you always spy on women at night?" she asked crossly.

"I... no, I just saw a strange light," he said, fully aware that was hardly an excuse.

Birdie didn't respond.

Jax knew he was in trouble, but since he was already here, he figured he might as well just ask about what he'd seen.

"That light," Jax began, "what was that?"

Birdie's frown faded as she looked to the ground and at a mirror she was holding in her unlit hand. Where she'd gotten it from Jax had no idea.

"It was nothing," was her answer. "It's just something I do sometimes."

"Which is...?" Jax prodded.

Birdie chuckled inaudibly, but her expression was clearly pained. "I'd really rather not talk about it. I know it isn't healthy — wanting to be something I'm not."

Jax was confused. "I'm not sure I'm following."

Birdie put her mirror down, craned her head back, and sighed. "Look, if you must know, I sometimes conjure up the appearance of other people. It's... an escape — pretending to be someone else for a while."

"Conjure up an appearance? You mean like, your actual appearance?"

Birdie looked up at Jax. Before another word was spoken, a dark aura flashed around her, and Jax was no longer looking at the same Birdie. Sitting on the ground in front of him was an older looking woman with long blond hair. Then, with another quick flash, Birdie was back to herself.

Amazed, Jax ventured to step into the room and sit down. "That's incredible," he said in awe. "I've never seen anyone use that spell like that."

"Like what?" Birdie asked, eyebrow cocked.

"You know, that easily. Everyone in the Light Guard who could do that always had to close their eyes when doing it."

Birdie shrugged.

"I don't understand, though. Why are you doing this?"

Birdie shook her head. "I don't expect you to understand. You can go wherever you want. Me? I can't go into human cities anymore — not out in the open anyway. If the wrong people saw me...."

Jax frowned. "I don't see what the problem is. With an ability like that, can't you just wear a disguise? No one would be able to recognize you!"

"Anyone with high perception skills can see right through those kinds of illusions," Birdie replied irritably.

"Maybe," returned Jax, "but it's not like the whole world is looking for you. What are the odds one of those people will be in the same place you are and have that kind of perception?"

"What difference would it make?" Birdie nearly shouted. "Whether I'm hiding in the shadows or hiding behind a mask, I'm still hiding!" Birdie threw her mirror against her bed and put her hand over her face. "That stupid Heart."

"The Heart?"

Birdie sighed in frustration. "Every moment it taunts me. Ever since you told me what it was, I've wished that I could use its power, but I know that I can't. With its power I could make all of my troubles disappear, but as it is it might as well be a damn rock!"

Jax had never seen Birdie this way before. He'd never have imagined that behind that cocky personality she was haunted by these kinds of thoughts. Remembering what she'd told him the night before, he supposed he couldn't blame her. If a group of people had come to Marisol seeking his head, and the city had tried to hand him over, he'd probably be pretty scarred by it, too.

"You know, I get it," he said after a moment.

Birdie glanced over at him from behind her fingers.

"I also wish I was someone else sometimes. I wish I was someone strong enough to take on Dezeroth. If it was possible, I'd use that Heart on myself in an instant and bury him over and over again, but like you said... it's not. The Heart belongs to the Dark Radiant Eclipse, and no one else can use it."

Birdie took her hand away from her face, her eyes a bit more relaxed, but clearly still upset.

Jax shook his head. "You know, when I left Marisol, I had it in my head that if I just kept at it, fighting every monster I came across, I'd get strong enough to beat him. I knew it was impossible, but a part of me wanted to believe it. The truth is, no one is strong enough to beat him, at least not a nepac like me."

"Oh, shut up," Birdie stated flatly, looking Jax in the eyes. "Dezeroth may be strong, but he's not invincible."

That response caught Jax off guard, but he quickly recovered. "Really?

And how do you propose someone like me can fight him? Only Lord Grandis and Lady Escalor are strong enough to defeat him."

Birdie shook her head. "Maybe on their own they are, but you don't have to fight him alone. No one does. I don't recommend you try it even with help, of course, but that doesn't mean it can't be done. He isn't one of the Masters, and that means he can be beaten. Even a Radiant can be defeated by nepacs if they work together."

Jax nearly chuckled at that — the thought of nepacs beating a Radiant — but then he saw the look on Birdie's face and knew she was being serious.

"You really think it can be done," Jax stated.

"I know it can," she replied.

Jax glanced sideways in thought before returning his eyes to Birdie. "I don't suppose you'd be interested in helping me, would you?"

Birdie raised an eyebrow. "Helping you? Defeat Dezeroth?"

Jax nodded.

Birdie took a moment to consider. "Well, I suppose after this I won't have anything better to do, and I wouldn't want Ev to lose her brother."

Jax blinked. "Really? You're actually saying you'll do it?"

Birdie sighed, then shrugged. "I'll tell you what. If, once we're done with this Heart thing, you still want to kill Dezeroth, and no one else has done it, then sure."

Jax wasn't quite sure what to say.

"I hear his sword and armor are worth a fortune for those who slay him, anyway," she added with a wry smile.

Jax returned the smile. "Of course, it's all about the money for you, isn't it."

"Every time," she replied.

With that, Jax decided it was time to head back to his room. Birdie seemed to be feeling better, and he didn't want to say anything that might get her thinking about those people who were after her again. He wished her goodnight and, upon returning to his room, finally managed to drift off to sleep beneath the soft, warm blanket the gobbols had provided him.

Chapter 15

The following morning was the first time in what seemed like ages since Jax felt truly rested. Pushing aside his blankets, he stood and stretched, pleasantly relieved that the soreness he'd carried since the septipede was substantially lessened. He stepped out of his room to find Birdie already up, but he had to wake Gare and Ev himself. Once they were all set, they took their leave of the inn and set out to gather supplies for the road.

Whatever Birdie and Gare had hunted last night must have had some valuable parts for trade, because they had far more than enough money to buy up enough food to last them the rest of the journey. They used what was left over for a set of blankets, some arrows for Birdie, and some packs to carry everything in.

Once everything was in order, Jax checked in with the trader one last time to get directions to Roehelm, then led the way to the east side of town. According to her, they just needed to follow the road east, taking the southbound fork when they came to it.

"We're almost there," he said to everyone, adjusting the pack on his back. "Just three days' walk, and we've made it."

"Finally," Ev sighed. "It will be such a relief to see Gram after everything that's happened."

"I'm just looking forward to dumping that stupid you-know-what off on someone else when we get there," Gare added. "I'm sick of being chased around because of it."

"Agreed," said Jax, "but we aren't there yet. Dezeroth is still after us. He'll probably figure out we didn't head south soon, so we'll need to move quickly, and we'll stick to the trees so that when he does send scouts looking for us, they won't find us."

"Sounds good to me," shrugged Gare. "Lead the way."

Jax nodded, pulled the straps on his pack tight one more time, then set off down the road. Fortunately, the road ran right alongside a forest, so sticking to the trees wasn't that hard. Jax doubted that they were in much danger of being spotted yet. If Dezeroth had figured out where they were going, it would have been recently. Still, it didn't hurt to be safe, and there was always the chance they'd run into more questionable Divine if they stayed out in the open.

Jax's concerns weren't realized, however. The day passed by uneventfully, without a single sighting of a traveler on the road or scout in the sky. Comfortable that they were in a good position, Jax pushed the group to continue on until well after dark. The sooner they got to Roehelm the better, after all. If they pushed themselves hard they might even get those three days down to two.

The only monsters they encountered were a few packs of shark-toothed furballs like the ones they'd run into back in the mountains. Despite traveling on foot, the little beasts posed even less of an issue than before, though the fact that Jax used his sword this time and not just his magic probably helped with that.

Eventually, Jax spotted an open area in the woods near a river. The location was hidden from the sky and nearly so from the road, and he doubted he'd find a better place to set up camp that night.

The group cleared out the debris on the ground and unpacked their blankets and some of the food they'd brought with them. It was all fruit and bread since they didn't want to be starting any fires that might attract attention, but it was certainly an improvement over the nights where they'd had nothing.

Just as before, they set up a watch schedule, this time with Jax going first. He found a nice spot a bit outside of the clearing where he had a straight view of the road and settled in there for the night. Ev, Gare, and Birdie all snuggled up under the blankets they'd bought, with Birdie going so far as to cover herself completely.

The night was just as Jax had hoped it would be — as uneventful as the day had been. When at last morning arrived, he found himself being kicked awake by Gare.

"Hey sleepyhead, you're missing breakfast," Gare said with a grin as he tapped his boot against Jax's head.

"Hey, get off!" Jax yelled, pushing Gare's foot away.

"What? You're the one who wants us to get to Roehelm in a hurry," Gare said, holding up his hands in mock innocence.

Jax grumbled, grabbed a loaf of bread from a bag, and headed off to the river to do his business. When he got back everyone was in the process of packing up the blankets, including his.

"Well, it looks like you're all about ready to go, huh?" he commented.

Gare stretched and slipped his bag over his shoulder. "Yeah, I guess so. It just kind of stinks that we'll be getting rid of the thing without ever even seeing what it looks like."

"Are you still on about that?" Jax asked him.

"Of course I am," Gare replied. "We never got to see it at the citadel, Kelva didn't let us see it in the caves, and you haven't let us look at it since. Aren't you at all curious what the Heart of a Radiant looks like?"

"It doesn't matter what it looks like," Jax answered. "All that matters is making sure we get it to Roehelm."

"And how do we even know we're really carrying it if we haven't seen it?" asked Gare, crossing his arms.

"Don't be ridiculous; of course we're carrying it," Jax answered, refusing to let such a notion enter his head.

"But do you know that for sure?" Gare asked, arms wide.

Jax just rolled his eyes.

Gare turned to Ev and Birdie. "Come on, I can't be the only one who wants to see this thing, right?"

Birdie and Ev both looked away, leaving Gare without any support.

Jax tried to reason with Gare one more time. "Look, Gare, I get that you want to see it, but it's not worth the risk. If we dropped the thing it would disappear the second it hit the ground."

Gare was clearly frustrated, but he looked defeated. Jax figured it would be best to get moving before the conversation started up again.

"Right then," he began, "in that case—"

"Actually, that's not true," interrupted Ev.

Everyone turned to her.

"Say what?" asked Gare.

"That's not true," she repeated, looking squarely at Jax. "The Heart disappears after sixteen seconds if it isn't in a nepac's possession, and doesn't disappear at all if its Divine is nearby, so there's not much risk of losing it if we drop it here."

Jax opened his mouth to say something, but he knew Ev knew more about the rules of the Divine than he did. He also knew he'd lost his only reason not to take out the Heart. That fact was not lost on Gare.

"So that settles it then. Come on bud, when are any of us ever going to get a chance to see this thing again?"

Jax looked at the faces staring at him. It was clear from each of their expressions that they were all interested, and truth be told, so was he.

He sighed, then brought the bag with the Heart around to his front. "Fine, but let's make this quick. We still need to get back on the road to Roehelm."

"Alright!" Gare shouted, rushing over. Ev and Birdie followed more slowly behind him.

Jax sat on the ground with the bag in his lap as the others gathered around. Jax released the straps that had been holding the bag closed and pulled back the flap to reveal a dark gleaming sphere no bigger than his head. Carefully, Jax reached in and pulled out the Heart. It's surface was incredibly smooth and glossy, highlighted with a dancing iridescence especially prominent in the glowing cracks of its dark surface. A thick golden ring flanked by two smaller glowing rings wrapped around the center of the sphere, emitting a steady sparkling light. Another golden ring bordered a glowing mesh at the poles of the sphere, the lines of which were warm to the touch.

"Wow," said Gare, reaching a hand out to touch it. "So this is a Radiant's Heart."

Jax had to admit, he was in awe of what he was holding. Sure, he'd known he'd been carrying it, but there was something about actually seeing it that made it all the more real just what they were trying to prevent from happening.

Gare carefully put his hands around the Heart and pulled it towards himself. Figuring things would be easier to just let him have the moment, Jax relinquished it without protest.

"Heh," Gare chuckled, staring at the object in his hands. "Just think how much easier things would be if we could use this thing's power."

"Yeah, but we can't, can we?" replied Jax. "Now whenever you're done, we need to get moving again."

"Hold on," said Gare, pulling the Heart closer to him. "Ev and Birdie haven't had a chance to look at it."

He offered the Heart to Ev, who tentatively reached for it but stopped short of actually touching it.

"What's wrong?" Gare asked.

"I..." began Ev, seemingly unsure herself why she was hesitating. "It just doesn't feel right touching it," she answered at last.

Gare shrugged, then offered it to Birdie. "Come on, how many people can say they've actually held a Radiant's Heart."

Birdie hesitated almost as much as Ev had, and Jax had had enough. "Alright, Gare, this isn't a toy," he said, but before he finished Birdie had taken the Heart.

She stared at it transfixed, a look of unease in her eyes.

"Birdie, come on," Jax said, gesturing to get the Heart back.

Birdie looked up at him with a pained expression, almost as if she'd been scolded. Slowly, she handed it back to him, and he tucked it back inside of his bag.

"There," he said, standing up, "now everyone's seen it, so we don't have to worry about that anymore. Right?" he added, looking right at Gare.

"Yeah, sure thing bud," Gare replied with a smile, swinging his own bag up over his shoulders. "I'm happy now."

"Good," said Jax. "Then let's get moving already. We aren't at Roehelm yet, and we won't be safe until we are."

The group traveled as they had the day before, keeping just inside of the forest in case any scouts flew by overhead. The only exception was when they had to cross the river. With their armor there was no way they could swim it, so they took the bridge. As soon as they were across they went right back under cover again. So they continued until almost sundown, when Birdie stopped abruptly, peering up at the sky. Jax knew that couldn't be good.

"What's—" he started, but Birdie jerked her arm to silence him.

Everyone else stood still as well, looking up and listening, but not seeing nor hearing anything.

Jax crept closer to Birdie. "What's the matter?" he whispered.

Birdie pulled out her bow and notched an arrow, answering Jax while remaining fixed on the canopy. "Harpies."

"Harpies?" Jax repeated. "What are harpies doing in this region?"

"Exactly," returned Birdie.

Jax paused to consider the situation. Harpies weren't supposed to be part of Dezeroth's army, but by their reputation Jax could certainly see them allying themselves with the Undead King. Even assuming that was the case, Jax thought it unlikely that Dezeroth would have sent more than scouts into the area. Still, it was better to be safe than sorry. The group would have to move more cautiously from now on, but also quickly. The more time that passed, the more likely it was more soldiers would show up in the area. In either case, Birdie had lowered her bow, so Jax assumed that the threat had passed.

"Are they gone?" he asked quietly, not wanting to jump the gun.

Birdie glanced over at Jax but didn't answer, telling him that she didn't think so.

Jax returned his gaze to the treetops and spotted a large birdlike creature passing by through an opening in the leaves. Birdie readied her bow, and Jax drew his sword. Gare pulled out his ax, not that it would do him much good.

A moment later, another creature flew by overhead, this time closer, and Jax could clearly make out the half-woman half-bird figure of the harpy. It disappeared as quickly as it had come, but it soon circled back and hovered above the opening Jax was looking through, peering down. The harpy opened its haggard mouth and let out an ear-rending scream — a scream that was immediately echoed by countless unseen harpies in the skies above.

Birdie let an arrow fly, piercing the monster's chest and silencing the scream, though failing to bring it down. Jax fired a beam at the retreating creature and knocked it from the sky, but a second harpy soon took its place and continued the deafening blare. A second arrow and light beam brought it down as well. A third bird appeared just as quickly.

At that point Jax was certain these harpies weren't out for a simple hunt. They wouldn't keep throwing themselves into the line of fire if they were. They were calling others to the group's location, and judging by the cacophony above them there were more than enough of them to keep it up until whoever they were calling arrived.

"We can't stay here!" Birdie yelled, taking aim once again.

"Well, where are we supposed to go?" Gare yelled back, and he had a point. They were still half a day from Roehelm. The forest was the most cover they'd be able to find, and clearly that was insufficient.

"We don't have a choice!" Jax called back as he joined Birdie in taking down the third harpy. "Move!"

They did. They ran through the forest as quickly as they were able, but the harpies kept right with them. Jax and Birdie would turn to take shots at the cretins, but for every one they silenced, another was ready to take its place.

Suddenly, the shrieking ceased. Jax looked back out of curiosity and spotted their pursuers still there, hovering silently. A sinking feeling turned instantly to dread as an enormous shadow appeared overhead. Before his mind was even able to register what his gut was telling him, a wall of fire rained down from above, blocking their path.

Jax retreated from the searing heat, the forest before them engulfed in flame. He grabbed Ev's arm and pulled her to the left, shouting "This way!" to the group, but he was cut off by another wave of fire before he could even take three steps.

The only paths open to them were towards the road and back the way they'd come. Jax knew damn well the road was a death sentence, but before he could make another move the way back was also cut off.

Jax cursed and peered up at the sky, shielding his face from the burning leaves and ash raining upon him. His heart nearly fainted at the swarm of dragons soaring above the now open canopy. Another dragon swooped in and unleashed hellfire through the trees, forcing the group to retreat.

Jax cursed, but the forest had become an inferno on all sides save one, a single path to the road. As they drew near the open sky, Jax hesitated. They were fleeing right into Dezeroth's hands. Perhaps if they doubled back they could find a way through the flames.

A loud crash behind him signaled the arrival of a dragon on the ground as it knocked aside several trees to make room for its bulk. The beast roared, and a revenant mage on its back pointed a staff towards Jax and fired a dark ball of magic towards him.

Jax returned a blast of light of his own, but the dark magic overpowered it, forcing him to jump aside to avoid it.

He landed hard on the ground, his armor burning from the heat of the nearby fire. A powerful grip yanked him back to his feet as Gare pulled him away from the blaze and towards the road. The sound of trees falling behind him told him the dragon was following, though at this point he didn't know if it mattered. Once they were in the open it would be all over.

They burst out of the trees, the cool breeze a contrasting relief to the sight of the half dozen dragons forming a perimeter around them. The dragon in the forest crashed out onto the road behind them, knocking down trees and forcing them further into the open.

Jax knew they were done for, and as he desperately tried to think of some way to salvage their mission, his attention was captured by the arrival of a new dragon — black, and easily twice the size of the largest of the others.

The black dragon soared in a wide arc out over the field before returning to land directly in the center of the circle of red-scaled beasts, then bowed its head to let off a cloaked man with a jeweled rod. Jax had no idea who this man was. He was obviously not a revenant, but he was clearly high up in Dezeroth's army. The man approached the group alone, his gait exuding a confidence that warned Jax there was more to him than met the eye.

Jax lifted his sword defensively. Whatever this guy was, he was definitely some sort of mage, and Jax didn't want him getting within spellcasting distance.

The man didn't take the hint however, and Jax lit up his hand as further warning. "Stay back!" he yelled, and Birdie joined him by notching an arrow in the man's direction.

The man stopped, then tilted his head and smiled. "I'm afraid I can't do that. You have something I very much need, and I'd appreciate it if you handed it over."

"Not a chance in hell," Jax retorted as an idea began to take shape in his mind.

"It's a shame you feel that way," the man returned, "but I don't think you have a choice in the matter."

The man placed his hands atop his rod in front of him, his smile broadening. Jax readied for some sort of spell to be sent their way, but what happened next he could never have been prepared for. From behind the man's shoulders a pair of brilliant crystal wings emerged, and Jax found himself open mouthed at the sight.

"Wh... what? How?" Jax stammered, then shook his head. "No! It's just an illusion! A Radiant would never serve Dezeroth!"

The wings disappeared, and the man straightened his back. "You are correct. I do not serve King Dezeroth. I have allied with him. Allow me to introduce myself. My name is Exalted Lord Syrus, and I have come to restore my friend, Eclipse, to his rightful status as Radiant."

Jax nearly dropped his sword. He could hear Ev gasp. "No," he muttered. "That... you can't be. Syrus's Heart... it was at..."

"At Roehelm, yes," Syrus answered. "The place you are fleeing to has already been conquered, I'm afraid. I have to admit it was odd attacking what used to be my own citadel, but Grandis is good at stealing followers, if nothing else."

"No!" Jax shouted, his strength returning as rage filled him. "You lie! Roehelm isn't gone! It can't be!"

"And I assure you it isn't," Syrus replied calmly. "And if you hand over Eclipse's Heart, it will stay that way."

"Never!" Jax yelled defiantly, whipping his pack off of his back. "Even if it only buys another day, I will not hand over the Heart!"

"Jax, what are you doing?" cried Gare, but Jax had already thrown the bag to the ground.

Jax stood staring at the bag, waiting for it to crumple as its cargo disappeared, but nothing happened.

Syrus laughed. "A valiant effort, but I'm afraid that won't work. Even if it did we have soldiers waiting in Marisol for it."

"You... what did you do?" Jax shouted, but Syrus didn't answer. Desperate for answers, he turned to Ev. "Why isn't it disappearing?"

Ev stammered. "It... the only reason it wouldn't disappear is if..."

Ev couldn't bring herself to finish the sentence, so Syrus finished for her. "Is if Eclipse himself is nearby."

"What!" shouted Jax and Gare in unison.

Jax looked down at the bag on the ground, and in desperation lunged at it, striking it with his sword with all his might. With a loud clang his blade bounced harmlessly off of the Heart inside, only succeeding in breaking a large chip off of itself.

Jax reared back to try again, slamming the tip of his blade against the Heart, again to no avail. He tried again, and again, but all he managed was to tear apart the bag.

"Jax, stop," called Gare, and Jax wanted to scream.

Everything had been for naught. They'd come this far, they'd gotten so close, just to lose everything and find out that the place they'd journeyed to had already been conquered.

Enraged, Jax spun towards Syrus, pouring everything he had into a blast of light at the Radiant.

With a wave of his hand Syrus dispelled the attack, then pointed his rod at Jax.

Black flames erupted from Jax's skin and armor, and he fell to his knees, unable to stand or even lift his sword. The flames weren't painful, but he felt every ounce of strength draining from his body.

"Jax!" Gare shouted, running to his side.

An arrow shot past him from behind and connected with Syrus's face, but it simply bounced off, barely leaving even a scratch. A second later another burst of dark flame erupted to his side, and Birdie collapsed to her hands and knees, barely even able to look up at the Radiant steadily approaching them.

Gare roared and charged at Syrus. Jax tried to call out to stop him, but it was too late. The black fire engulfed Gare as he fell to the ground, leaving only Ev still standing.

Syrus walked past the fallen Gare and stopped in front of Jax. "Now then, how about we try this again."

Syrus lifted his hand and waved one of the dragons over. The great beast lumbered over and bowed its head as a revenant climbed off of it and hurried to Syrus's side.

Syrus addressed the undead soldier. "Guard Eclipse's Heart until I say otherwise."

The soldier ran forward and retrieved the Heart, placing it into a new bag and returning to her dragon.

Jax cursed. "You…" he panted, straining with all his might to stand again, "you won't get away with this. Grandis will stop you!"

"Perhaps he will," Syrus responded, "but for the sake of Doxla let us hope he doesn't."

Syrus raised his rod and aimed it at Jax's face.

Jax stared Syrus in his eyes, ready for the killing blow to land, but the confrontation was interrupted by a cry from Ev.

"Wait!" she called, stepping forward to Syrus. "Please, you don't have to do this!"

To Jax's surprise, Syrus lowered his rod and addressed Ev. "My dear, my brothers, sisters, and I have sacrificed everything for this fight, and now only I remain. Outside of this world, among our own kind, we have lost so much because of what we have invested in our cause. I will not falter now. I will not abandon our child to the fate Grandis intends for this world."

"I don't understand," replied Ev. "What child? What fate? There must be some other way to get what you're after besides reviving the Dark Radiant!"

"The one you call the Dark Radiant is the child I speak of, so no, there is no other way."

Ev gasped. "The Dark Radiant… is your son?"

Syrus sighed and lowered his rod completely. "I led the group of Divine who created Eclipse. He is a being that is between that of a nepac and a

Divine. He is a part of this world, yet has the potential and abilities of a Divine. You have seen for yourself how the Masters and Divine have abandoned this world. Assuming your world does not degrade into nothingness, we wanted to make certain that there would always be someone who could stand against Apollyon long after the rest of us have moved on."

"You lie!" Jax growled, his strength beginning to return as Syrus's curse wore off. "The Dark Radiant didn't come to save this world, he came to destroy it! He drove countless Divine away — the only protectors we have, and you expect me to believe he did that to save us!"

"Of course I don't," answered Syrus. "You are a servant of Grandis. You have been raised on the story he has told you to keep your loyalty until he can claim victory over me and what I represent. Soon, however, you will see his true colors."

Jax glared at Syrus. He wanted nothing more than to drive his sword straight into the Divine's chest, but he knew he couldn't harm the Radiant, and he didn't dare make him angry again. For whatever reason, Syrus hadn't made a move to kill them yet, and Jax didn't want to change that. As much as a part of him was willing to die to land a single blow on this monster, he didn't want to risk Ev's life by enraging their captor.

Still, his mouth couldn't help but spit out defiance. "The only thing we will see is the light of Grandis purging your evil from this world once and for all!"

The look Syrus gave Jax was one mixed with pity and annoyance, the sight of which angered Jax all the more. "If you are so certain of your master's nobility, then why don't you join him at the Altar of Restoration on the Day of Awakening for Apollyon. That is the day King Dezeroth and I will launch our assault — the day that we will restore Eclipse to power. Then you will see where your lord's loyalties lie, as he chooses to stay and fight to prevent Eclipse's restoration, rather than protect the world from Apollyon."

Jax opened his eyes wide. If Syrus was telling the truth, their world was doomed. If Lord Grandis fought to protect the Altar, Apollyon would end the world. If he fought to defeat Apollyon, Eclipse would be restored.

"You... you monster!" Jax yelled, the urge to strike rising in his veins.

"The monster is the one who would sacrifice this world for a feeble strike against the Masters," Syrus answered, pointing his rod at Jax once again. "Now if you'll excuse me, I need to render all of you unconscious so I can find out which one of you is Eclipse, since he doesn't seem to want to volunteer that information on his own."

"What the h—" Jax began, but a flash of light cut him off, sending him into darkness.

Chapter 16

Jax felt himself being shaken against the ground, his ears barely registering his name. He groaned, opened his eyes and, upon remembering what had just transpired, jumped to his feet, nearly knocking Ev over in the process.

The horde of dragons was soaring away in the distance, and Jax knew they had the Heart. Gare was lying on the ground, but breathing. Birdie was nowhere to be seen.

"Where's Birdie?" Jax asked Ev, who just shook her head, refusing to look at him.

"Ev, what happened?" he pressed.

Ev still didn't answer, and Jax realized he should probably check on Gare. He rushed over and shook his friend awake.

"Gare, are you okay?" he asked.

Gare pushed himself to his knees and rubbed his head. "I guess so. When that guy knocked you to the ground, I tried to stop him, but, he did something with his rod and, I can't remember what happened after that."

"He took the Heart," Jax said flatly.

Gare looked down and cursed. "I'm sorry, bud. I tried."

"I know." Jax took a deep breath. "I think they also took Birdie."

"Birdie?" Gare repeated, standing up. "Why?"

"I don't know," Jax answered, but he knew it couldn't be for anything good.

Gare cursed again, and the two of them stood in silence until Gare voiced another question. "Why didn't they kill us?"

Jax shook his head.

More silence.

"So, what do we do now?" Gare asked.

Jax clenched his fists. "The only thing we can do. We go to Roehelm. Maybe we can find a way to send a message to Grandis there." Jax looked

Gare in the eye. "We have to warn him what Syrus's plan is. We can't let him force Grandis to choose between protecting the Altar and defeating Apollyon."

Gare nodded despite his look of confusion, then noticed Ev, who still refused to look at anyone. "Is she okay?"

Jax followed Gare's eyes to Ev. "Probably not. I don't blame her. They beat us. They took the Heart. They even took Birdie."

"No..." Ev finally whimpered.

"It's okay, Ev," Jax tried to comfort her. "We'll make this right, somehow."

"NO!" Ev screamed, shocking Jax. "You're wrong! They didn't take her, she went with them!"

Jax must have heard her wrong. "What do you mean she went with them?"

Ev clenched her fists to her chest, but looked Jax in the eye. "After you and Gare were knocked out, Syrus was about to do the same to me, but Birdie stopped him."

"How—"

"She's Eclipse, Jax..." Ev stated, clearly forcing herself to say it.

Jax had no idea how to take what he was hearing. There was no way that was possible. "Ev, I think you're confused. Eclipse was a man, remember?"

"No, he wasn't!" Ev shouted, losing her composure. "He was a shade! Birdie's a shade! She can look like whatever she wants!"

Jax shouted back. "Ev, listen to yourself! Birdie isn't a shade, that's—"

"I saw her Jax!" Ev yelled, panting.

Jax stopped.

Ev continued. "When Syrus pointed his rod at me, she stopped him. She told him she was Eclipse, then she turned into a shade right in front of me!"

Jax stumbled to think of what to say. There was no way Birdie could have been Eclipse! "She must have used an illusion. She just wanted him to think she was Eclipse so we could get away."

"No, Jax," Ev said, tears in her eyes. "Syrus wouldn't have taken her if she wasn't, and... the things he said..."

"How would he even know—?"

"The Heart didn't disappear when you threw it, and he'd know if Eclipse was already on their side!" Ev cried, then shook her head. "Jax, the things he said... about the Divine, about the Masters, about Lord Grandis... they were awful! They can't be true!"

"Then they aren't," Jax replied, stepping forward and placing his hand on Ev's shoulder. "Syrus wanted to drive the Divine from the world. You can't believe anything he says about them."

Ev grabbed onto Jax's hand. "I know. But Birdie... I think she believed him. That's why she went with him."

Jax squeezed Ev's shoulder and leaned closer to her. "Ev, I'm telling you, there's no way Birdie is the Dark Radiant. She saved our lives more than once. Why would Eclipse help us when he could have just let us die and taken the Heart for himself?"

"Because she doesn't remember..." answered Ev, calming down slightly.

"What are you talking about?"

"Eclipse isn't a true Divine. If he... she, is split, the Heart survives, but the mind is destroyed. She's like a monster that way. When she revives, she's not the same being she was before."

Jax could hardly believe what he was hearing. He didn't want to believe it, but he couldn't help but start to. "How do you know this?"

Ev paused before answering. "They talked for a long time while you were out. I... I don't know how much of it Birdie believed. I just know she made Syrus promise he'd let us go if she went with him."

Jax couldn't think of anything else to say. If everything Ev had said was true, then that meant they'd fought alongside the very being they'd sworn to prevent from returning to power. He tried to think of anything he should have seen in Birdie that would have hinted at her being the Dark Radiant, but his mind was drawing a blank. He knew she'd always acted strangely, but she'd gone out of her way to save Ev. She'd rescued all of them in the Slime Pits. She'd fought alongside them against the shades in the mountains. Even if she didn't have any memories of her previous incarnation, that wasn't how Jax would have expected the Dark Radiant to behave. Which meant... the last Eclipse must have only been evil because Syrus had trained him to be evil. And now, he was going to try to do the same to Birdie.

Jax looked Ev straight in the eye. "We have to get her back."

"What?" Ev replied, her distress replaced by shock. "How?"

"I don't know," Jax admitted, "but Syrus has to bring her to the Altar of Restoration to turn her back into the Dark Radiant. If we can get there first, maybe we can intercept them. If we can get her away from Syrus, we can talk some sense into her."

"But what if we can't?" Ev asked.

Jax looked down and squeezed his fist. "Then we do what we have to." He looked back up at Ev to see she'd turned her head away. "It'll be alright. If she really is Eclipse, she'll revive, and we've already seen what kind of person she'll become if Syrus isn't there to influence her."

Ev stood still for a moment, but slowly nodded her head. "Okay, we can try."

Gare spoke up from behind. "Uh, not to burst everyone's bubble, but how exactly are we going to get to the Altar of Restoration from here, and how the hell are we going to get Birdie away from Syrus? You know he'll probably have Dezeroth with him, too, right?"

Jax was surprised he'd actually forgotten about Dezeroth, but it didn't make a difference. They needed to rescue Birdie from Syrus, and if they got the chance to take down Dezeroth in the process, then all the better.

"We'll figure out the details later," Jax answered. "For now, we need to get to Roehelm. We have to send word to Lord Grandis about what happened, and maybe we can find a way to get to the Altar while we're there."

* * * *

Night had long since fallen by the time the group arrived at Roehelm. The city walls had been badly damaged, evidence that Syrus's claim of the attack against it was true. Jax was happy to see that there were survivors, however, and enough of them to have fully guarded gates. As the party approached the western gate, the guards on the ground readied their spears while archers on the walls took aim.

One of the guards on the ground spoke up. "Hold it right there."

They stopped.

The guard cautiously approached the trio. "None are allowed entrance without proving they are human."

"Uh, hello," said Gare, "of course we're human, just look at us."

The guard was unfazed. "Hold out your hands."

Jax obeyed, and the guard eyed him with annoyance.

"Take off your gauntlet."

"Why?" Jax asked, growing suspicious.

"Only humans have human blood," the guard replied. "Take it off."

Jax didn't like where this was going, but he complied. The guard stuck his spear in the ground and pulled out a short knife, which he used to cut into Jax's hand. Jax winced, but held steady. The guard pulled the knife away and rubbed Jax's blood between his fingers, giving it a sniff.

"You may pass," the guard said. Jax stepped aside but didn't head in, waiting until both Ev and Gare had also been checked before proceeding. Once through the gate, Ev healed the wounds on their hands.

Gare rubbed his hand and grumbled. "It would've been nice of them to have their own healer for us."

"Let it go, Gare," Jax said, looking around the city, eventually pointing down the road to the right. "Gram lives along the south wall, so we need to go that way."

Jax led the way down the dark streets, the only light coming from the stars above and the occasional lamp flickering on the street corners. The damage wasn't as bad as Jax had expected it to be. Most buildings were completely untouched, except for the ones near the gates. Gram would be sound asleep when they reached her home, but Jax knew she'd want to know everything that had happened. She was their best bet of getting a message to Grandis, and of finding a way to get to the Altar before Apollyon awoke.

They arrived at a small townhouse built against the southern wall, where Jax knocked on the door. After a moment with no response, he knocked again, louder.

"Gram!" Ev called, "It's us! Eveline and Jax!"

The sound of wood creaking announced that Gram was up, confirmed by the lighting of a lamp shortly after. A window on the second floor opened, and a thin, gray-haired woman stuck her head out of it.

She was understandably shocked by their sudden arrival. "Eveline? Jax! You're alive!"

Before Jax had a chance to speak Gram had disappeared back into the house. Seconds later, the front door opened and she embraced Jax and Ev.

"Lords, when I heard Marisol had been attacked by Dezeroth, I feared the worst." She pushed herself back, her face serious. "Where's Ronan? What happened to your father?"

Jax rubbed his arm and looked at her apologetically. That told her everything she needed to know.

"Oh... no...," she said, hand over her mouth. Tears in her eyes, she put her arms around Jax and Ev once again.

Jax returned her embrace, but after a few moments pushed her back to look in her eyes. "We have to send a message to Lord Grandis. We know what Syrus is planning."

Gram looked sympathetically at Jax. "Oh, dear, we already know what he's after. As soon as we learned Marisol had been attacked, we knew he sought to revive the Dark Radiant."

Jax shook his head. "No, it's worse than that."

Gram looked from Jax to Ev, and even at Gare, registering the earnestness on each of their faces. She then looked around the street, then stepped back and, wiping the tears from her cheeks, beckoned the group inside. Her home was warm and cozy, if a bit lacking in light. Only a single lamp burned in the main room, where she offered seats to everyone. Jax really didn't feel like sitting, but he obliged.

"Alright," said his grandmother after she took a moment to compose herself. "You say that traitor Syrus is planning something worse than reviving the Dark Radiant?"

Jax took a deep breath and explained everything that Ev had told him about Birdie and Syrus, with Ev filling in where needed.

"Unbelievable," Gram said after they'd finished, shaking her head. "I can't believe you actually traveled with the Dark Radiant. How could you have been so careless?"

Jax went on the defensive. "We weren't careless. Captain Kelva only let her join us after she saved our lives, and even then we didn't trust her."

"I don't know who this Captain Kelva is, but it seems to me you trusted her too much," retorted Gram. "If you hadn't relied on an outsider to—"

Ev cut her grandmother off. "If we hadn't let Birdie help, we'd all be dead!"

Gram was taken aback, and Ev continued before their grandmother could speak again. "We'd be dead, and the Heart would still be with Syrus and Dezeroth. She saved my life more than once!"

"And she's kind of the reason they didn't get it sooner, too," added Gare, who'd stayed silent up until then. He turned to Ev. "Remember when Jax thought that shade was Diana, and she killed it?"

Jax didn't appreciate the reminder, but he did appreciate the support in sticking up for Birdie. "Birdie isn't evil. Whatever the Dark Radiant was before, that's not who she is now. Syrus is the one who wants to turn her back into the monster that slaughtered the Divine."

Gram looked around the group and sighed. "It seems pretty clear to me that you all truly believe this Birdie is on your side."

"She is on our side," Ev returned, nearly getting out of her seat.

"Perhaps she is, but perhaps she's not, and if she follows through with aiding Syrus, then guess which way it is."

Jax paused for a moment to think. "Maybe... maybe she thinks she can ruin his plans if she's closer to him."

"And if that is her intention, then all the better for us," Gram responded, "but we can't rely on that assumption. One must always prepare for the worst in case the worst is what happens."

Jax squeezed the arms of his chair. "We have to tell Lord Grandis."

"Of course, we need to tell him," said Gram. "I will speak to the acting captain as soon as the sun rises. He'll see to it that Lord Grandis learns of Syrus's intent."

"There's one more thing," Jax added. "We need a way to get to the Altar of Restoration before Apollyon's awakening."

Gram frowned. "I'm sorry, but I'm not sending my last living kin to their deaths."

Jax returned her frown. "If you won't help us, then we'll find another way."

"Why?" asked his grandmother. "For this Birdie? You hardly even know her, or him, or whatever it is."

Jax squeezed the arm of his chair again. He could see Ev was about to lash out, so he spoke before she had the chance.

"No, not for Birdie, for Dezeroth."

Everyone stared at him.

"Excuse me?" said Gram.

"Dezeroth killed our father," Jax responded, looking his grandmother right in the eyes. "I was there when it happened. I tried to stop it, but my magic couldn't even reach him."

"Jax," said Gram, "Dezeroth possesses the strength of a high lord. To fight him would be to throw your life away."

"I don't want to fight him," responded Jax. "I just want to be there when he dies, be it by my hands or the hands of Lord Grandis."

Gram continued to frown, but Jax could tell from the softening of her eyes that he was winning her over. "You aren't going to change your mind are you?"

Jax shook his head.

Gram sighed. "You're as stubborn as your mother and father combined. Very well, I'll see what I can do. I'd also like to see the monster who killed my son-in-law brought to justice. But if I do this, then you must promise me one thing."

"What's that?" Jax asked.

"You must promise me that you will not fight. Stay in the camps where it's safe. I'm not about to lose you and Ev again after all of this."

"Deal," said Jax. "If you help us get there, then we'll stay away from the battle."

Gram leaned back, clearly skeptical, but she was convinced enough. "Then I will arrange for transportation for all of us once I've talked to the captain."

"Wait, you're going too?" Jax asked. That wasn't part of his plan.

"Of course," Gram answered. "After all, I have to make sure you keep your promise."

Jax shrugged. "Suit yourself." He wasn't about to show he was bothered. As long as they were going to the Altar, that was what was important. They'd figure out a way around her when the time came.

Gram stood up from her chair. "Then, since that's settled, I suggest we all try and get some sleep, if we can." She turned to Gare. "I'm afraid I don't have enough beds for all of you, however."

Gare waved his hand dismissively. "I've been sleeping on rocks and leaves for a week. Just a blanket would be more than good enough for me."

Gram smiled sheepishly. "I'll see what I can find. Jax, Eveline, the guest room is where its always been."

Jax and Ev nodded, then followed Gram upstairs, wishing Gare goodnight on the way. They entered the old room they'd stayed in several times before. Jax wanted to talk to Ev about how they might be able to find Birdie once they reached the Altar, but he didn't dare risk their grandmother overhearing.

Instead, he pulled himself into bed, wished Ev goodnight as well, and welcomed the two hours of sleep he was able to get before morning.

Chapter 17

Beneath the full moon, north of the Windy Mountains, Dezeroth gazed impatiently towards the horizon as his army prepared camp for the night. In less than two weeks' time, Apollyon would awaken. If Syrus failed to return with Eclipse, then all they had fought for would amount to nothing. His Radiant ally was powerful compared to most, but pathetically weak compared to others of his ilk. The two of them alone would stand little chance against Grandis and Escalor, even with Dezeroth's horde supporting them. Even if somehow they did emerge victorious, without Eclipse there would be no stopping Apollyon once the battle at the Altar was finished.

Hours passed before at last a horn in the distance blew, announcing Syrus's return. Moments later, the dragon Tyranor soared by overhead and landed west of Dezeroth's tent. Unable to wait any longer, Dezeroth marched to where Syrus had set down. That fool had better have had good news.

What Dezeroth saw upon arriving was not what he'd expected. There, next to Syrus, was a black haired woman — hardly the imposing figure he'd imagined of Eclipse.

"What is this?" Dezeroth demanded. "Don't tell me this woman is Eclipse."

Syrus opened his mouth to speak, but the woman answered. "I am," she said, stepping forwards, "but call me Birdie. You must be Dezeroth."

Syrus tried to put his arm in front of her to stop her approach, but she pushed him aside.

Dezeroth sneered. "My, my, such fearlessness. Clearly you aren't aware you're speaking to the most powerful nepac in Doxla."

"Is that right?" replied Birdie. "Funny, I thought you were Dezeroth. Apparently you're Apollyon."

Dezeroth's sneer turned into a scowl. "You would do well to know your place before me."

Birdie put her hand on her hip and cocked her head. "Oh, I think I know my place. Syrus explained things to me very well. You need me, or you lose everything."

Dezeroth clenched his fist. The smirk on Syrus's face was a tempting target for it. The Radiant was enjoying his creation's bravado far too much for Dezeroth's liking, but the confidence of the being in front of him reassured him that it was indeed Eclipse, despite its guise.

Dezeroth relaxed his hand once again as he regained his composure. "Yes, we need you," he murmured, "or we all lose everything."

"I know," said Birdie.

Dezeroth took a step closer to Birdie. "Then you agree to join us in our assault."

"Considering the circumstances, I don't think I have a choice, do I?"

The faintest trace of a smile tugged at Dezeroth's lips. "No, I don't think you do." He looked towards Syrus. "Well done, Radiant."

"Oh, don't give me too much credit just yet," Syrus replied, his hands resting on his rod. "She's agreed to help us, but I believe she wants you to know something first."

Dezeroth returned his attention to Birdie, his eyes narrowed. "And what, pray tell, might that be?"

"Simple," replied Birdie. "I've made a few friends in these last few days, and the one that I care about most..." Birdie suddenly shifted into the form of a young girl, "...looks like this."

Dezeroth looked down at the small figure before him. "And? What concern is that of mine?"

"Take a good look at her," Birdie said in a child's voice, "because it is very much your concern. There's a chance she'll follow her brother to the Altar. If that happens, and if any harm comes to her, then if I find out you or your soldiers were responsible, Grandis will be the least of your worries."

Birdie changed back into her other appearance while Syrus looked on in amusement. "Amused" did not describe the feeling inside of Dezeroth, however. Dark Radiant or not, he did not take kindly to this threat. He brushed it off, however. A child such as that was no threat to him or his army. Even if she did try to stand against them, it would be little effort for even the weakest of his soldiers to incapacitate her.

"Is that all?" he growled.

"Almost," Birdie replied before shifting into a young man. She continued with a male voice. "This is that girl's brother. He's... not exactly my favorite person, but considering you already killed her father," the young man's eyes narrowed, "I highly suggest you don't take her brother from her, too."

Dezeroth's eyes narrowed as well while Birdie once again reverted to her regular appearance. "Tell me. These two... individuals," Dezeroth tilted his head slightly. "If I find them at the Altar, what is it that they will be fighting for?"

"Most likely?" Birdie tilted her head to match his. "They'll be fighting to stop you."

"And you expect me to spare them if they are in my way, knowing what will happen if we fail."

"Not really, no," answered Birdie. "I just want you to be aware that if you do hurt them, not even Syrus will be able to protect you from me."

Dezeroth stared Birdie in the eyes, then shifted his gaze to Syrus. "I do not appreciate how poorly you are able to keep your creation leashed."

Syrus shrugged. "I did warn you she'd be beyond my control."

Dezeroth returned his attention to Birdie, anger filling his veins. "Consider yourself fortunate that you are what you are. If you were any other and spoke to me the way you have today, I would scatter your inky remains to the far ends of Doxla." He leaned in close. "As for your friends... if they do not threaten my mission, they live, but I will not risk victory for the life of anyone. You would do well to keep in mind what is at stake here and know that your threats mean nothing to me."

"My, my," remarked Birdie. "Such fearlessness. Clearly you aren't aware that you're speaking to the one who's soon to be the most powerful nepac in Doxla."

Dezeroth moved forward to strike Birdie but caught himself. As much as he hated it, her words were an understatement. If they succeeded, not only would she become the most powerful nepac in Doxla, she would be the most powerful being in the world. Syrus clearly took concern with Dezeroth's aggression, however, as he quickly stepped in.

"Well, now that I think we're all clear on where each other stands," he said while pulling Birdie away, "why don't we find you a tent for the night? Maybe one on the other side of camp, hm?"

Dezeroth watched for a moment as Syrus and Birdie walked off into the distance before turning to leave as well. This disrespect was something he would begrudgingly have to bear. It was a small price to pay to preserve his immortality, after all, and a smaller price yet to reclaim the kingdom the Divine had taken from him so long ago. Besides, if he did have to be subject to a higher power, it was better that it be this false Divine than a true one. Even if she was created by those outsiders, she was at least born from this world.

Returning to his tent, Dezeroth hung up his sword, stripped off his armor, and poured himself a goblet of wine.

Only thirteen days remained before he would stand against oblivion, and he needed a drink to help cool his head. Even with every piece in place, any distraction from his goal could compromise everything. He would focus only on the task at hand, and deal with Birdie's threats after the battle for Doxla was over.

Chapter 18

Morning came far too soon, but Gram did her best to provide a hearty breakfast. It wasn't anything special: just eggs, potatoes, biscuits, and honey, but it was certainly better than any breakfast they'd had the past week. As soon as they'd finished eating, Gram took Jax to Roehelm's citadel to meet with the acting guard captain, Orwick.

Before meeting with the captain, she gave Jax a warning. "Now I don't want to hear you saying anything about traveling with the Dark Radiant. You tell Captain Orwick about Syrus's plans and nothing else, understand?"

Jax nodded. He already knew better than to mention Birdie. There was no way Roehelm's captain would either sympathize or care. No, he knew exactly what to say to get him, Ev, and Gare transportation to the Altar of Restoration.

Gram knocked on the door of one of the side rooms of the citadel. "Captain Orwick? Are you there?"

Jax heard shuffling and the sound of a chair getting pushed back along the floor. A moment later the door opened, revealing a diminutive gray-haired man with glasses. He was no taller than Ev, and arguably thinner, and Jax couldn't help but wonder if this was Captain Orwick or one of his attendants.

Whoever he was, he clearly recognized Gram. "Dame Ruthoree. To what do I owe this visit?"

Gram motioned towards Jax. "Captain, this young man is my grandson, Jax."

Orwick extended a hand and smiled as Jax shook it. "A pleasure, but please don't call me Captain. I'm only filling in until Sir Doyle returns from serving Lord Grandis."

Gram continued her introduction of Jax. "He, my granddaughter, and one other have just arrived from Marisol. They served in the Light Guard and were there during the attack."

Orwick's eyes opened wide as he adjusted his glasses, looking over Jax's armor. "I see. We'd just received word that Dezeroth had killed all of the Light Guard. How is it that you managed to avoid that fate?"

The reminder of what had happened back home made Jax want to look away, but he held his eyes steady on Orwick's. "We escaped with Captain Kelva and a group of others. We were trying to bring the Dark Radiant's Heart here to safety, but..."

Jax trailed off, trying to remember what he'd decided to tell Orwick, but it turned out he didn't need to, as Orwick finished for him.

"But you failed."

Jax nodded, not letting his anger show at having Orwick state it so bluntly. "We were attacked twice in the Windy Mountains and once on the road just west of here. We managed to escape the first two encounters, but the last we were attacked by Syrus himself. We didn't stand a chance against him or his dragons."

"I see," said Orwick, pausing to think. "So he spared you as well."

Jax wasn't sure what Orwick meant by that. "Yes, sir. For some reason he decided to let us go."

Another pause. "Jax, was it? Tell me, what impression did you get from Lord Syrus?"

Jax was surprised by the question. As he fumbled for words, Orwick reconsidered what he'd asked.

"Never mind," he said, waving his hand, "I suppose it doesn't matter. I assume you must have come here for more than to simply tell me what we had already feared."

Jax straightened up. "Actually, there is more. We learned what Syrus is after. He intends to restore the Dark Radiant's power on the day of Apollyon's resurrection, to force Lord Grandis to choose between stopping Eclipse or Apollyon."

"I see," said Orwick. "I can't say I'm surprised by that."

"Please sir, we have to warn Lord Grandis."

"Yes, I suppose we should," said Orwick. "He likely already suspects this plan, but delivering confirmation won't hurt."

"Then let me deliver the message," Jax said. "I, my sister, and my friend Garrison, we let the Heart fall into Syrus's hands. Let us do whatever we can to make amends."

Orwick stared curiously at Jax before turning his attention to Gram, who nodded in agreement. "Very well, then. I'm afraid we don't have any fast means of transportation. Lord Syrus killed our fastest mounts so we couldn't spread word of his attack as quickly, but we have a few work horses I can provide."

"Thank you, sir," Jax said, bowing slightly, "you have no idea what this means to me."

Gram spoke up. "And Sir Orwick, if it's alright with you, I'd also like to accompany my grandchildren on their journey."

Orwick tilted his head slightly. "Are you sure? You're not as young as you used to be, Pamella."

Gram bristled at the remark. "I'll have you know I can still best any other spearman in the Guard. Don't forget who put you on your skinny rear every time you entered the ring with me."

A bead of sweat appeared on Orwick's brow. "That was..." he began, but quickly cleared his throat. "Yes, that sounds like a reasonable request. I shall see to it that you are given transportation. Lord Grandis is presently guarding the Altar of Restoration with Lady Escalor and an army of his finest soldiers. Meet me at the stables at noon, and I will provide you with a letter of my blessing that should grant you audience with them. Best of luck to the two of you."

With that, Gram and Jax bid farewell to Orwick, with Jax taking away a bit of new admiration for his grandmother.

* * * *

A few hours later, Jax and Gram had gathered up supplies for the journey. It took another hour still to find Ev and Gare, who'd wandered off to the library for lords knew what reason. The delay made them late to meet with Orwick, but he didn't seem to mind. Once they arrived he handed over a sealed letter to Gram.

"Show this to the guards at the Altar, and they should grant you audience with Lord Grandis."

Gram tucked the letter into a pocket of her bag. "Thank you, Orwick. We truly appreciate your help."

Orwick nodded. "Be careful as you near the Altar. I expect Lord Syrus and Dezeroth will be gathering their forces in preparation for battle. It would not be well for you to encounter them."

Gram climbed onto her horse and faced Orwick. "That isn't something you need fear. I've lived seventy-three long years and have no intention of dying anytime soon." She kicked the sides of her mount to start it walking, and Jax, Ev, and Gare did the same. They waved goodbye to Orwick, then made their way out of the city.

The journey to the Altar was a long one. They stopped at several small towns along the way, and spent nearly a week on the road. During that time, Ev stayed unusually quiet, more so than even after their father had died. She spent her entire time with her nose deep in books of scripture she'd taken from the library. Anytime anyone asked what she was doing, her answer was simply "studying."

By the time they arrived at the mountain where the Altar waited, only one week remained before the awakening of Apollyon. The group was fortunate enough to have avoided any encounters with hostile forces, but Orwick had been right about them gathering. While they might not have run into any directly, Jax could see the smoke of enemy camps in the surrounding foothills as they marched toward the mountain of the Altar.

The mountain itself was well defended. Sheer cliffs surrounded all sides of the mountain, save for a single path on the northern side which led to the Altar at the mountain's summit. An army of thousands was camped all along that path, standing in the way of any attempt by hostile forces to attack on foot. At the top was the Altar itself, and Jax knew that was where Grandis would be waiting.

As soon as the group reached the edge of the outermost camp, several soldiers approached them. One of them with a spear stepped out in front of the others. "State your business!" she demanded.

Gram handed over Orwick's letter. "We are here to deliver a message to Lord Grandis regarding the traitor Syrus's plan of attack."

The soldier looked over the letter and signaled to the others, who approached the group. "Leave your horses here. I shall take you to Lord Grandis."

Jax and the others dismounted from their steeds.

"Follow me," the soldier said.

The soldier led them to the top of the mountain, past rows upon rows of tents and troops. Every soldier was adorned in high quality armor, be they paladins, knights, mages, whatever. Jax could only assume that they were all part of Lord Grandis's personal guard, and if so, each and every one of them was likely as tough and skilled as Kelva had been.

At the upper edge of the camps were two large, decorative tents, which Jax assumed belonged to Lord Grandis and Lady Escalor. Once past the tents, the group was led up a large flight of stairs to the Altar: a plaza of white marble surrounded by granite pillars, in turn surrounded by a lip of natural stone that hid the Altar from view of anyone who hadn't climbed to the summit. At the center of the Altar sat an ornate fountain encircling a pedestal. If Jax recalled properly, that was where split Divine would place their Hearts to have their power restored, and that was what Lord Grandis sought to defend.

A group of elite guards surrounded the Altar, wearing armor and weapons the likes of which Jax had never seen before, and he assumed they were likely the highest class of equipment that nepacs could wield. Behind them, atop the lip of stone, stood a towering figure in golden armor and fiery hair staring out into the distance. Jax knew the moment he laid eyes on the figure that he was in the presence of none other than Supreme Lord Grandis himself. To Grandis's left was a second figure in white and gold armor — a woman — leaning against one of the pillars and appearing very bored. That had to Esteemed Lady Escalor.

The soldier leading them approached the guards and motioned to Jax and the others. "These soldiers have brought news from Roehelm regarding the traitor Syrus."

Immediately, Lord Grandis turned to face his visitors, revealing a sharply trimmed beard that matched his hair. He leapt from his perch atop the stone precipice and approached Jax, who was standing slightly ahead of the others.

Instinctively, Jax bowed low, as did the others, until he heard Lord Grandis command "Rise."

Jax stood up straight, trying not to shake in awe at the fact that he was actually standing before Lord Grandis.

"What news have you of Syrus?" Lord Grandis asked, his deep voice resonating in Jax's core.

Jax bowed his head again without thinking. "Supreme Lord Grandis, we regret to inform you that Syrus has obtained the Heart of the Dark Radiant, and he intends to attack on the day of Apollyon's reawakening."

Lord Grandis snorted. "Is that so? How disappointing."

Jax was taken aback by that response and looked up. "Y-your Lordship?"

Grandis turned away from Jax. "An attempt to divide my forces in such a predictable manner... perhaps I shouldn't have expected better of him."

"You... you aren't concerned?" Jax asked, barely getting the words out.

"Of course not," Grandis replied, spinning back towards Jax. "Time is his enemy. If he cannot take the Altar before Apollyon's darkness arrives, it will consume him and all of his forces. Sending Apollyon back to the abyss afterward will be a simple matter."

Jax was taken aback. "But... what about all the damage Apollyon will cause before it reaches here? Our own troops would also be in danger. Isn't there anything you can do to stop it?"

"No," answered Grandis, leaning in close. "My light can protect those loyal to me. I must stay here, unless you wish the return of the Dark Radiant."

Jax gulped.

Grandis stood up straight again, looking down at Jax. "The damage the Dark Radiant would cause is far greater than that of Apollyon's partial return. Sometimes we must make sacrifices for the greater good. That is a lesson you would do well to learn."

"I... y-yes sir, Lord Grandis," Jax said, bowing once again.

Grandis turned halfway away from Jax. "We are done here. Your information is appreciated."

"Y-yes sir," said Jax again, "thank you sir! But—"

Grandis turned his head towards Jax.

"If it's alright with you, I have a request."

"Which is...?"

Jax swallowed and forced himself to look Grandis in the eye. "Dezeroth killed my father. If you would let us, we'd like to fight here alongside you when he attacks, to send him back to the grave he crawled out of."

Grandis stared for a moment, then nodded. "Very well." He then addressed the soldier who'd led them up to the Altar. "See to it that our messengers are outfitted with the best equipment we can spare, and find a place for them in the camp."

"Thank you, sir. We won't let you down," Jax said, bowing once again.

Their escort also bowed, then led Jax and the others away from the Altar. Halfway down the mountain, she stopped them. "Wait here until I find a tent with beds to spare."

Gram stepped forward before the soldier could leave. "Actually, we have a small tent and some blankets in the bags with our horses, if that makes things easier."

Their escort paused for a moment before pointing to the western side of the camp. "If that's the case, then you can set up camp over there. I'll see if we have any extra armor or weapons for you. If we do, I'll have someone bring them over."

"Thank you," said Gram, and the group set off back down to the base of the mountain to get their supplies from their horses.

Later that afternoon after they'd set up camp, received better equipment than they'd ever had before — including a healing staff for Ev — and after Gram stepped out to see about meal arrangements, Gare, Jax, and Ev finally had a chance to speak alone about the situation.

"Man," Gare said to Jax, "I can't believe you actually talked to Lord Grandis that way. You're crazy, you know that?"

Jax could hardly believe he'd questioned Lord Grandis to his face, either, but what Grandis had said about waiting for Apollyon — the fact that what

Syrus had said would happen was true — made Jax realize that they had to do more than simply rescue Birdie.

"We need to get the Heart back from Syrus," Jax said flatly, looking at Gare.

"Oh really?" replied Gare. "And how exactly do you propose we do that?"

"I don't know," answered Jax, "but it's our only option. We have to remove the threat of the Dark Radiant. It's the only way Grandis will leave the Altar to stop Apollyon."

Gare leaned back on the pile of blankets he was sitting on, placing his arms behind his head. "Yeah, well, considering that Syrus has the Heart, and we have no idea where he is, that might be kind of hard."

"That's why we need a plan for when he attacks. We need to be ready so we can find Birdie and get the Heart away from him. If we can figure out a way to take Syrus and Dezeroth down in the process, even better."

Gare sat right back up again at that. "Whoa, wait just a sec there, bud! Rescuing Birdie? Fine. Getting the Heart back? Maybe. But taking on Syrus and Dezeroth? Either one of them could wipe us off the face of Doxla just by sneezing."

"Yeah, I know," Jax answered, having well accepted the fact that he'd never be able to face either of them alone. "Birdie and the Heart come first, but if we get the chance, we have to try."

Gare sighed and leaned back again. "Alright, I guess, but shouldn't we figure out just how we're even going to get close to Birdie before we start worrying about anything else?"

Jax looked over at Ev, who was reading in the corner. "What do you think, Ev? You know Birdie better than any of us. How can we get her away from Syrus?"

Ev glanced up at Jax before returning to her book. "I don't know."

"What do you mean, 'you don't know'? Don't you care that she's being forced to become a monster?"

Ev frowned. "What makes you so sure she's being 'forced'?"

"Of course she's being forced! You... she... just think how much she's done to keep the Heart out of Syrus's hands!"

"She helped us keep it out of Dezeroth's hands," Ev said flatly, not looking up from her book.

"Same thing!" Jax returned. "Ev, come on, I know you're upset, but we have to focus if we're going to fix this!"

"I'm trying to focus," Ev retorted, looking up at him with a scowl.

Jax returned the scowl, prompting Ev to close her book and move towards the tent's exit.

"Where do you think you're going?" Jax asked her, moving to block her.

"Somewhere else," Ev answered, pushing past him and taking her book with her.

"Whoa," remarked Gare. "What do you think that was about?"

Jax huffed as he looked out after Ev. "I don't know, but whatever it is she needs to get over it. We've only got a week left to figure something out."

* * * *

That one week came and went all too fast. Despite spending every second they had away from Gram and the other soldiers, Jax and Gare couldn't think of any way they'd be able to get Birdie away from Syrus and Dezeroth. The best they could come up with was to wait near the Altar once the battle started. If what Ev had said about her being a shade was correct though, then even that might not be enough, as there was no guarantee Birdie'd take on the same form they were familiar with.

For as much as they were pulling their hair out trying to come up with a plan, they were practically banging their heads against the wall trying to get Ev to help. But no, she was too busy cramming her face into old scriptures. She'd barely said a word since they'd left Roehelm, and any time Jax tried to talk to her about it she'd leave.

The evening before the Day of Awakening, Jax had had enough. He was going to talk to Ev about her complete lack of caring whether she wanted to or not. As soon as Gram had stepped away from their tent, he approached her.

"Ev, we've only got one day left to figure out what to do. Are you going to help us or not?"

Ev just pulled her little book up closer to her face, hiding the sullen expression she'd formed.

Jax wasn't about to keep putting up with this. "Come on, Ev, don't you even care? What's in that stupid book that's more important than saving our friend."

Ev turned away from Jax, and that was the last straw.

"You know what, fine. If you don't care about helping, then don't! If all you want to do is just keep your face buried in a book, you should have saved us all a lot of trouble and stayed back in Roehelm."

Jax stormed out of the tent, ignoring Gare's call after him. He found a nice little nook in the rock away from camp near the edge of the cliff and plopped himself down there.

What was the point of even coming here? They didn't have a plan, they didn't stand a chance against Dezeroth's and Syrus's forces, and the person he thought cared most about helping Birdie clearly didn't.

Jax threw his head back against the rock in frustration and immediately regretted his action. Tired, frustrated, and now in pain, he buried his face in his knees.

He sat there until the sun began to dip behind the mountains far to the west, when the sound of footsteps prompted him to lift his head. To his surprise, it was Ev, still holding her book of scripture.

"What do you want?" he asked.

Ev looked down at the ground, then the scriptures in her hand, before looking back up to Jax. She sighed. "I'm sorry. I've just... I didn't want to upset you."

"Well you did a great job of that, didn't you?" Jax retorted.

Ev grimaced at that remark. "I'm sorry," she said again. "I should have just talked to you. I just... I still haven't even figured out what I think yet."

"That's why I wanted us to work together," Jax returned, swinging his arm out in exasperation. "None of us know what to do! Maybe if you'd helped us we could have figured something out."

Ev looked to her side, then back at Jax again. "Let me ask you something."

"What?" Jax spat.

"Why do monsters exist?"

Jax blinked. Of all the questions he expected that was perhaps the farthest from any of them. "What does that have to do with anything going on here?"

Ev paused before answering. "After Syrus knocked you out, he said... things."

Jax felt his anger begin to subside. "Things? About monsters?"

Ev paused again. "Not specifically. He told Birdie things about the Masters, the Divine... things about our world — things I knew couldn't be true, and yet..." Ev clenched her eyes shut, then opened them with new fortitude. "Everything he said... it answers questions we'd always wondered, questions about things we'd always been told not to worry about, that the Masters knew what they were doing, and we shouldn't question them."

Ev closed her eyes again, then opened them to stare Jax right in his. "I still don't want to believe it Jax, so tell me, please. Why do monsters exist if the Masters made them? Give me an answer I can believe instead of Syrus's...."

Jax looked into Ev's pleading eyes, completely blindsided by the whole conversation. "You already know why," he answered. "Monsters exist so Divine and nepacs can defeat them and grow stronger."

"But grow stronger for what?" Ev asked. "To fight more monsters?"

"To protect us from the likes of Dezeroth and Apollyon," Jax replied, as if it needed to even be said.

"No Jax," Ev answered, "Dezeroth only became the Undead King because of magic the Masters brought to this world. Apollyon first appeared fifty years ago, a hundred years after the first Divine."

"Ev, just listen to what your saying. Apollyon has existed since time immemorial. The Masters must have foreseen—"

Jax stopped. Ev was violently shaking her head. "And it's awoken consistently every five years since then? Why not sooner?"

"The scriptures say—"

"Then the Masters could have replaced its seal, but they didn't!" Ev was panting heavily, but quickly calmed herself. "I'm sorry Jax, but what the scriptures say doesn't make sense."

"Alright then," replied Jax, "then what magical insight has Syrus given you that does?"

Ev held the book of scripture close to her, appearing almost apologetic as she answered. "The Masters made all of this... just to entertain the Divine."

Jax audibly scoffed. "Come on, Ev. I don't know anyone who's studied the scriptures more than you. Do you honestly think—"

"Yes."

Jax stared at Ev. Before he could find words she continued.

"Like you said, I've studied the scriptures my whole life. Some things, they never made sense, but I always accepted them, because that's what I was told to do. But now, looking at everything again, it all makes sense. The rules, the trials, the monsters... even the Divine disappearing." She looked at Jax pitifully. "Don't you get it? They abandoned us because our world no longer entertains them..."

Jax stood up at this, enraged that his own sister would believe such nonsense. "Are you telling me that you'd rather believe a traitor like Syrus over scripture handed down by the Masters themselves?"

"Of course I wouldn't!" replied Ev. "Why do you think I've been going through all of the scriptures again? I want to find a better answer, but I can't!"

Jax threw up his hands and spun around. "That's... how... GAH!" He spun back around to face Ev. "This... it doesn't even matter! Who cares why the Masters did what they did? That doesn't change the situation! We still have to stop Syrus and Dezeroth and rescue Birdie before Apollyon gets here."

Ev looked away from Jax at the ground. "This is why I didn't want to tell you about this. I knew you wouldn't want to listen..."

"I am listening," returned Jax loudly, but he caught himself and lowered his voice, "but that stuff doesn't matter now. We can worry about the Masters after this is all over."

Ev glared sideways at Jax. "It does matter, Jax. That wasn't the only thing Syrus said, but if you're this upset hearing what he said about the Masters, then I'm not going to waste my time telling you what he said about Lord Grandis."

Jax felt an uncomfortable twinge run down his spine. Something about the way Ev said that told him he didn't want to know.

After a moment of staring at him, Ev turned and began making her way back to camp.

"Wait," Jax called. He took a deep breath and swallowed. "Just... out of curiosity, what did he say about Lord Grandis."

Ev didn't answer.

"I promise I won't get angry."

After a moment's hesitation, Ev walked back to Jax, then looked around to make sure no one else was in earshot. "Before I tell you, I want you to know that I know we can't trust Syrus." She took a breath. "But, after what he said — what Lord Grandis said about letting Apollyon devastate the land just so he can stop Eclipse from returning, I don't know if we can trust him either."

"Ev," Jax said, putting his hands on her shoulders. "What did Syrus say about Lord Grandis?"

Ev took another breath and met Jax's eyes. "He said Lord Grandis isn't going to stop Apollyon. He said our world is dying without the Masters or Divine to take care of it, and Lord Grandis thinks it's better to let it all end quickly than leave it to die slowly."

Jax looked down at his sister. He'd promised he wouldn't get angry, but he was surprised to realize that he genuinely wasn't. What Ev was saying was borderline blasphemy, and while he was upset, he was equally worried. Grandis's words had weighed heavily on his mind as well, making him recall what Syrus had told him, as much as he'd tried to repress it. Ordinarily he would have dismissed it all as nonsense, but here they were, only one day away from what could well be the end of the world, and the one he'd trusted the most to protect them had flat out dismissed his worries, citing sacrifice for the sake of the greater good.

Jax squeezed his sister's shoulders and sighed. "Believe it or not, I understand."

Ev was visibly surprised. "You do?"

Jax nodded softly. "I'm worried too. I don't know who to trust anymore either, but there's one thing I do know, and that's how to find out."

A spark lit up in Ev's eyes as she waited for Jax to continue.

"We find Birdie, we find the Heart, and we prove to Lord Grandis that the Dark Radiant is no longer a threat. If we do that, and he still doesn't leave to fight Apollyon, then we help Birdie get her power back."

"But... how?" Ev asked, looking around again to make sure no one was nearby. "We'd have to give the Heart to Lord Grandis to do that. We'd never be able to get it back!"

Jax smiled faintly. "Lord Grandis can't hold the Heart, and who said we'd even give him the real thing? If we get Birdie back on our side, she can create an illusion of it, right?"

"I... that seems like a really long shot," Ev replied.

"I know," responded Jax, "but I can't think of anything better. Now how about we head back to the tent. After Gram goes to bed, we can sneak out and try to figure out how to find Birdie. If we can do that, we might actually be able to pull this off."

Ev smiled for the first time since they'd been ambushed by Syrus, and the two of them headed back to the tent. Later that night, they, along with Gare, snuck out to try one last time to improve their plan.

Chapter 19

The day of Apollyon's awakening, the sun itself refused to show its face. Unnatural dark clouds like inky tendrils stretched across the sky, promising to swallow up Doxla in eternal shadow. During the night, Dezeroth and Syrus's army had surrounded the mountain of the Altar with numbers far greater than of those who defended it. Dozens of dragons and thousands upon thousands of undead, brigands, and other fiendish and corrupted beings pressed up against the base of the mountain. The horde made not a move as Lord Grandis's troops readied themselves for the battle that was to come.

Jax checked over his own preparations a third time before heading out to meet up with Ev, Gare, and Gram. The armor that they'd been provided was superb — enchanted lightweight plates that resisted magic and blunt weapons as well as blades. The weapons weren't lacking, either. All of them were instilled with magic that prevented breaking and magnified damage against dark creatures. Jax would have preferred his own sword, but he'd need every possible advantage he could get. The plan they'd settled on was sketchy at best, after all, but it was certainly better than nothing. Their orders to help guard the side of the mountain against shades and other creatures capable of scaling it also helped, as they'd be in a better position once the battle started.

"Is everyone ready?" he asked them as he approached.

"Not really," answered Gare, "but we don't really have a choice, do we?"

Gram frowned down at the encroaching force. "I never would have imagined Lord Syrus would be able to gather such a horrid following after his fall. If I'd known he commanded such an army I never would have allowed you kids to come here."

Jax took a position next to his grandmother. "With all respect, Gram, you wouldn't have been able to stop us."

Gram grumbled. "Perhaps not, but I certainly would have tried."

"Why?" Jax asked. "The entire world could end today. Would you really have kept us from doing everything we can to stop that?"

Gram gripped her spear tightly, sighing. "You really are your parents' son, Jax. If they were here, I know they'd be proud to see you standing alongside Lord Grandis... you and Eveline both."

Jax didn't respond. While he appreciated his grandmother's words, right now he was focused on the plan at hand, and the fact that the attack still hadn't begun was making him nervous. Lord Grandis had said that time was on their side, that they only needed to hold off Syrus and Dezeroth until Apollyon arrived, but if that was the case, then why hadn't the attack started yet?

As Jax pondered Syrus's plans, a sudden tremor shook the mountain, sending a cold chill down his spine. In the distance, far to the northwest, the horizon grew pitch black, lit only by purple streaks of lightning arcing from the ground to the sky.

"Jax..." Ev began, but she didn't need to finish. Everyone on that mountain knew what was happening.

What little sun had previously penetrated the clouds vanished. Only light from the torches around camp and the lightning in the sky remained. A cold wind blew across the mountainside, and an unearthly rumble shook the heavens as the Great Destroyer Apollyon awakened.

Immediately, the opposing army launched its assault. Enemy soldiers charged as swarms of zodiacs, harpies, and other flying beasts circled around the back of the mountain, the dragons following close behind.

One of those dragons or zodiacs had to be carrying Birdie. If they were going to have any chance of reaching her before she made it to the Altar then they needed to move now.

Jax gripped his sword to make sure it was secure and signaled to Gare and Ev. Without a word they turned and ran up the mountain.

"Jax! Eveline!" Gram shouted after them.

Jax shouted back. "They're heading for the Altar. We have to get there first!"

Gram chased after them a short ways before she had to stop and catch her breath. Jax felt bad about leaving her, but they had no choice. What they were doing was too important to leave to chance.

Jax led the charge as they aimed away from the main camp. They didn't want to risk anyone stopping them, so going around was their best bet. That idea was quickly scrapped, however, as Jax noticed a multitude of shadows gliding up the side of the mountain, followed by blue, horned oger-like creatures Jax recognized as onis. The great beasts somehow managed to scale the cliff twice as fast as Jax had been able to run up it. Jax, Ev, and Gare ducked between a pair of boulders, hoping the horde would pass them by. To Jax's amazement, the maneuver was successful, and after the invaders seemed to stop coming they slipped out again to continue up the mountain.

They didn't make it far, however, before one of the oversized onis, apparently late to the party, pulled itself over the precipice and spotted them. Immediately it rushed the group with lightning speed, a large club that it had carried on its back now swinging right at Jax's head.

Jax ducked beneath the attack and drew his blade, then quickly rolled out of the way as the club came crashing down where he'd just been standing. He fired a blast of light at the brute's face as Gare took the opportunity to deliver a blow to one of its legs, causing it to topple forwards. With a wide swing Jax lopped off its head, ending the skirmish.

Gare brandished his ax, ready for more. "Lords, how many kinds of monsters does Dezeroth have anyway?"

"There's more coming!" Ev shouted, looking towards the side as another wave of shades rounded the top.

"Damn it!" Jax growled, looking around for another path.

Most of the soldiers in the camp were busy firing upon the aerial assault or had otherwise engaged the shades and other creatures that had scaled the cliffs. Since they were all distracted, maybe running through the camp wouldn't be such a bad idea after all. There looked to be a break in the lines just fifty yards up where they'd be able to slip back in.

"This way," Jax ordered.

He lifted up his sword and forced the shades out of their puddle forms with its light, ensuring that they wouldn't be able to close the distance quickly. He then turned his attention forward. He blazed past combatants on either side of him, and as much as he wanted to stop and help his fellow soldiers, he knew the three of them were the only ones who stood a chance of finding and talking to Birdie before it was too late. He pressed onward, ignoring the shouts all around him as the battle waged, but he stopped when he spotted several dragons swooping in towards the Altar.

A barrage of magic and arrows brought down two of the dragons, but three of them survived to rain hellfire upon the soldiers firing up at them, scorching the mountain peak. Suddenly, a golden arc of light shot out from the Altar and cleaved one of the remaining dragons in two.

Gare froze next to Jax at the sight. "What the hell was that?"

Jax was at a loss for words. Only one possibility came to mind. "Lord Grandis..."

"No way..." murmured Gare. "No wonder he said beating Apollyon would be easy."

"Jax, we need to hurry!" urged Ev, and she was right.

More dragons were joining in the assault, most of them attacking the archers and mages near the Altar, the rest of them directing their attention to the Altar itself. Arc after golden arc sliced through the sky, tearing through the giant lizards, forcing them to flee or land below the Altar, beyond Lord Grandis's line of sight. Their way up was quickly being cut off by the growing wall of dragons, but maybe there was a way around them.

"This way!" he shouted, and he ran back towards the cliff to his right.

They wouldn't be able to take the stairs, but the rock face around them was rough, so maybe they could climb up that instead. The flow of enemies up the mountain seemed to have halted, which gave them an opening.

Ducking behind boulders to stay out of sight of the dragons guarding the stairs, Jax led the way to the wall.

Halfway there, a terrible roar followed a flash of golden light as another dragon was struck down. The great beast slammed into the ground at the top of the Altar, then toppled over the side to land in front of Jax. Its wings were severed and a glowing gash was cut deep into its back. The impact had knocked a huge chunk of rock free from the ledge above, forming a jagged slope that would be easy to climb, and the dragon's body was tall enough to serve as a stepping stool up to the broken ledge.

Jax couldn't believe the stroke of luck, and he ran towards the dead beast, its head cocked at an unnatural angle to the side. Gare and Ev followed quickly but cautiously.

Just as he reached it, the giant lizard opened one of its eyes, causing him to freeze. The dragon lifted its head and looked straight at him, revealing its other eye to be mutilated and burned with wounds resembling lightning.

The dragon opened its glowing mouth, and Jax jumped out of the way of the massive blast of flame that poured from it.

The fire grazed Jax's legs, but his armor's enchantments held. Seeing that Gare and Ev had avoided the flames as well, he jumped back up and drew his sword.

He heard Gare yell, "Jax! Are you crazy?"

"It's either fight or get roasted while running away!" Jax responded, and he dodged as the dragon lunged its head towards him, narrowly avoiding its deadly bite.

The dragon took another snap at Jax, but again it was too slow, and Jax noticed it was having trouble turning — its back legs seemingly unable to move.

"Look!" he continued, "It's hurt! We can do this!"

Jax ran around the dragon's side, forcing it to turn after him. Jax heard Gare curse and smiled as he saw his friend run around the opposite side.

The dragon turned back to face Gare, charging up a blast of fire. Jax took advantage of the distraction to rush in and slashed at the beast's underarm, severing tendons and causing it to collapse to the ground, its fire missing Gare completely.

The dragon roared and turned its head back to Jax, preparing another blast.

Jax bolted to the rear of the dragon and jumped behind its back leg as the flames overtook him.

His armor's enchantments weren't enough this time. The fire scorched his exposed face before he'd made it to safety.

Jax clutched at his face as he hollered in pain, but immediately regretted it as his gauntlets were nearly glowing with heat, having also been caught up in the inferno. Jax grunted and gritted his teeth, panting. The dragon roared again and its body spasmed, reminding Jax that the battle wasn't over yet. Forcing himself to ignore the pain, he pushed himself back up and ran out into the open once again.

The dragon's attention was back to its other side and Gare. It was even more sluggish than before and wasn't even able to lift its neck off the ground completely.

Jax gripped his sword and moved in for the kill, plunging it deep into the base of the dragon's neck. The massive beast gasped and jerked, the movement nearly throwing Jax to the ground, but he held fast to his blade, pressing it down and widening the tear in the dragon's throat.

In the midst of its death throws came a loud clank, and the dragon's head fell to the ground. Jax looked up to see Gare on the other side of its neck, panting, his ax buried deep in its spine.

Gare grinned. "Guess what, bud? We just slayed a dragon."

Jax couldn't help but return the grin, but his grin turned into a grimace as the pain in his face returned.

Ev ran up to the two of them. "Are you okay? Jax! Your face!"

"I'll be fine," Jax answered. "Heal me once this is over okay?"

Ev opened her mouth to say something but quickly closed it again and nodded.

Jax returned his sword to his scabbard and looked up at the ledge they needed to climb. He realized Ev was casting a healing spell on him anyway, but he ignored it. His focus was on the hoard of zodiac riders converging on the Altar, but they quickly proved not to be an issue as a great explosion of golden light blew them all away.

"Right then," he said. "We're almost there. Let's be careful not to get caught in the crossfire."

Jax climbed up onto the dragon's back and onto the collapsed ledge. He was worried the stone would be loose, but it proved to be sturdy enough. At the top he found himself behind the lip of stone that encircled the Altar. The waist-high stone was just tall enough for them to remain hidden from Lord Grandis if they remained crouched. Turning back to the ledge, he helped Ev and then Gare up the last few steps.

Gare leaned in close to Jax. "Alright bud, we're here. Now what?"

"We do what we said we'd do," Jax answered. "We try and get Birdie's att-AGHH!" he screamed as the tip of a black arrow penetrated his chest plate.

Jax yanked the arrow out, the wound fortunately not deep, and glared up at the revenant in the sky who'd attacked him.

Jax raised his sword as the revenant nocked another arrow. They fired simultaneously, Jax knocking the revenant from its zodiac and the arrow striking Jax's arm, fortunately failing to penetrate his armor.

Several new zodiac riders took the first's place, and an undead mage unleashed a bolt of lightning that struck the stone behind them, sending pieces of it flying in all directions.

Jax raised his sword to fire again when another arrow succeeded in penetrating his gut. Jax ignored the pain and fired beam after beam as he pulled himself over the stone lip for cover.

Ev followed after him as arrows rained down, and a second bolt of lightning struck Gare before he could climb over. He fell to the ground back on the exposed side.

Jax cursed and jumped back up, taking aim and receiving another arrow to his chest, this one breaking through his armor completely. Jax gasped and braced himself for the next lightning strike, trying to point his blade at the mage but failing to hold it steady. He fired a beam, but it missed completely.

The mage pointed his staff directly at Jax when another zodiac rider with a familiar bag slammed into the mage, knocking her from the sky. The other riders turned their attention to this newcomer. After a few wild gestures, the new arrival sent the others away, then looked down directly at Jax, pointing a bony finger at him. The revenant then pointed emphatically back down the mountain and flew away.

After a moment's confusion, the realization of what happened hit Jax like a brick. "Birdie, wait!" he shouted, but it was too late.

Well, at least she knew they were there. That meant she'd be watching them, so maybe if they could make it to the back of the Altar where the stone lip was high enough to hide them completely, she'd give them a chance to talk.

Jax pulled the arrows from his body and crawled back over to Gare, relieved to find him still breathing, though unconscious. Ev followed and immediately started healing him, her new rod lighting up as she pointed it at him.

"Ev," Jax choked, unable to breath well, "I saw Birdie."

Ev looked up in shock. "You did? Where?"

"She's the one who saved us," Jax answered. "We need... we—" he coughed up blood.

Ev stopped working on Gare and pointed her rod at Jax's chest. The relief was immediate.

After a moment, he pushed the rod aside. "That's enough," he coughed, still with blood in his lungs. "We need to try—"

A massive blast from the Altar interrupted him. Jax looked back over the stone lip to see the smoking remains of over a dozen revenants, with Lord Grandis, Lady Escalor, and a handful of his elite soldiers standing in the center of the carnage.

An ear-shattering roar echoed across the sky as an enormous black dragon swooped up from behind the summit and landed on the stairs of the Altar. Syrus and Dezeroth jumped off of it to the ground.

No one moved as the three Radiants and the Undead King stared one another down. Streaks of purple lightning etched across the sky above them as a freezing dark mist began to blow through the area.

Syrus pointed his rod at Dezeroth, and Dezeroth his hand at Syrus, each of them beginning to glow — Dezeroth white and Syrus black — with Radiant-tier enchantments. Lady Escalor responded by raising her spear and slamming its shaft against the ground, sending out a golden shock wave that enveloped her allies in a yellow glow.

The great dragon opened its jaws and bathed the Altar in fire. Jax ducked back behind the wall to avoid the searing heat. When the flames had passed, he looked back up into the plaza to see Grandis engaged in combat against Syrus and Dezeroth in the middle of a large circle untouched by the flame — the rest of the plaza glowing bright from the heat.

Lord Grandis swung his golden blade, every parried blow sending shocks across the summit. The soldiers with him had backed away to a safe distance, most of them choosing to offer ranged support to Escalor as she battled the dragon, her spear launching bolts of light that cut deep into its hide.

Jax turned his attention back to Ev. "Stay here and keep an eye out for Birdie. She's riding a zodiac and looks like a revenant, but you can tell it's her from her bag."

Ev grabbed Jax's arm before he could leave. "Whatever you're doing, it better not be stupid."

Jax squeezed her arm back. "I'm just going to keep watch for her on the other side. I'll be careful."

Ev released his arm, and Jax made his way around the outer wall of the Altar, scanning the skies for Birdie. At this point he honestly wasn't sure what he was hoping would happen anymore. If Grandis killed Syrus and Dezeroth, the threat would be over; Escalor would be more than sufficient to protect the Altar while Grandis dealt with Apollyon. If Syrus won, then they'd have no choice but to let him give Birdie back her role as Eclipse, as she'd be the only being strong enough to stop the coming apocalypse.

As Jax passed behind the back wall of the Altar, out of sight of the battle, a pained roar followed by a huge crash shook the mountain. Jax hurried to where the rock was low enough for him to see over again, where he was met with the sight of the black dragon lying dead on the ground, along with all but two of Grandis's soldiers, and even the survivors were heavily injured.

Another great crash exploded as Grandis brought his sword down hard on Dezeroth's blade mere feet away from Jax, causing the Undead King to stagger backwards. Jax had to suppress the urge to jump up and join in, the thought of avenging his father rekindling his thirst for justice, but he knew such an action would be folly.

On the far side of the plaza, Escalor had put Syrus on the defensive. He was clearly wounded from the battle, whereas Escalor still stood strong. An odd feeling welled up within Jax. He was now confident which way this battle would go. Yet, despite them winning, something felt wrong.

That was when Jax saw Ev stand up behind Syrus and point her rod at him. The rod started to glow, and the reality of what she was doing made his blood freeze.

She was helping Syrus.

Escalor noticed.

"Ev, no!" Jax shouted at the top of his lungs, drawing both Grandis's and Dezeroth's attention.

There was nothing he could do. Escalor's next strike bypassed Syrus and went straight through Ev's chest, the beam of light leaving a glowing ring around the gaping hole it left behind.

Jax dropped his sword. For the second time, he'd failed to protect his family. For the second time, he'd been completely useless....

Helplessly, he watched as Ev staggered, then fell against the wall. Yet, she held her head aloft, staring defiantly up at Escalor as she shakily lifted her rod towards Syrus once again.

An enraged Escalor turned her attention to Ev, whirling her spear around to finish the job.

The blow never landed, however, as a dark barrier appeared in the path of the spear, blasting it away. Escalor staggered, and the brief disruption gave Syrus an opening. A shadowy spire grew from the tip of his rod, which he plunged upwards into her underarm. Dark smoke erupted from her every inch of her armor, and her body exploded in a flash of light, leaving behind a glowing orb that fell loudly on the ground.

Grandis spun around at the sound and drew back his sword, a brilliant glow emanating from it. With a rage-filled roar he sent a golden arc directly towards Syrus, cleaving through the stone wall and leaving Syrus one arm fewer.

Dezeroth used the opportunity to charge Grandis from behind, jamming his twisted blade into the golden armor. Grandis shouted in pain, then spun around and backhanded the Undead King, breaking his jaw. Before Dezeroth could recover, Grandis brought his sword around and removed Dezeroth's sword arm. A second sweep, and Dezeroth found himself on the ground, separated from his legs. A final thrust, and the golden sword pierced clean through the black armor, leaving Dezeroth broken and barely moving.

Grandis locked eyes with Jax, who couldn't keep himself from looking over at his sister and Syrus, who in turn was gazing defiantly at Grandis while pointing his glowing rod at Ev.

Eyes still on Jax, Grandis held his sword out in front of him as it once again began to glow that brilliant light. With a flash, he spun around, and Syrus jumped out of the way as a golden arc blasted past him. One of the surviving soldiers lunged toward Syrus, tackling him. Syrus kicked the soldier away but was left vulnerable as Grandis unleashed a second arc. This time the arc connected, and when the light faded all that remained of Syrus was his glowing Heart.

And that was it. That was the end of the battle. There was no one else who could pose a threat to Grandis, but without Escalor to guard the Altar there was no way he would leave to stop Apollyon. The only chance would be if Birdie relinquished the Heart to Grandis, but Jax knew that would never happen, and that meant all of this had been for nothing. The battles, the pain, Ev's...

A tear slid down Jax's cheek. He'd given everything he had, and he failed, and Ev... why? Why did she do it?

Breathing heavily, Grandis walked towards Jax, kicking Dezeroth against the wall on his way. Jax barely lifted his eyes at the approach.

"Tell me, boy," commanded Grandis. "Are you the one who said he wanted to stay to kill this disgusting fool?"

Jax looked down at Dezeroth's pitiful form. The Undead King, the monster responsible for tens of thousands of deaths across his countless resurrections, now merely a crippled old man lying helplessly on the floor. His orange eyes glowed with rage and defiance even in defeat, but Jax saw more than that in there. He saw despair and desperation, things he never would have imagined an immortal despot could possess.

Jax turned his attention back to Grandis, and barely uttered, "Yes."

Grandis narrowed his eyes. "Well, then. Pick up your sword, and do it."

Jax looked down at the sword he'd dropped. Slowly he reached down and grabbed its hilt. Standing up again, he eyed Grandis warily as he climbed over the stone wall and took a spot next to Dezeroth.

The old king looked up at him, the fury gone, resigned to his fate.

Jax gripped his blade tightly, but kept it at his side.

"What are you waiting for?" asked Grandis, his tone mocking. "This is what you came for, isn't it?"

Jax turned his head toward Grandis, then looked back over to where Ev... was alive?

Jax opened his eyes wide and nearly dropped his sword again as he watched Ev shakily push herself up, her eyes pleading with him.

Grandis followed Jax's gaze, but he was losing patience. "I will not give you another chance. End this fool now, or I will do it myself."

After a moment's hesitation, Jax looked Grandis in the eye and lowered his blade. Maybe there was nothing he could do. Maybe it had all been for naught, but if he only succeeded at one thing this day, it would be to find out if his sister was right.

"Why?" Jax asked, prompting an immediate glare from Grandis. "What's the point? We're all going to die here anyway, aren't we? When Apollyon arrives, you aren't going to save us from him. You never were, were you?"

The next thing Jax knew he was flat on the ground next to Dezeroth, his helmet dented from the impact of the flat of Grandis's blade.

Lord Grandis took a single step forward and towered over Jax. "So you're finally willing to drop the act. I should have known when I first saw you that you were one of Syrus's servants." He raised his sword to point straight at Jax's head. "I don't expect you to understand, but your world should not exist. Its purpose was a lie. Nepacs and Divine alike were deceived. I do not know to what end, but I know that your world must end. Only ill can come from its continued existence. It is already dying regardless. I am only accelerating that fact. The Masters trust that the presence of a Radiant ensures Doxla will survive Apollyon. I will betray that trust as they betrayed so many. At least now, nepacs will be granted a swift death, and whatever villainy the Masters glean from Doxla will be ended."

A dazed Jax glared up defiantly at Grandis, panting with rage. Ev had been right. Everything he'd given and everything he'd lost because of this war, it had all been because he'd trusted in this man. Because they'd trusted in him. Jax's father, Kelva, Huxley, Diana, all of them... they'd given their lives fighting in his name, and all along his only plan had been to hand them over to destruction.

"Lord Grandis!" a voice shouted, and Jax looked up to see a soldier running towards the central fountain carrying a Heart with two other soldiers chasing after him.

The golden sword immediately moved away from Jax and launched into a flurry of attacks, sending arc after arc at the nimble warrior.

Grandis roared and charged towards the fountain, unleashing a mighty blast from the palm of his hand that exploded on the ground, sending the two soldiers flying and causing the Heart bearer to disappear in a flash of light.

Yet, despite his victory, Grandis appeared more on edge than ever, looking around frantically as if he was expecting more.

Jax spotted why. On the far side of the plaza, behind one of the pillars and obscured by the dark mist, was Birdie in her normal appearance, holding her Heart and casting one of her spells.

Another soldier carrying another Heart appeared from behind the wall. Grandis launched into another furious assault at the illusion, and Jax realized what Birdie was trying to do.

Gripping his sword, he pushed himself to his feet and pointed his blade at Grandis. "You traitor! You think just because you're a Divine you get to decide the fate of our world?"

Grandis immediately sent a golden arc in Jax's direction. The attack was so fast Jax barely had time to dive out of the way, the arc blasting through the stone wall behind him like paper.

Jax resumed his stance and fired a beam of light at Grandis. The attack bounced harmlessly off his armor, but Jax hadn't expected it to do otherwise. "Maybe we will die someday. Maybe the Masters did lie to us, but we aren't going to die because some otherworldly despot thinks he knows what's best!"

Grandis glared at Jax and raised his hand to fire a magic blast when one of the soldiers cried out. Grandis spun around in time to see Birdie running past the two soldiers, one of them now dead and the other nearly so.

Grandis pulled back his golden sword, his blade emitting the ominous light that portended his arc attack.

"No!" Jax yelled, channeling magic into his sword and feeling an unnatural power welling within him.

His blade and arms began emitting a dark aura, and from the corner of his eye he saw Dezeroth casting an enchantment in his direction.

Grandis swung his blade as Jax fired, the dark beam piercing Grandis's shoulder and knocking his attack off course. The golden arc grazed past Birdie as she sprinted desperately towards the fountain.

Grandis raised a glowing hand, but Jax had already raised his first, firing a dark blast at the ground in front of Grandis and obscuring his vision.

Grandis roared and slammed his sword into the ground, creating a massive explosion that enveloped the center of the Altar and nearly threw Jax over the wall as shards of golden magic shot through his body.

Jax crumpled to the ground as he felt the dark enchantment leaving him, but looking up, he exhaled in relief.

There, at the center of the Altar, was Birdie, glowing in a black and white aura, the crystalline wings of a Radiant extended behind her. She glowered at Grandis, who backed away from her, a mixture of rage and fear etched on his face.

"No!" he screamed, and he let loose a golden arc that missed Birdie completely.

Birdie waved her hand and Grandis cried out as if struck, spinning around and swinging his sword at nothing. He quickly turned to attack the air again before being hit by another invisible attack.

Birdie walked slowly toward him. "You disgust me. You betrayed everyone who trusted you. You exploited them, made them worship you, and now you want to kill them all."

Grandis pulled his sword back to slam it into the ground, but a shadow appeared behind him and grabbed his arm, interrupting his attack. He spun around to strike the assailant, but it disappeared.

"Enough of these tricks!" Grandis shouted. "Fight me like a-HRRGGHHH!"

Grandis was cut off as a black dagger pierced his neck from behind. Birdie had appeared out of his shadow in her true shade form, and the Birdie standing by the fountain disappeared. Grandis dropped to the ground on one hand, the other hand grasping his neck. Shadows wrapped around his legs and wrists, pulling him against the marble plaza.

Birdie leaned in close to him. "But more than that, you hurt the people I care about. You hurt my world." She grabbed his helmet and yanked his head back. "I'm going to split you now, and if you ever dare return to Doxla, I guarantee I will make you suffer in ways you can't even begin to imagine."

A dark spire erupted out of Grandis's back, and his body disappeared in a flash of light, leaving behind a golden orb. Birdie returned to the form Jax was familiar with and approached him, the wings and glow disappearing.

Jax looked up at her, neither of them saying a word as she helped sit him up against the wall.

A bolt of lightning striking the mountain reminded him that they weren't safe yet, though. "Birdie... or Eclipse, wh—"

"Birdie," she answered.

"You have to stop Apollyon," Jax pleaded. "If you don't..."

"I know," answered Birdie. "I'm going, but I'm not going to leave you here. If Grandis's soldiers find out what happened here—"

"We'll be fine," Jax interrupted. "When you stop Apollyon, they'll know you aren't evil. And besides, who'd believe a couple of cadets could have hurt Grandis anyway?"

"Jax—"

"Go," Jax said. "The longer you wait the more damage is done. Stop Apollyon, for all of us."

Birdie stared at Jax, then looked back at Ev. She nodded, then disappeared into a puddle of shadow that slid to the edge of the mountain. A moment later, Jax caught sight of a zodiac and a shade rising up into the clouds, the brilliance of a Radiant's wings lighting up the sky. A roar of triumph went out from Dezeroth and Syrus's troops, and the army of monsters withdrew from the mountain.

Jax felt himself slipping over, unable to keep himself upright. His face landed against the cool ground, and he smiled as he watched Birdie fly away into the darkness.

Chapter 20

"Hey Bud, pass me some water," Gare said, tapping Jax with the back of his hand.

"Seriously? We just left. Why didn't you get something in town?"

"I wasn't thirsty then. Come on, give it here!"

Jax rolled his eyes and reached into the back of the wagon behind him, digging out one of the canteens they'd packed.

Handed the water over to Gare, he asked, "Anything else, your lordship?"

"Maybe in a minute. I'll keep you posted."

Jax slapped the bottom of the canteen, causing Gare to spill on himself.

"Hey!" he shouted.

"Sorry, there was a bump in the road."

Gram turned back from her seat in the front. "If you two waste our water, then you're going to be walking to Marisol."

"Sorry, Gram," replied Jax. "It won't happen again."

Gram turned forward once again and gave the reigns a slight whip, prompting the horses to up their speed.

Jax leaned back into his wooden seat and turned his head back toward Roehelm. He didn't know why, but he was hesitant to go. Probably because he didn't want to go back to the empty house waiting for him at home. Not wanting to think about it, he turned his gaze to the north, towards the Altar of Restoration. What happened to Birdie after she'd left, he had no idea. All he knew was that she'd succeeded in defeating Apollyon, seeing as how they were all still here.

Closing his eyes, Jax settled in for a long, boring journey home. After everything that had happened, he welcomed the change of pace. He only had a few minutes of peace, however, before Ev interrupted his tranquility.

"Look!" his sister shouted, pointing to the sky.

Jax shielded his eyes from the sun as he followed her finger, and nearly jumped out of his seat when he spotted a large yellow fish-like creature flying straight towards them. The zodiac came in for a landing in front of their wagon, forcing Gram to pull the horses to a halt. From off the zodiac came Birdie and someone who looked like Lord Syrus.

Jax and Ev leapt out of the cart ahead of Gare and ran to meet them.

"Birdie?" Jax shouted. "You're alive! And... Syrus?"

Birdie smirked and placed her hand on her hip. "Of course I'm alive. Did you forget who I am?" She turned her attention to Ev. "I'm glad to see you're all okay, though."

"Yeah, we are. Barely," responded Jax, eyeing the man he knew had to be Syrus. "We're just lucky no one knew what happened up there. I doubt anyone would have healed us if they knew we helped split Grandis. People are still freaking out about it."

Birdie chuckled. "Yeah, well, then they're really going to freak when we go get Syrus's Heart back again. We were hoping maybe they'd just hand it over this time now that Grandis is gone."

"Excuse me," Gram's voice called from behind, and Jax was surprised to see her approaching Syrus. She walked steadily past Jax and stopped a few feet away from the Divine. "Lord Syrus," she stated, and stared him in the eyes.

"Yes?" responded Syrus, hands behind his back.

Gram frowned. "My grandson tells me that you are the one who saved my Eveline, that you stopped to heal her even as you fought Lord Grandis."

"My battle with Grandis was over by then," Syrus stated. "I could no longer battle him. The least I could do was aid the one Eclipse... I mean, the one Birdie calls 'friend.'"

Gram bowed her head. "I care not why you did it, but know that you have my eternal gratitude, and my apologies for turning my back on you when I thought you'd done the same to us. We should have trusted you and not the words of Lord Grandis."

Syrus bowed his head in return, but Birdie didn't wait for their conversation to continue. "So, where are you all headed off to?"

Ev answered for the group. "We're going back to Marisol. We never had a chance to say goodbye to Father."

"Oh..." replied Birdie.

"It's alright," offered Jax. "We've all had time to accept it. What about you? After you get Syrus's Heart back, then what?"

Syrus turned to the north. "After that, we hunt down Grandis and Escalor's Hearts and lock them away, just as they did to ours."

"Oh, that... might not be possible," Jax stated, rubbing his arm.

Syrus turned back to Jax, head cocked. "And why is that?"

"Well," Jax wasn't sure how to put this, "they kind of disappeared. No one knows where they went."

Syrus frowned. "What do you mean, 'disappeared'? As in actually disappeared?"

"Yeah," answered Jax. "I saw it myself. Not long after Birdie left, Escalor's Heart just vanished from the Altar, and Grandis's shortly after that. People were panicking about it."

"I see..." said Syrus, now smiling. "In that case, I suppose our job is already done. A Divine's Heart only disappears if they sever all ties with this world. Since it is currently impossible for new Divine to enter your world, that means Grandis is gone forever, at least so long as the Masters do not return and change things."

"Oh, right," said Jax, his mind recalling what Grandis had said to him. "About that. Before Grandis was defeated, he told me something about the Masters. He said they deceived even the Divine. He said our world shouldn't exist. What did he mean?"

Syrus gave Jax an odd, almost pitying look. "All Divine have laws they must follow — even the Masters. They lied about what your world is. They created it in a place no world should be. I can only guess as to their intentions, but I guarantee their goals are corrupt at best. That said, it is quite likely that they have already achieved said goals and have since abandoned Doxla entirely, so it isn't something you should worry about. Any trouble that might arise should be many years off, and the world will have ample time to prepare."

Jax nodded, then placed his hand on his hip like Birdie. "Alright. So what are your plans now, then?"

Birdie sighed and rolled her head back. "Ugh, apparently we have to try and convince Syrus and Dezeroth's armies to get along with the rest of the world. After that, who knows?" She turned her attention to Ev and Jax. "Maybe I can visit you?"

"Yes," said Ev, "I'd like that."

"As long as it doesn't start another war," added Gare. "Maybe don't show up looking like someone people will soon recognize as the Dark Radiant."

Birdie smirked. "I'm pretty sure you guys are the only ones who know what I am, but I'll try not to sprout wings when I'm out in public if that makes you feel any better."

"Didn't you just say you're going to help Syrus get his Heart back?" Gare asked. "You know they took that thing back to Roehelm, right? That place where people still don't like you?"

Birdie rolled her eyes. "Fine, then how about I look like this while I do that?" she asked as she took on the appearance of Gare.

"Agh, no!" shouted Gare.

"Please don't," Jax groaned, "I already have to look at one of him."

Birdie chuckled and changed back. "Don't worry. I don't plan on letting people connect my favorite appearance with my Radiant status. Maybe if they ever get over Grandis and realize I'm on their side, but definitely not any time soon."

Jax smiled, and Syrus approached Birdie and put his hand on her shoulder. "Well, we should get going. I don't want to leave my army unattended for long, and I'd rather not risk any confrontations with them without my Radiance to keep them in line."

Jax nodded, and the two groups waved goodbye to one another as Syrus and Birdie climbed back onto their zodiac. The golden beast lifted off the ground, and Birdie looked back to wave goodbye.

Jax, Ev, and Gare all returned the wave. Once the zodiac was out of sight, they climbed back onto their wagon.

"You kids all ready?" Gram asked.

"Yeah," answered Jax. "Let's go home."

Coming Soon:

The Mind of the Radiant

Birdie emerged from the shadow once again, now behind Apollyon, the eyes on its back still blissfully unaware that they should also be trying to see through an illusion. As she prepared a second strike at its base, her doppelgangers attacked its legs. They wouldn't do much damage, but it would keep Apollyon's attention as she slashed once more deep into its flesh.

Apollyon erupted in a gurgling roar, its eyes lighting up as it prepared to bathe the battlefield with explosive balls of energy.

Birdie was pleased with herself. She was doing much better than last time — already a quarter of the way through the first phase of the fight. She melted into shadow again and darted for cover when something strange caught her senses. It felt similar to a curse her creator Syrus had mastered, but… different. The curse flew past her and struck Apollyon just before it unleashed its onslaught.

Safely behind the largest standing structure she could find, she waited for the cacophony of explosions to ring out, but the cacophony never came. Instead of explosions, the balls of energy burst with loud pops, barely even marking the ground. Then, the ground shook as Apollyon crashed to the ground, barely able to hold itself up on its shaking limbs.

Birdie stepped out from her cover dumbstruck. Not at what she was seeing, but at what she felt. Apollyon's energy had almost completely vanished. Not just aboveground, but in the tentacles below as well. She took a brief glance in the direction the strange curse had come from but saw nothing. Whatever had happened, she couldn't waste this opportunity.

She and her doppelgangers rushed towards the fallen Apollyon, she slicing deep into its base while her other selves cut through its limbs without effort.

Apollyon struggled to fight back, but it was pointless. It wasn't able to move, and the only spells it cast were so weak any of her companions back on the hill would have shrugged them off.

She maneuvered one of her doppelgangers towards the ring of eyes that was her target, and with a single half-hearted strike ended the battle.

The Great Destroyer Apollyon ceased its struggle and melted down into a sludge that slowly poured back into the hole from which it had emerged. The tremors and lighting disappeared, and the sky lit up once again. In another five years, Apollyon would return again, but that wasn't Birdie's concern at the moment. Turning her attention back to where she was sure the curse had come from — a dead forest in the valley of two small hills — her disbelief of what had happened gave way to concern. There was no sign of Syrus or anyone else, which meant whoever had cast the spell didn't want to be spotted. That meant it couldn't have been Syrus who was responsible, and *that* troubled her to her very soul.

For more information about upcoming books in this
series and others, check out D. S. Kogler's website at

dskogler-books.com

While you're there, be sure to sign up for the mailing list
as well!